FitzDuncan's Inheritance

John J. Spearman

DEDICATION

This book is dedicated to all the teachers who helped shape me. Some of them were fortunate enough to know of their positive influence. There were others who never knew how much I appreciate them. Not all are academics —some of my most important lessons were learned in the corporate world. Thank you Frank Longstreth, John Breuker, Tony Chapman, Corinne Davis, Dick Baker, Dean Seiters, Professor Gilchrist, Tom Murdough, Bill Kurtzner, Bill Daugherty, and Skip Flanagan.

OTHER BOOKS BY THIS AUTHOR

The Halberd Series
Gallantry in Action
In Harm's Way
True Allegiance
Surrender Demand

The Pike Series
Pike's Potential
Pike's Passage
Pike's Progress

The FitzDuncan Series
FitzDuncan
FitzDuncan's Alchemy
FitzDuncan's Enlightenment
FitzDuncan's Fortune
FitzDuncan's Gambit
FitzDuncan's Hope

The Perseverance Andrews Series
The Defense of the Commonwealth
The Courage of the Commonwealth

ACKNOWLEDGMENTS

Many thanks to my editor, Martin Roy Hill, who has been of enormous help from the standpoints of both technical expertise and moral support.

Deepest gratitude for Thea Magerand, the marvelous artist whose artwork has brought Caz and Lucy alive. Every piece she has done for my books amazes me further.

Finally, Dear Reader,
You are the purpose of this and all my books. Thank you for reading. If you like what you have read, please leave a positive review on Amazon.com or goodreads.com. If you did not like it, I'm sorry.

If you would like to stay abreast of my latest activity,
please visit my website: johnjspearmanauthor.com

1

I suddenly saw our outpost at Bannock Hill from a lofty vantage point. Searching within, I found the node for Shasha, the sparrow hawk who had bonded herself to me.

Where have you been?

"I was injured. The past few days, I have been sleeping most of the time while my wounds healed."

This is not the time for sleep. People have come. This is important, yes?

"From over the mountains?"

Yes. They have come.

I sat bolt-upright in bed. "How many? When?"

You are alarmed. You should not be. They are already leaving. Their animals will not go back. You shared that people coming from over the mountains is important to you, so you should not sleep.

"Can you show me?"

Not now. I am at watchtower. This was then.

Shasha shared a memory with me. In it, I saw cattle grazing on the eastern edge of the Patker River. It was only a brief glimpse, but I reckoned there were about a hundred. Then she showed me five men on horseback with a two-wheeled cart heading eastward across the broken landscape just past where we surprised the nomads with an ambush earlier in the summer.

"When did you see this?"

Time was a concept where Shasha's perception was vastly different from that of a human. I sensed that to her, the past was all the same. She did not have a way of organizing recent events separately from those much earlier.

"How many times has the sun risen since you saw the memory you shared?" I thought, trying to help provide her a framework.

Oh. One, I think.

She was not accustomed to keeping track, so she was not sure. She shared more memories with me. In them, I saw the horsemen herding the cattle westward, close to the river at the foot of the mountains. Then she showed me the group further along, on the dry plain. Finally, I saw the cattle breaking for the river when they sensed water was near.

I have been trying to share with you, but you have not responded.

"Thank you, Shasha. As I mentioned, I was wounded and was sleeping."

This is important, so you should not be sleeping, yes? But not cause for alarm. I feel you are calmer now.

"It is very important, and I thank you. They may come back with more men. That will be a reason to be distressed if it happens."

Shasha left my mind. Now I had the problem of knowing there were a hundred or so cattle grazing near the Patker River and sending someone to collect them. I had never mentioned my connection to the supernatural with my father. Given that he saw both Fenwick and me appear larger than life a few days earlier when we both manifested the Goddess Bellona, this discussion was now overdue. I could then explain how I now had a sparrow hawk as a "familiar" who alerted me to the presence of the cattle.

"Lucy!" I tried to holler, but my voice was weak and cracked.

"Coming!" I heard her sweet voice call back.

While I waited for her, I slid to the edge of the bed and dangled my feet. I could tell I was still light-headed, so I did not try to stand. Nonetheless, I wanted a bath to wash any remaining blood off and to dress. With that accomplished, I could then tackle the difficult conversation with my father.

When Lucy appeared, I shared my wishes with her and explained what I learned from Shasha. Lucy agreed that it was time to inform my father of my abilities. She also mentioned that both he and Fenwick were still in the house eating breakfast.

"They can help fill the bath," she said. "And I think it might be an easier conversation with your father if Fenwick takes part. It will help your father accept what you tell him."

Lucy departed but Roberta came in shortly after bearing a tray with a huge breakfast on it. There were eggs, sausages, strawberries, and muffins—enough for two or three men. I inhaled it all. Roberta started to leave, but when she saw how quickly I was eating, she decided to stay to collect the tray and save herself another trip up the stairs.

Fenwick arrived not long after, and I heard the squeak of the pulleys from the hoist in the hallway. He appeared with two buckets of water and dumped them in the tub. While he waited for the next two, he sat next to me.

"Do you have anything pressing today?" I asked.

"Not until later," he responded. "Why?"

I shared with him my desire to discuss my abilities with my father, adding, "Lucy and I think it might be easier for him to come to grips with it knowing that you and I have the same dominant."

"I'm happy to help, Caz," Fenwick said, "but I don't think you have a cause to worry. Your father certainly knows about Lucy and has at least a strong suspicion about the two of us. He has never struck me as being as uncomfortable with the supernatural as His Majesty is."

When the bath was full, Lucy came and helped me to the tub. She removed the bandages from my thigh and left palm. Once I submerged, she began helping me clean the dried blood away. There was quite a bit, and the water had a definite reddish tint when I stood up.

Lucy put fresh bandages on my wounds and helped me dress. She tried to steer me back to bed, but I refused. We headed downstairs at my insistence and with her help. I was pretty wobbly. Fenwick and my father were in the parlor.

"Sir," I said, "there is something I need to tell you."

He recognized the sobriety of my tone and sat up straight. I took a seat in an armchair facing him. I cleared my throat nervously.

"Fenwick believes you already have figured this out," I began. "I need to let you know I have ... abilities."

"I had my suspicions," my father responded with a faint smile as his posture relaxed, "but there was no doubt left in my mind after seeing the two of you a few nights ago. Suddenly, both of you appeared physically larger and more powerful, matching the size and strength of your opponents."

"We summoned the Goddess Bellona," Fenwick explained. "She took control of our bodies."

"How long have you been able to do this?" my father asked.

"It is a fairly recent thing, in my case," I explained. "I was unaware I had any potential until after I started seeing Lucy. Being near her 'woke' my connection."

"Tell me more," he requested.

"My dominant bond is with Bellona," I said. "I also have links with Eir and Njörun."

"Is your dominant Bellona as well?" my father asked Fenwick.

"Yes. That's why we both were able to manifest the Goddess," Fenwick replied. "My other, lesser connections are different."

"Fascinating," my father whispered. "And you, my dear?"

"My dominant is Freyja," Lucy answered. "And I also have links to Eir and Njörun—one of the reasons Caz and I are so compatible."

"That explains it," my father said with a hint of triumph. "At the festival, I would have sworn Freyja herself was present. She was, wasn't she?"

"Partly," Lucy admitted. "I did not allow her to gain full possession of me, but she was sharing my body, if that makes sense."

"I must say, sir, you are accepting this better than I hoped," Fenwick said. "It's a subject that makes many uncomfortable—like His Majesty."

"Pah," he spat. "It's nothing to fear unless you run into someone who practices the Dark Arts. Most people who have supernatural ability are assets to their communities. Your mother's mother was a hedgewitch, you know," he said to me.

"I did not know that," I said.

"She was. Your mother was disappointed she did not inherit her mother's ability. Anyway, why are you bringing this up?"

"Like some people with this kind of ability, I have an animal—"

"A familiar," my father interjected.

"Yes. She is a sparrow hawk from the area near Bannock Hill," I explained. "She has been keeping watch for anyone coming from the east."

"Oh," my father said, his pleasant demeanor fading quickly.

"Five men and about a hundred cattle arrived a few days ago," I said. "The men are already on their way back home. The cattle refused to go back with them."

"Oh?" my father's mood improved. "So, we need to send someone to collect them?"

"Yes."

"I'm sure we can pick out a handful of men to do that," my father said. "What do you plan to do with them? Another festival?"

"I have not thought that far ahead," I admitted. "I don't think a festival so quickly after the last would have any impact. Part of me wants to keep them and pasture them between Oritur and the Patker River. But you and I both have our hands full right now, and taking on another project seems foolhardy."

"Just sell them to Williamson and be done with it," my father said. "Now, you say your sparrow hawk is watching the approach from the east?"

"Yes."

"If a larger force comes, we will have advance notice?" he asked.

"At least four days before they would reach the Patker," I replied.

"Enough time to raise the alarm and recall the armsmen," my father stated. "Getting the militia back in position will take a few days longer, but every town has enough veterans that could fill in for the two or three days. I will need to communicate with them."

"I thought you would want to pull the men back immediately," I said.

"A month ago, that would have been my preference," he said. "Not anymore. Certainly, I am unwilling to let any of our towns fall, but I also have the king's commitment that he will respond in force if the nomads return. He is quite serious about ending that threat, just as Albert said. A thousand men or more would respond to our summons."

"I must say, Lord Easton, you are far less troubled by all this than even I would have dared to hope," Fenwick commented.

"The time I spent in Mr. Farquahr's custody, with those two goons beating me for his amusement or their own, had a strangely beneficial effect on me," my father said. "I have had a glimpse of the future, and it seems much more promising than the past. Embracing it will produce better results than fighting it, don't you think?"

"I would certainly agree," Lucy said.

"Good. Anything else?" my father asked. "I was planning on leaving for Easton this morning. It's a bit later than I hoped, but I can still make a full day's journey."

"What are you planning on doing?" Lucy asked.

"I need to find some idle hands to round up some cattle," he said. "Mr. Balboa should have a list compiled for me of what construction he wants to tackle first. I will meet with your Mr. Pruitt, who did such a fine job restoring the manor and engage him to build for us in Port Charles."

"Starting when?" I asked.

"His Majesty informed me the dredging of the harbor will be far enough along that Traval will be able to unload the materials necessary to construct a wharf by the end of the month. Mr. Traval has committed that the wharf will be ready to receive shipments by the fifth of Twiman. I will have Pruitt place his order for materials immediately and have Traval deliver them in Port Charles on the fifth."

"You and Mr. Traval seem to be working together well," Lucy commented.

"He feels indebted to you, Caz," my father said. "Your advance notice of the project has given him time to prepare, and he has pounced. Hawkins is kicking himself because he ignored the information his younger son passed along about it. He mentioned it during our meeting. Coombs seems indifferent. Based only on his posture and demeanor in our discussions, I would not be surprised if Coombs' business is slipping quite badly."

Fenwick responded to this comment by laying his finger beside his still-swollen nose. My father saw the gesture and nodded. My father then rose.

"Caz, when you are well enough to travel, I will be in Easton or out checking on the progress of the various work sites," he said. "Send someone to fetch me. I'm sure by the time you arrive, we will have much to discuss."

After my father departed, Fenwick lingered. He joined me in the parlor. Lucy came in a moment later with a hot cup of qava for me.

"I'm glad your father has decided that change is coming, and it is better to welcome it than fight it," Fenwick said. "It would be difficult for him to resist, with so much coming along in the last year and even more promised."

"His attitude toward the supernatural caught me by surprise," I said. "We never discussed it, but I assumed he would have views similar to the king's. Speaking of the king, what is the mood in the castle?"

"One of profound relief," Lucy stated. "You were unconscious during her visits, but Lily has come to the house several times to assist with your recovery. The king and Albert are both aware they are further in your debt, and it even applies to Fenwick—to a lesser extent."

"In what way?" I asked.

"His Majesty remains my sole employer," Fenwick said, "and I continue to be at his beck and call. My status no longer seems to be one of indentured servitude, though. Though we have often joked between ourselves about my position and title, I am beginning to feel as though I truly am more of a confidential advisor with a unique set of skills and less the Royal Assassin."

"Well, you've definitely shown him that you are capable of far more than simply killing people," Lucy said.

"That still has great value to the king," Fenwick stated, "but he is aware that I have potential in other areas. Speaking of which, the sacks we bought in Mooresa have arrived. They are in one of Traval's warehouses."

"What is the overall progress on the restoration of the river and harbor?" I asked.

"From the reports His Majesty shared with me, the obstacles in the river have been eliminated," Fenwick said. "The landings are being rebuilt. The three trading houses are building boats they will transport to Port Charles for the river traffic."

"And the harbor?"

"The goal is to restore a minimal degree of function this year," Fenwick said. "They will have a channel cleared that will serve the Traval wharf from both the river and the sea. There will not be much of an anchorage in the harbor, and it will probably be necessary to warp boats out."

"What does that mean?" Lucy asked.

"A ship carefully lowers her anchor into a smaller boat," Fenwick explained. "The smaller boat rows forward and then drops the anchor. The ship then pulls itself forward, using the anchor, then the process is repeated."

"I get the impression the dredging work is moving more slowly than planned," I said.

"You are correct," Fenwick said. "The boat dredges are only effective to a certain depth. Beyond that, the silt has had over a hundred years to settle and is too solid for the dredge ship to work. Using cofferdams has been successful, but the work crews lack men and materials. The king is aware, and they are planning on continuing to work through the winter. There is another problem, though."

"Which is?"

"The fact that Port Charles is uninhabited," Fenwick said. "Traval is planning to include some living quarters in his warehouse, but those workers will be Port Charles' only residents."

"That will be a problem for the construction my father mentioned," I said. "Pruitt's workers will need food and shelter."

"There will be others who come," Fenwick warned, "and someone will need to maintain order. There will be disputes over property ownership. You and your father will need to have some sort of constabulary in place, and it would be best if one of you were nearby to prevent any disputes regarding the land from escalating."

"Is there a list of who owned the different plots?" I asked.

"His Majesty's people are compiling it, along with a map," Fenwick said. "You will need a copy. The king will need to have a magistrate nearby who can issue definitive rulings."

"Fenwick, you keep bringing up more problems that make my head hurt," I complained. "Do you have anything cheerful to balance the scales?"

"As part of His Majesty's loosening of my reins, he has given me permission to marry Julienne if I wish," Fenwick said.

"That's wonderful," Lucy exclaimed.

"I meant cheerful for me," I said.

Lucy cuffed me on the back of my head.

2

It was another five days of mostly sleeping and eating before I felt I was ready to attempt the three-day ride to Easton. This was the second time I suffered a dramatic blood loss. My connection with Eir, the Goddess of Health, helped prevent me from dying and sped my recovery, but the toll it took let me know how close death had been. Unlike physical wounds, where I could summon Eir's power to speed my healing, I did not know how to use her assistance to replenish my blood supply.

Before I left the city, I remembered to write the Duke of Caurus to tell him about the Port Charles project. At the king's winter solstice gathering, he asked to be alerted if there might be an opportunity to invest. It was of special importance to him since his territory was one which needed to import food. I explained that the king would soon release the list showing the last known owners of the property in Port Charles. Unclaimed land would be subject to escheatment and sold. That might be an opportunity for the duke.

Lucy and I enjoyed fair weather all three days of the journey to Easton. Fresh air and sunshine also seemed to help me recover. By the time we reached the manor, the one lingering effect of my injury was my ravenous hunger. From experience, it, too, would fade over the next few days.

When we arrived, Madame Hernandez and Mr. Balboa were present. My father was not. According to our groom, my father was visiting worksites. According to Madame Hernandez, before he departed, he met with Mr. Pruitt and engaged his services to begin rebuilding the farmstead just outside of Port Charles.

Mr. Balboa was quite excited. The first two structures Pruitt would build were going to be a massive barn and a small house for Mr. Balboa. Apparently, Pruitt was already on his way to Port Charles with a crew of workers. He would clear the debris from the foundations and see if they could be repaired for use.

My father returned the next afternoon, joining me on the veranda. After Hazel brought him a glass of water, he settled into his seat with a satisfied expression. He took a minute to organize his thoughts, then began.

"The work crews I visited are all now in the process of cutting the trees and pulling the stumps from the roadbed," he said. "The men are happy enough. Though the work is hard, they can see how much progress they have made and what is remaining to be done. Another month should see the roads cleared—just in time for the harvest."

"Did you send some men to collect the cattle?" I asked.

"I did, and they have all returned," he said, impatiently waving the question away with annoyance. "Williamson gave us a fair price for them."

"I apologize. That was a stupid question," I said. "From your tone just now, I suspect you have something else you would rather discuss. Please go ahead."

"You're right," he admitted. "While I was checking on the road work, I also stopped to see what was being done on the river. These are separate work gangs, employed by the crown and supervised by the engineers. They report that the river is clear from the Quinn's Ford landing to the harbor. The two groups I saw were busy repairing or rebuilding the landings. In addition, they were building a barn and a cottage at each landing."

"I understand the need for a barn," I said. "What is the cottage for?"

"The local agent for the trading company," my father replied. "My understanding is that the port fees a trading company pays also cover the cost of this lodging and use of the barn for storage. The buildings are owned by the crown. There is so much involved with the resumption of trade along the river that I would never have guessed. It's a pity our people did not keep better records."

"Perhaps they did, but after a few decades, no one saw the point in keeping them any longer," I suggested.

"You're probably right," he agreed. "One thing for certain, though, reopening the river will require other changes."

"Such as?" I inquired.

"Lumber," my father responded. "We need to alert every sawmill in the March that there will be a demand for lumber over the next few years. For instance, in rebuilding the farmstead outside of Port Charles, Mr. Pruitt will order the first shipment of lumber from Aquileia. Once the roads to the river are open, it would be cheaper to buy lumber from providers in the March. A significant part of the town of Port Charles will be rebuilt in the next two years, and that requires lumber, nails, tar paper, and other items."

"I would imagine the cost of things we buy from elsewhere in the kingdom will also drop," I said. "Transporting goods on the water must be significantly less expensive than wagon loads traveling overland."

"Yes," my father agreed, rubbing his hands together excitedly. "It might take a few days longer for them to reach here by water, but the cost to move it from one place to the other will be far less. When you also consider that all our farmers will have new markets for their surplus crops, the future looks bright for the entire March. It benefits us as well. Our tenants pay us a fixed percentage of their crop. New markets will increase our income, too."

"That's nice," I said, "but it was never part of my thinking process."

"I know," my father agreed. "Just as I am certain none of this would have happened if you had not returned to the March. The circumstances when you arrived just over a year ago could not be more different than they are now."

"I think you give me too much credit, sir," I protested.

"No, I think you give yourself too little," he responded. "Your ideas, your perspective, and your actions have changed things more dramatically than anyone could have predicted. I am certainly aware of it. So is His Majesty. You are making him look like a genius for putting you in place."

"Fenwick pointed out some other needs we will have after you departed the city," I said. 'We need to rebuild the bridge over the river that fell in. The workers, like Mr. Pruitt's, need a place to sleep and eat until more of the town is rebuilt. Some form of constabulary needs to be in place, and there should be a magistrate of the king's nearby to rule on property disputes. It might also be wise to keep one of the surveyors on hand to help the magistrate settle such arguments quickly and completely."

"Pruitt is building a temporary wooden bridge. It will be too low for boat traffic to pass underneath, so it will be taken down once he has his materials across. Traval's warehouse is on that side of the river, thank all the heavenly beings. Regarding housing, though it sounds unnatural, Pruitt is planning on having his men move into the loft area of the barn as soon as it is finished. That way, they will have a roof over their heads when the weather turns," my father answered. "But for others, it sounds like an inn should be constructed as soon as feasible. When I met with His Majesty, his people showed me another piece of land we owned in what was the center of town, one block away from the waterfront. There is enough property for an inn with a small stable."

"Do you want to be an innkeeper?" I asked my father mischievously.

"Majors and Minors, no!" he blurted. "I wouldn't mind being the landlord, though. As far as a constabulary, we can use some of the armsmen. I'll ask for volunteers. The magistrate question will need to wait for the king to appoint someone and probably for the inn to be built. So many things to consider, and we probably have only scratched the surface."

Our conversation was cut short by the arrival of Madame Hernandez. She selected a chair between my father and me. When she asked what we were discussing, my father started to tell her. Within a few minutes, I could tell I was no longer needed to continue the conversation. My father was waxing rhapsodic about the future, and Madame Hernandez was listening attentively. I rose quietly and stole away.

The following day, I decided to tour the work sites to the south. As my father said of the groups in the north, they were all engaged in removing the last full-grown trees from the road. Each one they pulled meant another few feet of progress. My last stop, after being gone a week, was Commerford, the river landing nearest to Easton.

Here, the crew had only four trees remaining. I rode to the landing. There was already a dock built using the existing stonework from over a hundred years earlier. A small three-pulley crane was anchored into the ground next to the dock. With it, two men could lift hundreds of pounds of weight.

The workers were busy with the barn. They were constructing the roof trusses. I watched, fascinated by how smoothly the men worked together. They were using a larger, five-pulley hoist to lift the heavy beams into place. The foreman explained that they would take the crane apart when they were finished.

"It won't be worth anything by then," he explained. "We built it with green wood from right here. It's already beginning to warp. It only needs to last a couple of days more."

One thing I noticed for the first time in Commerford was the raised bank on the east side of the river. The work crews had cleared it of brush and felled all the trees on the river side of the embankment. Where trees grew on the top, they cut them nearly flush to the surface but did not pull the stumps.

"What is this?" I asked.

"The towpath," the foreman replied.

Seeing that I did not understand, he continued, "Boats coming upriver can be towed or poled, depending on the time of year. Well, they can be towed anytime, I should say. In spring and early summer, the current will probably be too strong for poling. After that, until mid-autumn, poling is usually quicker."

"I'm sorry, but I still don't quite understand," I admitted.

"We yoke a pair of oxen and attach a line to the boat. They pull the boat upstream. The boatman's job, then, is to keep away from the bank. When the current is slower and the river less deep, the boatmen propel themselves by shoving with poles against the river bottom. It's quicker than the oxen but a goodly amount of work."

From Commerford, I headed back to the manor. The road was restored all the way to Easton. As Andy and I rode through fields of ripening grain, the hard-packed gravel surface showed only a few scars where tough-rooted weeds had been. Other than the heaps of sod lining either side, it was otherwise impossible to tell that the road had lain forgotten for over a hundred years.

After the guard at the gate let me in, I saw Fenwick sitting on the veranda with Lucy. I waved and proceeded to the stable. I saw Fenwick's attractive piebald horse, Davy, but I did not see my father's mount. George Collinwood met me and held Andy's reins while I slid out of the saddle. Most of the time, I groomed Andy myself, but with Fenwick visiting, I allowed George to take over. I slung my saddlebags over my shoulder and headed into the house.

No sooner was I through the rear entrance when Hazel met me, bobbed the slightest curtsy, and asked for my bags. I handed them over, and she trotted up the stairs with them. Continuing through the center hall, I reached the massive front door. It was open, and I could hear Fenwick speaking.

Stepping outside, I interrupted him. Lucy rose in her graceful way and came to embrace me. After sharing a quick kiss, I walked over to sit. As soon as I did, Lucy slid into my lap.

"Hello, Fenwick," I said. "What brings you to Easton?"

I was fearful he had an errand for the two of us from the king. More and more, though, his visits were purely social. If I were lucky, that would be his purpose today.

"Milord," he replied but then stopped when he saw my astonished expression.

Fenwick *always* made fun of my recent jump in station to the nobility. I was born my father's illegitimate son—a bastard—but the king changed that not quite a year and a half earlier. His Majesty declared me legitimate, made my father adopt me and name me as his heir, and gave me the title of Lord Oritur after one of the towns here in the eastern March. In all that time, Fenwick had *never* addressed me as "milord"—the standard honorific for my degree of noble rank.

Fenwick's address broke through my guard. I learned as a boy to keep my facial expressions under tight control. Only rarely did I allow my emotions to manifest, and it was usually Lucy who would get me to break my impassive façade.

"Milord," he began again, "I come on a personal matter of importance. Miss Traval has accepted my proposal of marriage. Her father and mother have consented to the match, and we plan to marry on the next summer solstice. Would you please do me the honor of standing with me as my bridesman?"

The tradition of a groom having bridesmen predates our written history. The story handed down is that bridesmen were friends of the groom. Supposedly, their job was to prevent the bride's father from apprehending the groom after he abducted the girl. Since the custom of kidnapping one's wife-to-be had also stopped long before the history books were written, no one knew if this were true.

Of course, the idea of teasing Fenwick immediately sprang to mind. Fenwick got the better of me so many times with his quick wit and sharp tongue. This was a golden opportunity but one I dismissed as quickly as it came to me.

"Mr. Fenwick," I replied in a serious tone, "I would be honored."

At my pronouncement, Lucy held her hand out to Fenwick, palm up. Fenwick reached into the money pouch attached to his belt and fished out a wheathead—our smallest denomination coin. He placed it in her palm.

"What's that about?" I asked.

"We had a bet," Fenwick sighed. "I lost."

"What was the bet?"

"That you could not resist the chance to get one over on Fenwick," Lucy said with a giggle. "He was convinced you would taunt him. I was equally sure you would respond with politesse and a measure of decorum. I won."

"The stakes weren't very much," I commented.

"The money doesn't matter," Fenwick said with a gloomy tone. "It's the losing."

"Doesn't it make you happy that I agreed?" I asked. "How many other bridesmen do you have?"

"You were my only choice," Fenwick said.

Here was another opportunity to skewer Fenwick with my wit, but Rose came out that very instant to inform us that lunch was ready. The moment was gone. Lucy saw the disappointment on my face and began to laugh.

"Rose," Lucy hollered when she quit chuckling, "we'll take lunch out here."

"Where is father?" I asked.

"He, Madame Hernandez, and Mr. Balboa have gone to Port Charles," Lucy said. "They want to check on Mr. Pruitt's progress."

"I don't think their presence will speed things along," I said.

"Mr. Balboa has been very eager," Lucy commented. "He does not have much to do here, and I believe he wants to earn his pay. It would not surprise me if he starts preparing the fields in some way."

"There are some saplings," I commented.

"Let's hope they keep him busy so your father can spend time with Madame Hernandez," Fenwick said.

Fenwick teasing me about my father's obvious attraction to Madame Hernandez almost brought a testy response from me, but in the middle of forming the words, another thought came to mind.

"What business did you say she owns in Aquileia?" I asked

"A restaurant."

"Do you think she could run an inn?" I asked.

"I don't see why not," Fenwick shrugged. "Why do you ask?"

"In talking with my father, we felt one of the businesses Port Charles will need most quickly is an inn," I said. "Until houses are built, there is nowhere for people to stay unless they are willing to live rough or ride back and forth to Hillstead. Father said we own some land in the town big enough for one, but we don't want to try to manage an inn along with everything else. We would be happy merely being landlords."

"Are you thinking of building an inn or merely renting the property?" Lucy asked.

"Majors and Minors!" I exclaimed mildly. "It was idle conjecture. I have no conception of what to do."

"Don't get excited, dear," Lucy cautioned. "An inn is an excellent idea, that's all. Not only will it be vital in the early days of re-establishing Port Charles, but once the harbor opens to regular traffic, it will surely be a profitable venture."

"Father and I thought so as well," I said. "Neither of us wants to be an innkeeper, though."

"I may know someone," Fenwick offered. "Not Madame Hernandez. Running an inn in a port town requires skills she does not possess."

"Keeping drunken sailors in line?" I asked.

"Exactly," Fenwick agreed. "If all you wish is to merely rent the land, I might be willing to make the investment in the building after I speak with the man I think would run it."

"Feel free," I said. "What sort of person is he?"

"He was a sailing master until a couple of years ago," Fenwick explained. "Rhetian pirates tried to take his ship. They did not succeed, but they did leave one of their axes in his knee. He ended up losing his lower leg, and his sailing days were done. He has been working for a chandler in Aurora, but I believe he might enjoy this far more."

After lunch, I asked Theo to have the maids prepare a hot bath for me. Fenwick, Lucy, and I chatted on the veranda, discussing a variety of things, none of which concerned Port Charles. Then Gladys announced my bath was ready.

After spending the week in the saddle, a hot bath was just the restorative my body craved. I eased myself into the water and sighed. My mind drifted in random directions, thinking not very deeply about anything.

I was entertaining an idle thought that my father might move to Port Charles. The remnants I saw of the largest dwelling on the property there indicated it was probably a stately home, built of wood instead of stone as the manor here in Easton was. If my father decided to hand management of the March over to me while he contented himself by playing gentleman farmer, I would not stand in his way.

Of course, so much depended on the damned nomads from over the eastern mountains. If we could end that threat, all kinds of possibilities would open up for both my father and me. It would benefit every resident of the March as well.

3

The month of Twiman arrived, heralding the denouement of summer and the beginning of the season of harvest. The last trees were removed from the old roads quickly when the crews which had been working on the river joined the militia and armsmen pulling stumps. Other crews engaged by the crown also cleared the road from Hillstead to Port Charles. By the beginning of the second week of the month, boats were already coming upriver, delivering the sacks that would be used to hold grain for shipment. All the members of the militia were released in plenty of time to bring in the crops.

My father spent a couple of weeks at Port Charles, overseeing the construction of the barn and Mr. Balboa's quarters. He returned and reported back that Traval's warehouse had been erected almost overnight. More interestingly, he told us that the work crews employed by the crown had devised a double drawbridge to cross the Pheas River in town. The design of it was such that a man on each side could easily raise and lower it.

I took some small journeys to the river and soon found every river landing bustling with activity. At one of my first visits, to the town of Quinn's Ford, the mayor shared that there was a shortage of wagons to carry the sacks of grain to the landing—another unexpected obstacle. Fortunately, a spirit of cooperation prevailed, and neighbors helped one another get their grain to the landings.

Returning from Commerford, my sight of the road in front of me vanished. Instead, from a distance and great height, I suddenly saw two men on horseback accompanied by a woman driving a two-wheeled cart. They were climbing the nearer riverbank at the foot of the eastern mountains. Shasha, the sparrow hawk who bonded with me, was still keeping watch. I went within myself and found the reddish-brown node that connected us.

People are coming.

"So I see," I replied to her in my mind.

Shasha glided closer to them. As she neared, I noticed the two men were better dressed than the warriors I was used to seeing. Instead of a tunic and trousers made of rough homespun, theirs appeared to be of tightly woven cloth. The leather vests on their chests were embellished with silver studs, and the leather itself was tooled in ornate designs. The woman on the cart, however, was clad in homespun like the warriors wore. Based only on the appearance of the two men, I guessed they were probably significant in the nomads' hierarchy.

There were two water barrels on the cart, along with other baggage. The woman was fair-skinned, as most people in the March were, while the men were the more weathered shade common to the nomads. I wondered if she was a captive, taken from the March during the nomads' successful raids two years earlier.

"Thank you," I communicated to Shasha. "I think this will be important."

I thought as much. Now you have seen, I must go. I may not hunt here, and I am hungry.

With that, the connection between us was broken. With my knees, I urged Andy to a trot, wanting to return to the manor as quickly as I could. I hoped my father would be there. I wanted him with me to meet these visitors. Whatever the purpose of their journey was, my father was Earl of the March. Any negotiations must include him.

Arriving at the stable, I saw my father's horse. I handed Andy to Tom Collinwood. In my haste to find my father, I even left my saddlebags for someone else to bring in—something I almost never did.

I found my father in the study with Lucy. From what I overheard the last few steps, they were planning for the harvest fair this year. The arrival of the people from across the eastern mountains might interfere.

"Sorry to interrupt," I said somewhat breathlessly. "I was on my way back from Commerford when I saw some people coming from the east."

"Your familiar?" my father inquired.

I nodded.

"How many and where?" my father asked, immediately concerned.

"Only three—two men and a woman," I replied. I explained where they were, how they were dressed, and my guess that the woman was a captive.

"They are probably bringing her to translate," Lucy remarked.

"I hope so," my father said. "In all these years, I don't think I know anything in their language except the curses and insults they've hurled at us."

"Maybe you will finally learn what they mean," Lucy retorted.

"Why would they be coming?" my father asked, ignoring Lucy's quip.

"It probably has something to do with the losses we've inflicted on them the last two campaigns. They probably want to complain," I added snarkily.

"Let's hope they want a truce and aren't coming to threaten retaliation," my father said.

"Either way, we should take them to the capital," I said. "His Majesty will want to be involved."

"I'll write him immediately," my father said as he withdrew a sheet of paper from his desk. "If I get it in the post before tomorrow morning, a letter will arrive a few days before we do. I doubt Mark would be pleased to simply have us appear without warning."

Quill already in his hand, he bent to the task. Lucy stood. With her uncanny grace, it seemed as though she flowed upward from the settee. With a tilt of her head, she indicated I should accompany her.

"We were discussing the Harvest Fair," she said quietly.

"I know," I said. "I overheard as I came in."

"Should we still plan for it?" she asked, a faint line of concern appearing on her forehead.

"It seems unfair for the burden to fall entirely upon you again this year," I said. "I have a feeling these visitors may consume all of my time for the next few weeks."

"Having done almost everything in organizing last year's," she said with a hint of cheek, "the second time around will be less trouble. Besides, I kept notes. I'll be fine."

The previous year I had been called away to participate in an exchange of rare stones between our government and the Grand Vizier of Scaramouche. Scaramouche possessed some gemstones of a material known as tan-zyan, and wished to trade for some electrum, of which King Mark possessed an abundance and the Grand Vizier owned none. The importance of the tan-zyan stones was not their beauty. Indeed, they resembled sapphires, only slightly duller.

The reason we wished to acquire them is that tan-zyan was a conduit for the asomatous energy Fenwick and I could access through our connection with the Goddess Bellona. Having a ring made with this stone allowed us to draw off and store this energy in diamonds placed in the pommels of our swords. We could draw upon that power at another time when we needed it. Without those stones and the ability to store this numinous power, Fenwick and I would have been killed not long ago when we confronted two assassins who possessed our same affinities with Bellona.

This year, instead of the Grand Vizier of Scaramouche, it appeared as though the nomads from the east would keep me busy during the month leading up to the fair. The mountain range was at least a five-day ride due east from where I was in Easton. It took two days for a rider to reach the desert, then three days or more to reach a river at the foot of the mountains. The nomads came from somewhere on the other side of those peaks.

For hundreds of years, predating any written history of the region, the nomads had appeared in the middle of every summer. They generally brought between four and five hundred men, setting up camp on the east side of the Patker River. From there, they raided the towns and villages of the March until the first snow of winter stuck on the ground.

If they managed to break through the defenses, they would sack the town. Until two years ago, this hardly ever happened. Strangely enough, beyond the rare breakthrough, they caused little damage. They left the crops undisturbed in the fields.

Even so, the necessity of protecting the people of the March from rapine and pillage consumed a great deal of time and attention and carried a large financial burden. My father, and my other Barry ancestors before him, managed to keep the depredations of these nomads under control to the point that the king had no real knowledge of the burden it caused. Three years ago, my stepmother nearly bankrupted the March, indulging her own spending sprees and those of her irresponsible and spoiled sons. My father reduced the number of armsmen by a third and cut the pay of the remainder because of the financial shortfall.

That summer, the nomads ravaged three of our towns. They killed all the men and took everything of value—including some of the women. These calamities brought the Eastern March to the king's attention. He summoned my father and my two half-brothers and delivered an ultimatum—that they had six months to show they could defend the March properly. My half-brothers responded to this challenge by complaining to their mother, who thought I was the king's choice to succeed my father. She hired an assassin to kill me—the bastard son.

The king, as it turned out, was not planning on having me replace my father at that time. The assassin hired by my stepmother, Fenwick, nearly succeeded, however—twice. In our second meeting, I managed, with great difficulty, to subdue and capture him. I was not terribly pleased when I learned the king allowed Fenwick to live, provided he fulfilled the duties assigned to him by the king—he became the Royal Assassin, as it were.

Not long after that, other events, unrelated to the March, transpired that resulted in the king decreeing that I was hereby legitimately born, officially adopted by my father, and was now his legitimate heir. My stepmother and two half-brothers met untimely ends, though not before one attacked me at a religious festival in full view of thousands. Fenwick, on the orders of the king, arranged for them to suffer fatal accidents.

Following the king's decision, I returned to the March a year and a half ago and took command of our armsmen. Each of our border towns was walled and protected by militia, but the armsmen were necessary to break up the nomads' attacks and drive them away. Without the armsmen, the greater numbers of the nomads would prevail.

Despite being outnumbered at the beginning of the campaigning season, I had been able to anticipate the attacks mounted by the horsemen from across the mountains. My approach was aggressive—perhaps even reckless at times—but our unexpected ferocity yielded excellent results. Later that season, when we restored the number of armsmen to previous levels, I led a night raid on the nomads' camp. I would guess only a hundred of them survived after that, and they returned from whence they came immediately—several months earlier than usual.

This past spring, I studied the possible approaches available to the nomads. Aided by heavy cavalry supplied by the crown and commanded by Prince Albert, we ambushed them and left none of the invaders alive. I had been anticipating that the nomads would have returned in greater numbers this year because of what took place the year before, but there were about a third fewer.

While no one knew for sure why the nomads attacked every year, my father and grandfather suspected it was some sort of rite of passage for their young men. From the diminished numbers this year, and judging by the youth of the corpses, I believed that might indeed be the case. It also influenced me to believe that the population of the nomadic nation or tribe was not much more than a hundred thousand people. When the visitors arrived, I supposed we might learn a great deal more.

My father had finished his letter. He came out of the study and called for me. When I came down the stairs, he took me by the elbow.

"Ride with me to post this," he said. "We need to discuss how we will handle these uninvited guests."

Tom and George Collinwood, our grooms, quickly saddled our horses. We swung up into the saddles and walked down to the gate. My father waited until we were clear before speaking.

"Should we ride out to meet them east of Oritur?" he said. "And where?"

"The best place is probably where we laid the ambush for them a few months ago," I said. "If you don't like the idea of sleeping on the ground for a night, we can wait for them in Oritur. That will probably be the first village they approach."

"On second thought, I would rather have them come to us instead of going out to them," my father said. "We should not appear too eager, I think."

I shrugged. He made a good point. Besides, meeting them that far out would raise the question of how we knew they were coming. It would be better not to become mired in that topic. Even meeting them in Oritur might provoke curiosity. I mentioned it to my father.

"Hm," he mused. "I like that even better. Let them find their way to us. Yes. Still, damme, I'm anxious to know what they want."

"I said it as a joke, but I'm honestly beginning to believe they might be coming to complain," I said.

My father looked incredulous, then barked a short laugh.

When we returned to the manor, my father found Lucy, and we began discussing the Harvest Fair. As before, we would hold it near the end of the month of Haustman. The location would be slightly different, as we anticipated this year's would be larger, so we needed more space.

Over the next five days, while we were waiting for the nomads to arrive, my father showed a side of himself I did not remember seeing as a boy. As with the beginning of the road projects, he showed he possessed a gift for organization. He had already arranged new assignments for the armsmen. Some were sent to the river landings to provide security for the traders stationed there. Each trader's agent had chests of money with which to pay the farmers. Though banditry was uncommon in the March, these traders might be targets too tempting for someone to ignore. A few men were posted to Port Charles. The remainder he pressed into service to help with preparing for the fair.

In the midst of this, we received a letter and a proposal from Fenwick, asking for a lease on our property near the center of Port Charles. He intended to build an inn and wished to get the roof up before the winter set in. Fenwick told us he intended to visit for the Harvest Fair, bringing Julienne Traval and the man he planned to have manage the inn, Toby Penfrew. My father and I agreed this was a good idea, but we did not have a clue what to charge for a lease.

During this period, Shasha kept me apprised of the progress of our visitors. She wasn't following them. Instead, she flew overhead occasionally and, when she saw them, connected with me.

I would have been interested to see their reaction when they encountered the remains of the large funeral pyre in which we cremated the remains of the three hundred men we killed in the ambush five months earlier. Bones don't burn. Skeletons of men and horses were left when the fire burnt out. With only a thin layer of soil on top of the rock below, we could not have buried them.

They reached Oritur on the fifth day, moving a bit slower than I anticipated. I warned my father and Lucy to expect our visitors the next evening. Over dinner, we discussed how to treat them.

"Should we offer them dinner and rooms for the night?" Lucy asked.

"I've fought against them my entire adult life. Generations of our family have done the same. Welcoming their arrival is simply not something I am prepared to do," my father said. "I will not have them under my roof."

"Even if they come as supplicants, begging for clemency?" Lucy asked.

"I doubt very much that they will adopt that posture," he said. "If they do, any pardon will need to come from His Majesty—not from me."

"Earlier today, I warned the Tawny Lion to keep two rooms free tomorrow evening," I said. "Like father, I do not feel comfortable inviting them into our home. After we take them to the capital and learn more about the purpose of their visit along the way, perhaps my feelings will be less cold toward them. For now, a cool reception is the best I feel we can offer."

My father, Lucy, and I were all distracted the next day by the impending arrival. We accomplished little of note. I knew from Shasha that the nomads spent the night outside of Oritur. They did not attempt to enter the town, probably fearing a harsh reception.

From Oritur to the manor was a full day's ride. I wondered if the woman they brought was indeed a captive who knew the way to Easton. We would find out when they arrived, I supposed.

As the afternoon wore on, I gave up even pretending to try to work. It was a pleasant fall day, and I moved to the veranda. My father joined me not long after. Together we waited in companionable silence. Lucy tasked Gladys with bringing us each a mug of fresh cider, then sat with us shortly afterward.

"The two of you could not appear more different in mood," she commented. "Father, you look fierce. Caz, you look hopeful."

"I have defended the March against these bandits from the time I came of age," my father hissed. "Years upon years, my life has been consumed by them. They have killed friends—good men I have known, who were husbands and fathers. Not long ago, they killed hundreds when they took Alessa, Gambion, and East Norton. Things have gone against them for the first time I know of in these last two years, thanks to you, Caz. And they dare to come calling!"

"Father, I cannot gainsay what you've experienced," I said. "It is a tragedy I have known about all my life, but I did not have to live mired in it as you did. We have inflicted heavy losses on them recently, and what's more, you have King

Mark's promise of assistance in the future. I see the possibility that this long nightmare may end. Majors and Minors! Surely the Gods are smiling upon us if what I hope comes to pass."

"We'll see," my father grumbled. "We'll see."

4

The bells in town rang five o'clock not long before Jon Sinchak came huffing and puffing up from his post at the gate of the manor. He caught sight of us on the veranda. I could see his sigh of relief when he realized he would not need to run all the way to the house.

"There are three people at the gate, milord," he called. "Two men and a woman. The men look like nomads. The woman looks like one of us."

"Send them up," my father replied.

"Lucy, have one of the girls fetch the armsmen," he asked. "They need to wear breastplates and helmets, and to bring their swords."

The two men were on horseback while the woman drove the small cart. They stopped about fifteen yards short of the veranda. The woman set the brake on the cart and slid out, striding forward in front of the two men. One of the two began speaking in the bird-like tones of the nomad's language.

"We wish to treat with the warrior-mage," the woman translated.

"What's your name, child?" my father asked in a kindly tone. "You look familiar."

"My name is—used to be—Patsy Campbell, milord," she responded shyly.

"Doug Campbell's wife?" father asked.

"Yes, milord."

"Come closer, Patsy," he said.

She shuffled forward a couple of steps, clearly fearful of the two men and what their reaction might be. My father glared at them, almost daring them to object. They met his gaze coolly.

"Would you like to see your husband? I can arrange it," my father said.

Patsy twisted her hands together in worry.

"Don't be frightened," my father said. "They cannot harm you now."

"I—well, he— I'm not the same woman I was before, milord," she said quietly. "They've— He might not want me."

"Patsy, I've known Doug longer than you have," my father said. "I know he has not taken up with anyone else since you've been gone. Whatever happened to you is certainly not your fault."

"Milord, you don't understand," she said morosely. "I had a child. A boy. He's still with them."

The look on my father's face was frightening. I never saw him so angry—as though he would explode. The muscles in his jaw clenched, and I watched his ears turn red.

"Then they will need to bring the boy to us," my father said tensely. "These men with you—they are some of the leaders of the nomads?"

"The one is the head man's brother," Patsy said. "The other is a cousin. Both are important men among their people."

"I see," my father said. "Tell them the warrior-mage they seek is my son, but he is not the lord of these lands. I am the Earl of the March, and they must treat with me."

Patsy turned to the two and began explaining my father's instruction that they needed to speak with him and not me. The tone of the discussion was shrill. Patsy pointed to me, then to my father.

While the argument continued, the six armsmen who would spend the winter in the quarters above our stable appeared on the veranda behind us. All six were wearing breastplates and helmets. Their swords were buckled on at the waist, and all six had their hands on the grips. The two nomads saw them appear, and the argument they were having with Patsy died down.

"Milord, I explained to them the way things work here in Aquileia," Patsy said. "They did not want to speak with you. You are known to them—for many years. In all that time, you never accomplished what your son did. That is why they want to speak to him. I told them that what they want is impossible according to the laws and customs of Aquileia. They finally conceded that they will deal with you."

My father's eyes were glittering with rage, but his voice was controlled as he replied, "Tell them they have dishonored me and angered my son. There will be no further conversation this evening. Do you remember the Tawny Lion, Patsy?"

"Yes, milord."

"There should be two rooms set aside for them," father said. "The armsmen men will accompany you to the inn. After you help these two arrange their lodging for the night, you are welcome to return here. The armsmen will make sure you are allowed to leave to join us for dinner and to spend the night."

"Milord, it will make them very angry if I leave," Patsy said.

"I don't give a good goddamn about how it makes them feel!" my father thundered. "I care about you, Patsy. Your life surely has been like being in one of the seven hells since they took you. I don't want you to spend another minute under their thumbs."

"Milord, I—"

"Tell them they have dishonored me, and our conversation for the evening is over," my father said.

Patsy translated. The two men were clearly angry. One nudged his horse forward in Patsy's direction.

"Stop!" my father bellowed, getting the man's attention.

"Tell them there are rooms arranged for them. You will help translate for them to arrange this, then you will return here. The armsmen will escort you."

As she relayed the words, my father gestured to the armsmen. They advanced and surrounded Patsy. The two nomads were furious. One began responding in a harsh tone.

I decided to put an end to this disagreement. They came to see the warrior-mage. I would show him to them. I climbed down the steps, placing myself in front of my father.

Within myself, I found my connection to the Goddess Bellona. Touching my ring with the tan-zyan gem to the diamond in the hilt of my sword, I allowed the asomatous energy I had stored to flow into me without restriction. At the same time, I opened my connection to Bellona completely. My body seemed instantly larger—though I knew it was some sort of magical illusion. Otherwise, my clothes would have ripped apart. Incredible strength filled my entire body. My nerves thrummed with exhilaration.

The nomad who was speaking stopped with his mouth still open, struck mute by my changed appearance. Their horses began backing away, wanting to twist their heads and bolt. If they had not been well-trained, they would have been halfway to the gate already. The other nomad quickly held a hand up in a gesture of compliance and stammered something.

"It will be as you say," Patsy translated for him after she recovered from her own shock at my changed appearance.

Upon hearing that, I severed my tie with Bellona. The illusion of my immense size dropped away, though the singing of my nerves and muscles took several moments to fade. The two nomads, the armsmen, and Patsy, were all still slightly stunned at what they had just witnessed.

Patsy returned riding in front of one of the armsmen less than an hour later. My father met them and asked if any of the men would volunteer to ride to Quinn's Ford the next day to summon Doug Campbell. All six raised their hands.

"Work it out amongst yourselves," my father said. "Chances are Lord Oritur and I will set out to escort these visitors to the capital in the morning. Doug will need to catch up to us."

Lucy took Patsy into the manor. A bath was already prepared for her. Rose, one of the maids, was of a similar size and shape to Patsy, and Lucy borrowed some clean clothes from her for Patsy to wear.

My father asked me into the study. After I entered, he closed the door. He poured us both a glass of sherry and sat down heavily.

"Over dinner, we'll ask her what their intent is," he said. "Majors and Minors, they brought out my choler! I have more than half a mind to send them packing."

"I will admit I am surprised as well," I said. "Whatever they came here seeking, they are certainly not approaching things in a conciliatory manner. Don't send them away just yet, though, father. If you do, our hope of permanently ending their attacks goes with them."

"You're right, of course," he said with a sigh. "As unpleasant as this might be, let's get them to the capital. That may take some of the temper out of them."

Lucy appeared in the doorway. "Dinner will be served soon," she said. "Wash up."

When we finished scrubbing our hands, we found Lucy and Patsy in the dining room. Patsy was wearing one of Rose's uniforms. It fit reasonably well.

The immense table was set for only the four of us. The thirty-two empty chairs stretched down its length on either side. My father sat at the head, of course. Lucy placed Patsy at his side, and Lucy sat closest to her. I was opposite Lucy, on my father's right. Gladys brought in the first course.

Patsy's eyes were wide, and she looked uncomfortable. Even if she was never captured by the nomads, sitting to dine beside the Earl of the March was quite a jump from her previous experience. With what had to have been a difficult life the last two years, I knew she was overwhelmed.

"Patsy, don't be nervous or frightened," I said softly. "You're among friends. And I promise we won't fuss about manners and such. We are happy to have you with us."

"Thank you, sir," she said stiffly.

"Oh!" Lucy said. "You have not been introduced. Patsy, this is Casimir FitzDuncan, Lord Oritur, my husband."

"You said he was your son, milord," Patsy commented. "But he's not either of the two I remember."

"Caz was born before I was married, Patsy," my father said as a blush crept up from his collar.

"Ohh," Patsy said, recognizing the awkwardness of his confession but still not quite understanding.

"A great deal has changed here in Easton since—" Lucy began, then faltered as she searched for the right words. "Since you've been gone."

"And Lady Easton and the other two?" Patsy asked.

"No longer on this earth," my father said. "By the king's decree and my own wishes, Caz is now my legitimate son and heir, and a full member of the Barry clan."

"And you're the mage they came seeking, obviously?" Patsy asked. "What you did out front—"

"I am."

Patsy almost involuntarily made the warding gesture common throughout the kingdom, the tips of her middle fingers touching, with the ends of her index fingers on the second knuckle of the other hand's middle finger. She caught herself doing it and hid her hands under the table. Lucy chuckled.

"It's alright, Patsy," she said. "Nothing to be afraid of."

Noticing Patsy's discomfort, my father weighed in.

"If you don't mind my prying, Patsy, what do these nomads hope to accomplish from this journey?" he asked.

"They are powerful unhappy, milord," she said. "You killed more 'n most of 'em they sent last summer, and this summer, you slaughtered 'em all. One of the few who survived a year and a half ago came back and spread the word that it was the work of a warrior-mage. That's you, innit?"

I nodded.

"They don't think that's fair," she said. "Course, they dint ask me. I always heard 'All's fair in love and war.' They come making war, they need to face whatever."

"So, it's acceptable for them to come sack our towns, but not for us to kill them?" my father asked, growing slightly heated in his tone.

Patsy nodded. "Like I said, they din't ask me. A few weeks back, when they found out what happened, they were a might vexed. Me and the other women they took were having a hard time keeping the smiles off our faces at first, but then they started taking it out on us."

My father's anger was about to bubble over. Lucy saw it. She tried to relieve some of the pressure.

"What kind of people are they? How many are there? What sort of lives do they lead?" Lucy asked.

"They're simple folk," Patsy explained. "Where they live is a grassy plain that goes as far as you can see. They have some small villages up and down a river where they grow some vegetables, but mostly they herd cattle and some sheep for wool. The women and children stay in the villages, in huts they make out of the sod. The men come and go, taking turns tendin' the livestock and keepin' an eye on the neighbors."

"The neighbors?" I asked.

"There are other groups just like them, further east," Patsy said. "They try to steal each other's cattle and horses."

"How many people are there?" my father asked.

"I don't rightly know," Patsy replied with a shrug. "I only saw a couple of villages. They're about a league apart, along both sides of the river. Don't know how many they are. Could be fifty? Could be a hundred? I dunno. After the news came back that you killed everyone they sent over this summer, a few of the important men rode off for a couple of days. My master is the head man's brother. His name is Bynar. He returned with his cousin, Polim. They collected me and we set off."

Gladys came in and took away the soup bowls from the first course. She returned with some bread and cheese. She also brought cider.

"Oh, praise all the heavenly beings," Patsy murmured. "Bread!"

"They don't have bread?" Lucy asked.

"Not like this they don't," Patsy said. "They make hard little loaves of barley bread and this other flat stuff that about breaks your teeth. Oh! And cider! They don't have cider. Got cheese, though."

"And they are coming to complain?" my father inquired, trying to nudge the conversation back to what he wanted to know.

"Mhm," Patsy responded, her mouth full. She held up her finger, indicating she had more to say but wanted to finish chewing first. "They want things the way they used to be."

I could tell my father was angered, so I intervened.

"Why do they come all this way?" I asked. "If they have neighbors they fight with, why travel so far to bring war upon us?"

"Please don't take offense, milord," Patsy said, "but they don't see you as being as threatening as their neighbors. They send the youngsters this way to give 'em a taste of fighting. When they war against the neighbors, they tell me it's thousands of both sides."

"Do they treat the neighbors the same?" Lucy asked. "Taking captives?"

"It works both ways," Patsy said. "They don't fight big wars against the neighbors but every five years or so. Every summer, there are raids and small tussles, though. If the neighbors get to a village, they take the women and kill the men, same as what happened to us."

"Well, we intend to slaughter every last one of them that comes near," my father said in a steely tone. "The king himself has pledged to send whatever troops we need. He had no idea until recently how much of a drain it has been to fend these nomads off every year."

"Well, they won't like that," Patsy said.

5

After dinner, my father quickly sat down in the study. When I asked what he was doing, he held up his hand. When he finished writing, he looked up.

"We are going to bring four of the armsmen with us to the capital," he said. "I have no intention of providing those people with an opportunity to steal Patsy away again. That means I need to move others around to handle the duties I assigned to the four who will join us. I don't think our visit with His Majesty will take more than a day or two. We should return in plenty of time to help prepare for the Harvest Fair, but I assigned certain tasks to the armsmen. I will not ask Lucy to cover for their absence."

"Should I expect the armsmen to stay at our house in the city?" I asked.

"Majors and Minors, no!" my father retorted, "They can stay in the barracks with the Castle Shield. Might do them some good, associating with the king's own troops."

"What about the nomads?"

"His Majesty is better equipped to entertain foreign visitors," my father said with a sly smile. "We will need to explain about Patsy, though."

We collected the two men from the Tawny Lion the next morning. Both wore unhappy expressions. The one Patsy called Bynar began complaining as soon as he saw her. Patsy did not repeat his specific verbiage.

"He says dinner and breakfast were difficult because they don't speak the language," she reported with a shrug.

The first argument was over where we were going.

"Patsy, we are going to the capital and will see His Majesty," my father instructed.

She translated and reported their response was, "Why?"

"Explain to them as best you can that the king rules all these lands, and that lords like me serve him," my father said.

"I told them what you said in terms they could understand," Patsy reported after a lengthy discussion. "Their people are spread over a broad area and have sub-chiefs who manage things on a more local level. It is less structured than Aquileia, I think. The sub-chiefs all need to give hostages to the overall leader."

"Hostages?" my father asked.

"The sub-chief must send his oldest son and daughter to live with the leader's entourage," Patsy explained. "It is a way of keeping the sub-chiefs loyal. Otherwise, the leader kills the children. Not that they are well-treated—their status is almost as low as mine."

"What if the sub-chief has no children?" I asked.

"Then he cannot be the sub-chief," Patsy said.

The next disagreement came regarding the two-wheeled cart and whether to bring it. Patsy ended the argument by admitting she was not very skilled at riding a horse, even though we had provided her a gentle mount, and that she would be more comfortable driving the cart. I arranged with the innkeeper to return the horse to the manor later.

When we started off, the four armsmen with us positioned themselves around Patsy. My father took the lead, and I rode alongside him. The arrangement discouraged further conversation with Bynar and Polim. He later admitted to me that he did this on purpose.

"Any substantive discussions we have with these *people*," he said, "will include His Majesty. I do not intend to speak with them any more than is absolutely necessary."

Arriving at Commerford, we saw a riverboat being loaded with sacks of grain. We stopped and chatted briefly with the agent of the trading house. Hawkins & Company managed this landing.

"My storehouse is still quite full, though not up to the rafters any longer," the agent said with a grin. "We were almost overwhelmed at first, then worked out a delivery schedule with the farmers. The in-gathering will be complete by the end of Haustman. Before the month of Gorman is over, we plan to have emptied the storehouse here. Otherwise, we run the risk of the river icing over."

"Business is good, then," my father commented.

"Well, they tell me that every bit of produce I collect is already sold elsewhere," the agent said. "Good fortune passes all along the river. We've already shipped enough to have filled the storehouse once more in addition to what you see now, and I'll collect that much more before we are finished."

He showed us his storehouse—a large barn-type building—and it was indeed comfortably full. He had three young men, in their mid-teens from the look of it, moving the material from the storehouse to the boat. They loaded a wagon with the sacks of grain, then a mule pulled the wagon to the river. Next to the river was a three-pulley crane. A rope net was spread on the ground, and the youths piled the sacks on it, then gathered the corners of the net and attached them to a hook on the crane. Using the mule to pull on the rope, the crane lifted the bundle, and the youths swung it over the boat and lowered it gently. The boat crew then quickly moved the sacks off the net while the boys returned the wagon to the storehouse for another load.

I must admit, the amount of material in the storehouse struck me. Knowing that there were fourteen other landings like this one, and the amount of material already shipped from here and still to come—it was staggering. And this was only the first season that farmers would have increased production. With the success this year, I imagined all of them would plant even more next summer.

Bynar and Polim were peppering Patsy with questions. She translated what the agent said and asked a few questions of my father to clarify. When she had answered the nomads' questions, she had many for us.

"When did this happen?" she asked.

My father told her about the project of reopening the river and Port Charles. Though Patsy was married to an armsman, she grew up a farmer's daughter. As a result, she understood the importance of restoring the river and port, especially in light of grain shortages elsewhere in the kingdom.

"I would imagine every farmer in the March who was smart enough to plan ahead will be pretty happy right now," she said.

"It has increased prices for bread and basics here in the March," my father admitted. "In the past, our usual surplus kept costs down locally, but now that extra is being sent away. I think the amount of money brought into the March will more than offset that minor inconvenience."

Our nomad visitors were quiet the rest of the day. I think they were beginning to realize that the kingdom of Aquileia was bigger and more powerful than just the March. At least, I hoped that was what they were thinking.

Alas, their thoughts returned to what brought them here by dinner time. We arrived at the first town on the journey and found an inn with three rooms available. My father and I shared one, the two nomads another, and Patsy took the third. The four armsmen would sleep in the stable loft. They assured me they would be quite comfortable, and that a cozy bed of straw was greatly preferable to the cold, hard ground.

At dinner, Bynar and Polim were grumpy. The innkeeper told us roast mutton was the menu for the evening. Patsy translated for them. Both the nomads scowled and muttered.

"They do not eat sheep," she explained. "Sheep are for wool. Mutton is only served to their captives."

"Then they can go hungry, for all I care," my father replied.

Patsy translated. Bynar then began speaking, glaring at my father as he did. He went on for a couple of minutes.

"I blooded myself twenty summers ago against you and your people, old man," Patsy translated. "The best you could do was hold us off. Three summers ago, we routed you, taking three of your villages. Send away your warrior-mage, and we will see how long your haughty arrogance lasts."

She added, "There was more that he said, but that is the heart of it."

I expected my father to kindle into rage. He did not. Clearly, he had prepared himself for this.

"The defeats you suffered these last two summers have stung, haven't they?" my father responded with a smile. "Otherwise, you would not have troubled yourself to journey to us. You want things to return to the way they were, don't you? That will not happen. Whether my son is here to oppose you does not matter. The king, my lord, has pledged that you will never again trouble the

March as you have for years upon years. We are going to meet him so he can deliver that message to you himself."

After Patsy relayed this to them, the two men looked at one another. Bynar was silent. Polim was the first to speak.

"Why? What has changed? Why now, after so many generations?"

"Because until three summers ago, the king—and the others before him— were not aware of how much effort we spent in keeping you at bay," my father said. "Up to that point, we held you off, as you said. My failure brought it to his attention."

"And he sent you the warrior-mage," Bynar sneered.

"The warrior-mage is my son."

"Why has he not been present before?" Polim asked. "Was he a hostage to your ruler?"

My father now looked uncomfortable. There was no reason to share our unpleasant family history with them. I decided to step in.

"We do not take or furnish hostages in Aquileia," I said. "Besides, what does that matter? I am here now, and here I will stay. Know this—whatever force you send over the mountains and across the river, I will destroy utterly."

"Even if we came by the tens of hundreds?" Bynar asked in a threatening tone.

"Then the piles of your people's scorched bones would be left as an even more ominous warning to any who would try in the future," I said.

When Patsy translated this for them, I could see the reaction on their faces. Patsy had told us that seeing the remains of men and horses that survived the pyres shocked them. Seven hells! It bothered me when I saw it.

"But why now?" Bynar asked.

"This entire land," my father said, sweeping his arm around in an expansive gesture, "is our mighty king's to rule. I, and my family before me, have governed our portion of it on his behalf. He has many other lords who do the same elsewhere throughout Aquileia. It is because of my failure three summers ago that he learned how much effort we spent in fending off your annual attacks. The king has more important things for us to do than dealing with a bunch of flea-ridden nomads from across the eastern mountains."

"Even if we ride with tens of hundreds?" Polim remarked.

"Then the king will supply us with tens and tens of hundreds to destroy you," I said.

"And my son, the warrior-mage, will lead them," my father added. "Your people will be ruined—a carcass for your neighbors to pick apart like jackals and vultures."

The remainder of the journey did not bring further discussion. As we neared the capital, the towns through which we passed grew larger, their streets cobbled, the dwellings visible symbols of widespread prosperity. That made an impression on the two nomads as much as the threats we delivered. On the afternoon of the third day of our ride from Easton, we saw the city of Aquileia as we approached. Realizing that there were several times greater population in the one city than the number of their entire people must have been sobering for the two.

We rode up to the city walls and through the gate. Once inside, I could tell the two men were trying not to gawp at the size of the city. It became more difficult the further we went.

"I've never been here myself," Patsy admitted as we rode, speaking loudly to be heard over the rattle of her cart's wheels on the cobblestones, "and I am amazed at how big it is. Bynar and Polim must be stunned."

Even more impressive than the size of the city, the way the king chose to meet them must have been even more difficult to grasp. Obviously alerted to our impending arrival, the king mustered the two thousand members of the Castle Shield—his personal troops—to meet us. The small square in front of the bridge, which connected the castle to the rest of the city, was jammed full.

The soldiers and horses were in full armor, gleaming in the late afternoon sun. The long lances were pointing to the sky, their butts in the rests connected to the stirrups. There was a small passage between the men, forcing us to proceed one at a time.

Once through the cordon, the sergeant-at-arms asked us to dismount. Patsy translated his instruction to the nomads as my father, the armsmen, and I slid from out from our saddles. Patsy climbed from the cart, surreptitiously rubbing her bottom, probably made somewhat numb from driving an unsprung cart over the cobbled streets.

A squad of fully armored foot soldiers led us across the bridge to the castle. Our armsmen stayed behind. When we reached the far end, the seneschal instructed us to surrender our weapons. While Patsy was translating this, Bynar and Polim saw my father and me complying, unbuckling our swords and handing them to one of the soldiers. With great reluctance, the two nomads surrendered the jeweled daggers they wore in their belts.

With weapons handed over, the seneschal then led us into the castle. From the entrance he used, I knew he was taking us to the throne room. Two more soldiers in full armor were at the doors. When we arrived, they swung them open.

The throne room was massive. The floor was black-and-white squares of marble. The ceiling was so high you almost expected to see clouds. On either side were statues of previous kings and their queens. At the far end, atop a raised platform, were the massive thrones of the king and queen.

King Mark and Queen Liliana were wearing their full regalia. Scarlet robes with ermine trim were draped over their shoulders. Heavy crowns of gold, encrusted with large jewels, sat on their heads. It was a sight designed to impress, and it did not fail in that regard.

My father and I approached and went down on one knee at the base of the thirteen steps of the platform on which the thrones rested. Patsy stopped a few paces behind us and went to both knees, bowing her head. Bynar and Polim did not know what to do. Polim began to kneel, but Bynar stopped him. The king observed them with a cool, detached air.

"Rise, Lord Easton and Lord Oritur," the king commanded.

"And you, too, my child," he added to Patsy, seeing that she had not moved. "You translate for them?"

"Yes, Your Majesty," she replied.

"You are from the March," the king commented. "Were you taken captive?"

"Yes, Your Majesty," she said. "Three summers ago."

"You will be their captive no longer," the king said.

"We have already informed them, Your Majesty," my father said.

King Mark smiled. "Good," he grunted.

"Your name, child?" he asked.

"Patsy—Patsy Campbell, Your Majesty," Patsy uttered.

"Patsy, we will allow you to assist these two until we have them situated in their quarters for the night. After that time, we will want to speak with you. You will dine with us this evening."

"Yes, Your Majesty."

"Please tell them we will have them taken to their quarters. Warn them that they will be under guard. We will see to their needs but do not wish to speak with them until morning," the king stated.

Patsy translated. When she finished, a page appeared to lead them away. In the shadows, waiting for them, I saw Fenwick. He followed them as they departed down a corridor.

Once the nomads left, the king and queen stood. Several other servants appeared and began taking away their regal vestments. Queen Liliana let out an audible sigh as the heavy crown was lifted from her head. When the king gave her a sharp look, she shrugged.

"It's heavy," she commented.

"So is this one," the king stated, "and you don't hear me complain."

"That's because your neck is stronger from having to support the weight of your thick skull all the time," Liliana quipped.

The king laughed. With a smile, he offered his arm to his wife, and they departed. The seneschal indicated my father and I were to follow.

We arrived at a cozy sitting room after a brief walk. A servant offered us a glass of wine. After checking to make sure the king and queen were also drinking, my father and I accepted. Their Majesties sat on a sofa, and the king gestured for us to sit as well.

"Tell us what has transpired with these two so far," the king asked.

It did not take long for my father to share what had taken place over the past few days. Both the king and queen nodded appropriately at different spots in the narrative. The only sour note was when we informed them that Patsy had given birth to a child while in captivity.

"When we meet with them tomorrow," the king said, "we will reinforce the things you have already brought up. They are never to attack the March again. In addition, they will surrender all captives who wish to return and any children like the one of Patsy's you mentioned."

"Your Majesty, I believe they will find these terms intolerable," I cautioned. "Not these two—I believe they have seen enough to know not to anger you—but their countrymen have not."

"Then we will convince the rest of them," the king stated flatly. "Duncan, in an ordinary year, when did the nomads leave to return home?"

"Usually a few days into the month of Ylir," my father said. "About three weeks before the winter solstice."

"I would imagine the snow in the mountain passes dictated that," I added.

"Hm. If we sent a thousand men, would that be enough to convince them to comply with our wishes?" the king mused.

"I don't know," I replied. "Patsy Campbell might be able to tell you."

"Then we will ask her later," the king stated. "I am thinking of sending Albert, along with half of the Castle Shield, plus Fenwick and you, after the beginning of Gorman—in three weeks or so. That should give you enough time to return before the passes through the mountains close. We may send some surveyors with you. We know precious little about that part of the world and should correct that ignorance. I am not opposed to establishing friendly relations with these people, but there will be no more raiding."

"Understood, Your Majesty," my father replied.

"Now, more important, Duncan—we wish to express our gratitude for your part in the swift completion of the reopening of Port Charles and the Pheas River," the king said.

"It is apparent that all the Gods and Goddesses and other heavenly beings shone their favor upon this venture from the start," Queen Liliana added.

"Our clerks have given us estimates of the amount of produce that will be gathered from the March," the king continued. "The Gods' favor is clear. Agricultural production in the rest of the kingdom fell slightly short of last year's numbers. Without the contribution of the March, the shortfall would have drained our grain reserves to dangerous levels. In addition, the shortages would have encouraged speculation, inflating prices and creating potentially dangerous instability throughout our realm."

"Instead, there is no crisis," Liliana commented. "Prices are stable or even slightly lower than a year ago. Our grain reserves will be untouched this winter."

"Work on the harbor will continue without cease," King Mark added. "As you know, we just released the list of last-known property owners in the town of Port Charles on the first of Haustman. Relatives and assigns were given six weeks to submit their claims to a royal magistrate. We are also assigning a magistrate to stay in Hillstead until suitable accommodations are ready in Port Charles. As agreed, the auction of unclaimed parcels will take place in Easton on the first of Ylir."

My father nodded. He and the king discussed this weeks ago. Then, with a smile, the king introduced a small surprise.

"As a measure of our gratitude, we have commanded that the normal terms of escheatment for unclaimed property in Port Charles be reversed for one year, beginning on the fifteenth of Gorman, a few weeks away. On any unclaimed properties sold during that year, the March will claim the two-thirds share with the crown due the final third."

"That is most generous, Your Majesty," my father acknowledged.

"A calculated risk," Mark smirked. "We think only a few adventurous souls will invest so quickly. Most will wait until Port Charles proves itself. If we are wrong, it proves we have more for which to be grateful. Should Fortune find a home there more quickly, how can that be a bad thing?"

"Finally, Duncan, we would like to invite you to join us for the upcoming celebration of the winter solstice. Caz has been the last two years, but it is time for you to come. You may even bring a guest if you wish," Liliana said with a sly smile.

6

They dismissed us not long after, instructing us to return by eight o'clock in the morning. My father and I returned to the far side of the bridge to find our horses waiting, already groomed. The sky was nearly dark, so we rode to the Foaming Boar, where we would stable our mounts. I thought we would also have dinner since it was unlikely that Roberta, the housekeeper who looked after our home in the city, would have anything to prepare for us.

A former sergeant in the Rangers, Carl Stensland, owned the inn. He bought it with his retirement savings and was enjoying success. Carl participated in a few of my earlier adventures.

Andy, my horse, recognized when we were drawing close to the inn. Jerry, the stable boy, used to care for Andy when I lived in the city. The two of them had a bond.

Jerry was an orphan. Carl caught him hiding in the stable a few years back and gave the lad quarters in the stable loft and fed him. He put Jerry to work tending the guests' horses and insisted that Jerry attend school. The last time I saw the boy, he had begun to sprout up. I was better prepared this time.

We entered the small yard, and Andy gave a whinny. Before we came to a stop, Jerry slid down the ladder from his loft. I swear he was another two inches taller.

"Andy!" he called out, his voice cracking on the syllable from low to high.

I laughed in spite of myself. Jerry paid me no attention as he held out his arms, and Andy laid his head beside the boy's. The two shared an embrace for a moment.

"Milord," Jerry said in his deeper voice, remembering his manners.

He gave my father the same greeting, knuckling his forelock as well. I reached over and rumpled Jerry's hair. He squirmed away with a squeak of protest.

"Cor—pickin' on a poor lad," Jerry said.

"I missed you, Jerry," I replied.

"And I missed Andy, Mr. Caz, milord," he teased me.

"Mr. Caz is fine," I commented. "Majors and Minors, Jerry! You've grown again since I last saw you. Your voice is changing, too. How are you? How is Thunder?"

"I'm doing well, Mr. Caz," Jerry replied. "And Thunder is simply the best horse in the whole kingdom."

I looked past Jerry and could barely see Thunder in his stall. Thunder was a large black gelding. If he did not move when he heard his name, I might not have been able to spot him.

"How is Aster, milord?" Jerry asked, referring to my father's horse.

"You remember his name? Good for you, son," my father said. "Aster is fine and probably looking forward to your attention."

My father's hand darted out quickly and rumpled Jerry's hair. Jerry was not expecting it, so he was doubly surprised. He quickly ducked away.

"Not fair!" Jerry cried, his voice once again in the higher registers. "Two against one!"

My father chuckled and pulled his saddlebags off. I did the same. We headed inside.

It was the beginning of dinner time. Carl saw me immediately, and his face lit up. He bustled over to us.

"Two for dinner?" he asked.

When I nodded, he took our bags and placed them behind his counter, then led us to a table. He scurried away as soon as we began to sit, returning quickly with three mugs of cider. The third was for him, as he sat down and joined us.

"It has only been a few months since I last saw you, Cap'n," Carl said, "but knowing your life, I imagine you already have stories to tell. What brings you to the city?"

My father answered before I could. He shared with Carl how the river project and reopening of Port Charles had progressed. Then he mentioned the arrival of Bynar and Polim, and the reason for their visit.

"That's a bit of cheek, milord, if you don't mind me saying so," Carl responded.

My father raised his mug in agreement.

"His Majesty agrees with you, Sar'nt," he said. "He intends to put a stop to their annual raids."

"What about your soldiers, milord?" Carl asked. "Some of them just joined you a year and a half ago."

"They will all have continued employment for years to come," my father reassured him. "It might not be as exciting as tussling with the nomads, but there will still be a need for them."

"As soldiers?" Carl asked.

"I think more as roving constables," my father said. "The reopening of the river and port will bring increased wealth to the March. I am not naïve enough to think that won't attract some opportunists. They will still need to train the militia every year as well. That is an obligation we have to the crown that will not end."

Carl was soon called away by his duties. Our food was delivered not long after, and my father and I ate quietly. When we finished, he pushed back from the table with a gentle sigh.

"I'm sure it has not escaped your notice that I find Madame Hernandez attractive," he said.

"It has not," I admitted. "Is your interest returned?"

"It is," he answered. "There have been no professions of everlasting love to this point, but it is clear we enjoy one another's company."

"Intimately?" I prodded.

My father said nothing, but the flush on his face gave me the answer I sought.

"If His Majesty is successful in convincing the nomads that any future raids will be met with swift and harsh retribution, I may consider stepping aside and putting the care of the March in Lucy's and your hands next year," he announced quietly.

"Sir! Father—" I began to protest.

"I've spent my entire adult life defending us against them," he said. "With that threat eliminated, my usefulness diminishes."

"But, sir, there is much more you have to offer than that," I said. "You have a genius for organization. I could never have planned the different projects as carefully and competently as you did."

"I did not say I was sailing off to Nagah, boy," my father retorted. "I'll probably be no further than Port Charles most of the time."

"You're planning on rebuilding the plantation house, then," I observed.

"I am. The idea of settling into the life of a gentleman farmer appeals to me," he said, "even though I never heard of jute until a few months ago."

"But we've hired Mr. Balboa to run the plantation," I objected.

"Even better," he said with a wide grin. "He will still do that. I want to travel. In my lifetime, I've seen precious little of Aquileia, and I have never been overseas. It would be nice to visit old friends and restore those bonds, and adventure to see new lands."

"With Madame Hernandez," I commented.

"If she is willing. Don't worry, Caz. If you and Lucy ever begin producing grandchildren, you will see more of me than you might like."

"Grandfather stayed with you to the end," I said.

"He had nowhere else to go," my father replied. "Plus, he felt guilty for arranging such an awful match. I think he stayed to make sure things did not fall apart. They certainly did after he died."

I had nothing I could add to that. Finding Carl, I settled our bill, also giving him money for two days' worth of board for the horses. My father and I retrieved our bags and walked to the house Lucy and I owned in the city.

We frightened Roberta half to death, arriving in the dark, unannounced as we did. She recovered quickly, and hastily scurried upstairs to make up beds for us. When she came back down, we apologized again for giving her a scare and then climbed up and retired for the evening.

The next morning, the creak of the hoist woke me before the sun was up. I stumbled out of bed and saw my father in his nightshirt. He was whistling through his teeth as he pulled two buckets of steaming water out.

"Good. You're awake," he said. "I asked Roberta to boil water for baths. We can't show up at the castle today smelling so much like horse. You'll need to draw some water for yours, though. It wouldn't be fair to ask her to do all the work."

I went downstairs. By the time I walked past the cupboard where the hoist was concealed, I could hear the two buckets my father emptied coming down. I waited for them before joining Roberta in the kitchen.

"Good, you can help," she said.

A fire was blazing in the stove, and steam was rising from the large pot on top. Roberta handed me some mitts so I could lift the pot without burning my hands. I poured the hot water into two waiting buckets, then carried them to the hoist.

"Ready!" I called up, and my father began to pull them up.

I took the two empty buckets to the well and filled them. Returning to the kitchen, I placed the large pot back on the stove and emptied the buckets into it. By then, I heard the clatter of the hoist and went to get the other two buckets. When I filled them, I went straight to the hoist.

"Sir? Are you still there?" I called up.

"I am."

"Would you mind pouring the cold water into my bath? It will save me a trip." I asked.

"Lazy bones," my father snorted, but he began pulling them up.

I took the other two buckets and filled them from the well and brought them into the kitchen. My father returned the two empty ones on the hoist. Now I just needed to wait for the water to heat. While I was waiting, Roberta offered me some bread and jam. By the time I finished nibbling, the water on the stove was steaming. I emptied the pot, then filled it. Putting the two buckets of hot water on the hoist, I went upstairs and pulled them up, then dumped them in the tub.

The tub would hold six buckets of water. Two would be cold, straight from the well. Four would be heated to near boiling. The combination produced a full, hot bath without danger of scalding oneself. I sent the two empty buckets down, then went down myself to pour the last two. After I emptied them into the tub, I stripped off my nightshirt and climbed in.

If you have read my earlier stories, you know that I feel the pleasure of a hot bath is one of the greatest gifts the Gods have given mankind. Not only does it remove grime and odor, but it is also restorative to the soul. In addition, I feel I have done some of my best thinking while soaking.

No momentous ideas came to me. I pondered the question of my father stepping aside, but it did not trouble me after he explained his intentions. There would clearly be much we would need to discuss when the time came, but it could wait until later. I was happy he seemed to have found someone in Madame Hernandez.

His mention of children stuck with me. To be honest, I was puzzled why Lucy was not already a mother several times over. We engaged in highly enjoyable intimate relations as often as we could. I decided, with her knowledge of medicines and potions, that she was avoiding pregnancy.

In truth, I could not blame her. Since we met and fell in love, I have nearly been killed more than a handful of times. The number of dangerous situations into which I thrust myself was even greater. If the king convinced the nomads to cease their attacks, perhaps we could discuss becoming parents.

Our bathing completed, we dressed for our visit to the castle. It was easier for me since I kept clothing in the house. My father had only what he brought with him, but it was presentable.

We walked to the Foaming Boar and retrieved our horses. Jerry was in a hurry. He told us he needed to get to school. We sent him on his way and finished saddling the horses ourselves.

When we arrived at the guard house at the bridge, they were waiting for us. They took our horses, and a page led us across. The seneschal met us and took us to the throne room.

The seneschal continued to accompany us and explained we would be on the dais with the king and queen. He placed my father on the king's right and me on the queen's left. Patsy entered, wearing new clothing.

No longer in Rose's uniform or the drab homespun, she was wearing a blue dress. It was not fancy, but it fit well and seemed appropriate. I imagined it was probably similar to the type of things she wore before being captured.

Patsy waited at the bottom of the steps, where she would translate for the nomads. They entered, led by a page, and followed by two members of the Castle Shield bearing halberds. Neither Bynar nor Polim looked happy.

"We understand you speak for your people," the king stated.

After Patsy translated, they agreed.

"Then hear this," the king stated firmly. "Your attacks on our borders will cease."

"But it is our custom," Bynar objected. "We have been blooding our young men this way for generations. It is the way it has always been."

"Find a new way," the king said emphatically. "We have no wish to bring the horror of war upon a distant enemy, but we will respond to any attack in the future in the most harsh and violent way possible. You have seen only the smallest portion of the men we command. We will send them over the mountains by the tens and tens of hundreds if you violate our command."

Bynar and Polim looked at one another with miserable expressions. Whatever they hoped to gain from their journey, this was probably not the outcome they sought. Finally, Bynar shrugged.

"It shall be as you command," he said reluctantly.

"You will return all captives you have taken from our lands who wish to return. Along with them, you will return any children they have produced during their time as your prisoners," the king pronounced. "A ten of hundreds of our soldiers will accompany you upon your return to ensure this happens immediately."

Bynar and Polim reacted physically to this statement. They might have been prepared for the king to forbid them from attacking us. Returning their captives must have been more like a nightmare for them, judging by the way they flinched. Before they could speak, the king continued.

"We understand from speaking with your former captive," the king nodded at Patsy, "that your nearby rivals may hear of this and become more bold in their aggression against you. We do not wish for your reputation to suffer among your neighbors on the plains where you dwell. In exchange for the captives and their children, we will give you a hundred suits of armor similar to what these guards are wearing."

When Patsy finished translating this, a look of hope replaced the despair evident on Bynar and Polim's faces. The two of them began speaking between themselves in hushed tones. The discussion took a couple of minutes.

"They also request a hundred sets for horses," Patsy translated, "and two hundred long lances with iron tips."

King Mark appeared to consider this, but I sensed it was just for show. I suspected he was prepared to offer more. Finally, he nodded gravely.

"It shall be so," he said. "Further, we understand that wood and iron are difficult for your people to obtain. We would encourage trade between our two peoples instead of war. The cattle you were accustomed to driving across the mountains to feed your raiding parties would be suitable to trade for wood and iron in the town of Oritur."

This provoked another discussion between the two men. From their earlier pained looks of disappointment, their expressions now were showing signs of suppressed excitement. They would not be returning to their people with empty hands and threats of violence. Still, a thought occurred to Polim.

"Who will determine a fair rate of exchange?" he asked.

The king looked to my father. My father nodded his agreement, then indicated me as well. The king smiled.

"The Earl of the March or his son will make sure you are not cheated," he said.

7

The meeting ended shortly thereafter. The journey back to Easton would begin the next day. Half the Castle Shield would accompany us, along with wagons carrying the armor and lances agreed upon.

I returned to the house to change clothes. My father stayed behind to speak with the king. By the time I came downstairs, I could hear Fenwick speaking with Roberta in the kitchen.

"There you are," he said. "Have you considered my proposal?"

Proposal? I thought. I wracked my brain. *What proposal is he talking about?* Then I remembered.

"Your letter came in between the time we learned the nomads were coming and when they arrived," I explained. "I apologize. I have not given it the consideration it deserves. My father and I agree that we would like to establish an inn in Port Charles as soon as possible, but we have no idea what a fair rate for the land would be."

"I suspected that might be the case," Fenwick said, "from the timing of your father's letter warning His Majesty of the nomads' arrival. If you don't mind looking at this, I took some time to learn what comparable rates are in Aurora, Newcastle, and here in Aquileia."

He offered me a sheet of paper from a leather portfolio he was carrying, listing different plots of land in the different port cities and the terms of the leases. As one would expect, rates were highest in Aquileia, the kingdom's largest city and busiest port. Aurora was the smallest. I hoped Port Charles would be of similar size in a few years.

I took the paper and sat on the sofa to study it. My father and I did not have a pressing need for income from this parcel of land. Port Charles would need an inn in order to grow more quickly, and a good inn would be even more beneficial. I could let Fenwick have the land for nothing, but that did not seem right.

The listings for Aurora were the ones I examined most closely. One was a close match in terms of its size and proximity to the harbor. The lease covered use of the land and was for a thirty-year term.

"This one," I said, pointing to it. "Fifty percent of that rate for the first five years, seventy percent for the second five, and ninety percent for the balance— thirty-year term."

"Fair enough," Fenwick said, and he extended his hand.

We shook, and he added, "Done."

"We should have my solicitor draw up the necessary documents," I suggested.

Fenwick gave me a sly smile and retrieved other papers from his portfolio.

"Do you have a pen?" he asked.

"In the study," I said as I stood.

Looking over his shoulder, I could see he was holding a lease agreement already prepared by my solicitor, Graham Throckmorton. There were blank spaces for the numbers, but Fenwick clearly anticipated the sort of terms I would offer. It made me chuckle.

"How many different versions of the agreement are in your satchel, Fenwick?" I asked.

"Two others," he admitted as we entered the study. "But this was the one Graham and I thought would be closest to your way of thinking."

Fenwick entered the numbers I proposed in the appropriate blank spaces on the three copies of the agreement. When he finished, he asked me to initial them. He then did the same.

"That's a relief," he said.

"Why? You must have known I would not be unreasonable," I said.

"Well, I did count on that," he said. "So much so that I already engaged a builder. He and his crew, along with the materials they need to get started, left on a Traval ship yesterday."

"Awfully cocksure to have set your plans in motion before we reached agreement," I commented.

"I was counting on your oft-demonstrated sense of fairness," Fenwick smirked.

Fenwick then withdrew some papers showing the plans the builder drew up for the inn. It was to be a sizeable establishment, making use of every inch of the property. The inn proper would have fourteen good-sized rooms. Above the stable, Fenwick showed me smaller quarters for another dozen guests—rooms not much more than enough to fit a bed and a washbasin.

"The inn will cater to two different types of clients," he explained. "Well-to-do guests will stay in the inn. Transients, like sailors, will be able to afford the lesser accommodations above the stable. There will be two different dining rooms as well, but only one common room."

"It seems well planned," I remarked.

"I've had help," Fenwick admitted. "I found the man who will run the place, and I would like you to meet him this evening. I hope you are available for dinner?"

"You know I have not had the opportunity to make any plans," I said, shaking my head.

"Excellent! Please join us for dinner," he said.

"Where and when?"

"The Brass Frog, at half-past six?" he offered.

I arrived at the Brass Frog, one of the better inns in the city, precisely on time. Fenwick was waiting and took me to a private dining room. Julienne Traval was there, along with a barrel-chested man who looked like the former sailing master he was. Captain Toby Penfrew's hair was black, though gone gray at the temples, and had a face toughened by wind and sun. He stood to shake my hand when Fenwick introduced me. His hand was one used to hard work, but his grip was firm without being overwhelming. When he spoke, his voice was surprisingly soft, though. Despite missing his lower right leg, he moved quite nimbly.

Over the soup course, he shared his plans for running the inn. In many ways, he reminded me of Carl Stensland. Carl was enjoying great success as an innkeeper, and I hoped Penfrew would as well.

After the soup was finished, Julienne shared with me the figures she compiled of the different foodstuffs that had either already shipped from Port Charles or were sitting in the warehouse (or in storehouses at the landings) awaiting shipment. As the king shared earlier, in all cases, production exceeded the estimates I provided the king months earlier before the work began. It was different seeing the actual numbers, especially since they were in the millions of modia. We actually met the figures provided by the mayors and head men and women except for peas, which fell slightly short.

"The king shared with me that the grain from the March has helped keep prices stable," I said. "Is that your understanding as well?"

"Yes, and thank all the Heavenly Beings," Julienne said. "There were some speculators who lost huge sums, but they are profiteers of misery, and any sane person rejoices at their misfortune. Anyone looking to profit from the pain of others deserves an unhappy outcome."

Fenwick turned to the topic of the land in Port Charles. Before the end of the month of Twiman, which was the equinox, the king's clerks sent letters to every mayor or head of a village throughout the kingdom to be posted publicly. The letters listed the last known owner of every plot of land in Port Charles. Every royal magistrate was provided with a copy of the map of Port Charles prepared by the surveyors that identified each plot.

We ourselves learned of four other pieces of land our family owned in Port Charles from this posting. My father already had me file our claims with the magistrate. The clerks verified them quickly and had already issued updated deeds.

"My understanding is that very few claims are being put forward, meaning most of the land will be available for sale," Fenwick said. "It is no secret that Traval wishes to buy additional land adjacent to their warehouse. Hawkins & Company will attempt to purchase enough harbor front property for their own warehouse and wharf. Coombs appears to be asleep."

"We do not anticipate a huge windfall from the sale of the land," I remarked. "His Majesty reversed the normal terms of escheatment for a year, but I think most investors will wait to see whether Port Charles will succeed."

"On that issue, I do not think you need to worry," Julienne stated. "Though the necessity of warping in and out of the harbor slows things in a minor way, the workers in our warehouse have been hard-pressed to keep up. Port Charles will clearly be successful. In addition to Hawkins looking to purchase land, there are others who want to establish themselves as soon as possible. One of the difficulties we are facing is that more and more of our warehouse space is being taken up by building supplies that arrive on every ship. The auction scheduled for the first of Ylir will be interesting."

"In addition to the businesses Julienne has told me about that are hoping to build in Port Charles, there will also be land speculators, hoping to snatch up properties to sell at inflated prices later," Fenwick said. "You and your father would be wise to set minimum prices for all the parcels to hinder them as much as possible."

"Where would I even start?" I pleaded.

"Graham Throckmorton," Fenwick said. "We worked on compiling the list of properties I showed you and the lease rates. He also has information on recent sales in Aurora, Newcastle, and Aquileia."

"Aurora is the most similar," I said.

"And I think your valuation of ninety percent of the value is probably accurate as well," Fenwick added. "Write him a letter and ask him to compile the figures. It should not be difficult."

"Why could I not simply visit him tomorrow?" I asked. "The Castle Shield does not need me to help them return the nomads home."

"Perhaps he did not make himself clear, but His Majesty intends for you to join me on the journey to nomad-land," Fenwick said. "Mr. Penfrew will also be riding with us as far as Easton. He will then head to Port Charles and oversee the construction of the inn."

"Fenwick," I whined. "That means all the work of organizing the Harvest Fair falls on Lucy again. Last year you dragged me off to Mooren—"

"And what a successful trip that was!" Julienne commented. "I've been wondering if I could hire 'Lord Compote' to assist me with other tricky negotiations."

"That's not the point, Julienne. It's not fair to Lucy," I said.

"Do you think she will be bothered by your absence?" Fenwick asked.

"No," I admitted. "But that's because she has the kindness and patience of a Goddess."

"She is also extremely capable. I think she also understands the unique nature of your position," Julienne offered. "Not just in the March, but also in terms of your importance to Their Majesties and His Highness."

"Flattery will not help me feel better," I groaned.

"It's not puffery," Fenwick said firmly. "You do not grasp how critical your role has been in the last four years. I know of at least three different points during this time where you have prevented the ship of state from foundering. You might not understand it, but I assure you the king, queen, and Prince Albert do. Lucy does also, as a result of her unique relationship with Her Majesty. They now rely on you, and, if I may flatter myself, me as well."

"This is an awfully long-winded way of telling me I can't excuse myself from traveling," I complained.

"It will be fun," Fenwick said. "Just like all the other adventures we have enjoyed together."

"As I recall, I almost died twice on our first visit to Scaramouche," I pointed out.

"Fine. Just like all our other adventures except that one," Fenwick amended.

"But 'Lord Compote' won't be with us," I said. "He's been something of a good-luck charm."

"Except his first appearance," Fenwick said, "when that Parkinson fellow nearly killed you."

"When did I tell you about that?" I asked.

"You didn't," Fenwick replied. "Lord Rawlinsford did."

"Oh."

"He doesn't normally complain like this," Fenwick explained to Penfrew. "He's usually standing in the stirrups and ready to go. By the way, you should attend the Harvest Fair in Easton at the end of the month. It's one of the best in the kingdom."

When I returned that night, my father was sitting in front of a fire. We discussed the idea of minimum prices for the plots in Port Charles. He agreed with the strategy.

"You'll be pleased to learn that His Majesty is absorbing the cost of the armor we are providing to the nomads," he said.

"I had not considered that," I admitted. "It's a substantial expense."

"It is, but he feels it is well worth the investment," my father said. "He wants nothing to interfere with the flow of grain from the March."

"What else did you discuss?" I asked.

"I mentioned that I was thinking of stepping down if we achieved peace with the nomads," he said. "His Majesty is supportive."

"Anything else?"

"Nothing I am at liberty to mention," my father said with a slight smile.

Before retiring, I wrote a letter to Graham Throckmorton, explaining the information I wished him to compile. The following morning, I rose early. I was due at the castle by seven o'clock. That was the hour set for our departure.

I left the letter with my father, asking him to post or deliver it. He told me the night before that he was not leaving Aquileia today. He did not share what was keeping him in the city. I figured if he wanted me to know, he would tell me.

When I arrived at the small plaza before the bridge to the castle, I found it crowded. A thousand members of the Castle Shield were mounted and ready. Bynar and Polim were there, as was Patsy in the two-wheeled cart. Prince Albert rode at the head of the Castle Shield and beckoned me over to ride with him.

We set off exactly on time. Albert and I took the lead, with Fenwick riding alongside Bynar and Polim. Conversation would be impossible until we left the city. The cobbled streets and the accompanying rattle of the cart's wheels on them would prevent Patsy from being able to translate.

About halfway to the east gate, we climbed a small rise. I turned to look at our procession. The Castle Shield rode four abreast, and the glitter of the armor stretched nearly a half-mile. Behind them came a train of two hundred wagons pulled by four-mule teams. I could not see the end of the procession.

When we left the city behind, Fenwick struck up a conversation with the two nomads. I knew the reason why. One of Fenwick's lesser affinities was to Mielvanir, our God of travel and commerce. From this connection, Fenwick had the uncanny ability to learn other languages quickly. I reckoned by the time we reached Easton, he would speak the nomad tongue fluently.

Albert wanted to talk to me about marriage. He was three years older than me, and his father was beginning to make noise about Albert's need to find a suitable mate and begin production of the next generation of the royal family. The problem Albert faced was that he did not like any of the leading candidates that had been proposed to him. He shared with me a list of names his father put forth—all daughters of important and influential members of the nobility.

"They are all shallow," he complained. "All of them like the idea of becoming queen very much, but none of them realize that the position requires work and effort. Freddy, Fenwick, and you have all found women who would be great queens, but none of them were of high enough station to be suitable for me—according to my father and his grasp of politics."

"Have you spoken with your mother about this?" I asked.

"Not yet."

"Please do," I suggested. "Your father's understanding of political realities is amazing, but I think your mother has much greater insight into human nature. If you involve your mother in the search, I think the two of you will find someone who will make you happy. The woman might not be as highly placed as those your father has suggested, but your mother will assist you in winning your father over."

"It is very difficult for me to oppose my father's wishes," Albert admitted. "Especially after—"

"You are not that person any longer, Your Highness," I said. "Your father realizes this as well as I do. He may even be hoping that you demonstrate a bit of resistance—to show you can stand up for yourself. If that is not the case, you can hint that he is pushing you into a marriage like the one in which my father was trapped. That should scare him."

Albert looked at me sharply, trying to figure out if I was teasing. I must have given away enough. He began to chuckle.

8

Halfway through our first day of travel, we encountered Doug Campbell riding toward us. His reunion with his wife Patsy was heartwarming. I stayed out of earshot but recognized when she was telling Doug that she had delivered a child while she was a captive. Doug clearly understood that she had been forced to submit to her captors and embraced her. He later informed me that he would accompany us across the mountains to bring "his son" back to the March. I raised an eyebrow at his choice of words.

"They didn't give her no choice," he said. "He's her son. She's my wife. That makes him my son, too."

"You're a good man, Doug Campbell," I said.

Our ungainly procession, over a mile in length, moved without difficulty all the way to Easton. I split from the group briefly to inform Lucy of where I was going (and to pick up fresh clothing). She greeted my news with a smile and graciously accepted my apologies for not being present to help prepare for the Harvest Fair. This indicated to me that she already knew about it somehow. There was a hint of sadness in her eyes that did not match the rest of her expression, and it puzzled me. I guessed the hint of sadness was over my being away for the Harvest Fair. She sent me on my way with a warm embrace and an incredibly passionate kiss. As I rode to meet the group at Bannock Hill, I wondered whether Lucy knew of my impending absence from one of her clairvoyant visions or had received warning in some way from the queen.

When I arrived, I saw the area where our main group of armsmen would customarily be stationed was now overwhelmed by the thousand men and horses of the Castle Shield. I could never have imagined it so crowded. Yet, despite the mass of people, everything seemed organized and calm.

We continued the following day, passing Oritur and reaching the spot on the Patker River where the nomads were encamped when we conducted our nighttime raid a year and a half earlier. The soldiers filled hundreds of barrels with water in preparation for our trek across the desert. Patsy started to fill the barrels on her little cart, but as soon as he saw what she was doing, her husband and some soldiers took over for her, glaring at Bynar and Polim for expecting a woman to do this for them.

The next day, we reached the place of the ambush we laid in early summer. We slaughtered all the nomads who came to raid us. Our huge group encamped in the same place where Prince Albert and I had established our troops. Bynar and Polim were clearly uncomfortable, being so near to the remains of their countrymen. They stayed on the side of our bivouac, furthest from where the funeral pyres had been.

The day had been fair and pleasant, but when the sun went down, the temperature dropped sharply. I retrieved an extra blanket for Andy and pulled my cloak from my saddlebag. The men of the Castle Shield were complaining since their officers would not let them build big fires. We would not have the ability to collect more wood until we reached the banks of the river at the foot of the mountains. With the many wagons slowing us down, we were at least five days away. Even when we reached the riverbank, all we would find was what Patsy described as "scrub"—stunted trees that clung to the rocky ground. The men were going to be horrified when they learned what the nomads used as fuel for their fires—dried animal manure, according to Patsy.

My first encounter with the desert was only a few months ago, when I scouted the terrain in search of a likely place to lay in wait for the nomads. I remembered being struck by how different it was from the lush greenery of my country, Aquileia. Here, the color palette was reds and browns. At first, I found it interesting. After four days, I was heartily sick of it, along with the lack of available water, the freezing nights, and the monotony of the landscape.

The mountains to which we were heading seemed to remain as far off as ever until one remembered how they appeared in the morning of each day. By the fifth day, they were now looming ahead. As sunset neared, we caught sight of the river. The men cheered.

Foraging parties were sent in search of wood, instructed to range far from our current location before cutting down any trees. That way, future travelers would not be inconvenienced by our passage. Those men returned as twilight ended, and the officers allowed the men to build fires as large as they wished. The warmth of the fires put smiles on their faces. If they knew we had only just completed the easier part of the journey, I doubt they would have been quite so cheerful.

In the morning, we crossed the river. We were able to leave the wagons carrying water barrels behind. Along the way to the pass, we would find many small streams, so water would not be an issue. We also left a number of wagons full of food behind. Not trusting that the nomads would be willing to provide us with supplies, we left the capital with enough to carry us through our return to the March. The wagoneers stayed behind to watch over the mules and our material. There was enough forage near the river to feed the mules until our return.

Prince Albert kept me by his side, but our conversation failed as we climbed toward the pass. The track we followed grew narrower the farther we went. It also ascended steadily upward. Maneuvering the wagons around the corners when the track reversed on itself was the most difficult part. There was not enough room for a four-mule team to turn. We needed to unhitch the leading two, then manhandle the wagon around the bend. We would then put the mules back in the traces until the next switchback. This process slowed us considerably. I now understood why the nomads used two-wheel carts instead of wagons.

Darkness fell before we reached the area where there was enough of a saddle in the terrain for us to set up camp. Winding our way on the narrow trail by the occasional torch light, usually with a steep drop on one side, was nerve-wracking. Added to that were the cold and the wind. By the time we stopped, we were exhausted.

We started again at first light, climbing to the pass. Again, the sun set before we reached our stopping point. The area at the pass was crowded with men, animals, and wagons. I was so tired I did not bother to try to erect my canvas shelter. Grabbing blankets and wrapping myself in my cloak, I huddled under one of the wagons.

The third day of our mountain trek brought wretched weather. It was snowing when we started for the day, but not quite cold enough for it to accumulate. The snow changed to a fine drizzle after dawn, bringing the type of chill that seeps into one's bones.

I stayed with the prince, and I will say that he never once complained about the conditions. In fact, when we rounded a corner, and a blast of wind greeted us, whipping the cold mist into our faces like a thousand needles, he turned to me with a sardonic grin. There was no longer any trace of the spoiled aristocrat left in him.

Our journey from the pass down to the plains was speedier than our climb up, if only because we did not need all four mules to pull each wagon. That meant we could negotiate the switchbacks without stopping. Of course, it did not take long before we could smell the scorched wood of the brakes on the wagons. Once we reached the plains, they would all need repair for the return journey.

We reached our stopping point before darkness fell. The cold misty drizzle continued unabated, though. As I did the night before, many others skipped setting up shelters and simply curled up under wagons. I shared the cover of mine with two other men.

On the fourth day since we left the river on the other side of the mountains, the sky cleared mid-morning. The wind was brisk and in our faces, but the sunshine helped us dry out from the day before. With the rain gone, we could see the magnificent vista of the plains stretching out before us. After a series of low rolling hills, the ground was flat and featureless as far as our eyes could see.

"Bynar and Polim have seen that there is a party waiting for us," Fenwick said, after he rode to where the prince and I were in the procession. "We will reach them before the end of the day."

"Majors and Minors," Albert sighed. "I hoped for at least a day to get my feet underneath me before—"

"Don't worry, Your Highness," Fenwick assured him. "Caz and I will make sure the discussions begin on the most favorable terms for you."

I looked at Fenwick, my eyebrows raised in question.

"The same way you closed their mouths back at Easton when they first arrived," Fenwick said. "With an added twist."

"How did you know about that?" I asked. "Did Patsy tell you?"

"I haven't seen Patsy or her husband, except at a distance, since we left Oritur," Fenwick replied. "Bynar and Polim were talking about it."

"You speak their language?" Albert asked incredulously.

"It's a gift, Your Highness," Fenwick said modestly. "Foreign tongues come to me quickly."

"That's why father sent you," Albert remarked wonderingly, as the missing piece of the puzzle fell in place in his mind. "I was puzzling why, and also troubled about using Patsy as our translator. These nomads will not want to listen to what a former captive says."

"Agreed," Fenwick stated. "I will serve as your translator."

"And how will you make sure they are prepared for the terms I will pronounce?" Albert asked.

"Aw, don't make me ruin the surprise, Your Highness," Fenwick answered. "It will be fun, I promise. The Castle Shield can help. You'll have them form up in ten ranks, a hundred men across."

"That part I understand," Albert said. "I was thinking of something like that. Do you know what else he's talking about, Caz?" Albert asked.

"I do."

"Will you tell me?"

"If you so command," I said.

Albert looked at me, then looked at Fenwick. Fenwick was still sporting a slight grin. Albert turned back to me and opened his mouth to say something, then shut it.

"It won't offend them?" he asked Fenwick, turning back to him.

"No," Fenwick stated firmly. "But it, with the might of the Castle Shield behind you, will start the discussion on the proper note."

In the early afternoon, we stopped in order that the Castle Shield could equip their horses and themselves with the armor they had been carrying. Albert donned his own armor, and the men took care of his horse. Suitably impressive, clad in gleaming metal, our procession continued to where a sizeable party of nomads was waiting.

Fenwick brought Bynar and Polim to the front of the column. They joined Albert and me. We stopped short of the nomad encampment.

"Make them ride to us, Your Highness," Fenwick advised. "Have the Castle Shield form ranks behind you now."

Albert turned and hollered the command. Officers picked it up and repeated it. As the nomads began to ride toward us, the Castle Shield assembled behind us with their lances upright. They wheeled into place before the nomads reached us.

The soldiers were, I must admit, an awesome sight. A thousand men and horses glittering in the late afternoon sun in a huge, seemingly unbreakable mass. One would need to be blind not to be impressed with the show of force.

One of the nomads called out to Bynar and Polim as he approached us. Fenwick spoke to the two nomads with us harshly, preventing them from replying. With a nod, Fenwick indicated I should move forward with him. I gave Andy the slightest squeeze with my knees, and he stepped off.

Fenwick stopped. I reined in next to him. He began speaking in the nomad tongue. He later told me what he said.

"You sent your two emissaries to treat with the warrior-mage, who slaughtered your raiders the last two years. The impudence to demand we allow your attacks on our land to continue as in the past! We have no intention of allowing you to attack us ever again."

At this, the one nomad in the center began to protest. We learned later that he was their chief—Bynar's brother. Fenwick did not allow him to get more than a few words out before nodding at me.

As I did in Easton, when I wished to awe Bynar and Polim, I touched my ring with the gem of tan-zyan to the diamond in the pommel of my sword. Accessing my link to the Goddess Bellona, I allowed the stored energy in the diamond to flow through the tan-zyan and into that connection.

Both my body and my horse Andy appeared dramatically larger. It is a magical illusion, though Andy did not know that. His wild-eyed, nostril-flared look made him seem incredibly menacing. What was not an illusion was the tremendous strength I felt flow through my entire being and the pull I felt for action. Out of the corner of my eye, I saw Fenwick and his beautiful piebald mount, Davy, exhibiting the same awe-inducing appearance.

Whatever the chief intended to say stuck in his throat. His horse, and the others in his group, reared in fright. While the nomads were struggling to control their mounts, I closed my connection to the Goddess and returned my appearance to its usual state. Fenwick did the same. He waited for the nomads to calm their horses.

"This man," Fenwick said, indicating Prince Albert, "is the son of our mighty king. Both of us owe our allegiance to him and to his father. As he commands, so we will do. Hear now his decrees!"

Fenwick then told Albert, "I told them to listen to your orders. You can list them now, and I will translate."

"Majors and Minors, that was amazing," Albert muttered to us in a whisper. Drawing himself upright in the saddle, he then said loudly, "The troops you see before you are only the smallest fraction of the numbers we command. We have no desire to visit war upon you, but we pledge to destroy you if you attack our people again."

The chief began to protest, but Fenwick held up his hand and glared at him. The man flinched slightly. Albert resumed speaking.

"You will return all captives you have taken from our lands who wish to return. Along with them, you will return any children they have produced during their time as your prisoners."

The chief was stunned to silence, too angry to speak. He finally opened his mouth, but Fenwick hissed at him like a snake. He closed his jaws with a snap.

"Bynar and Polim did not fail in their mission," Albert continued. "They do not return to you with empty hands. Our kingdom has no wish to weaken you in the eyes of your rivals here on the plains. In demonstration of that, we present you this gift."

While Fenwick was translating, Albert yelled back to the wagons, "Bring the armor forward."

As the wagons began to rumble toward us, Albert said, "In these wagons are a hundred sets of armor, as you see my soldiers wearing. There is also armor for a hundred horses and two hundred lances with iron tips."

The chief was silent while his brain absorbed what Albert said. Meanwhile, the wagons proceeded, passing us and heading to the nomad encampment. The chief could not help but stare at the armor as it rolled past. He also noted the eyes of the others in his group as they fixed their gaze upon it.

"You have presented terms both harsh and generous," the chief said finally. "I must speak with Bynar and Polim before I give you an answer."

"Speak with them now," Albert replied. "But know that we will not rest until we have your answer."

Saying this, Albert gestured with his arm. The officers of the Castle Shield saw this and barked orders. A thousand lances were lifted from their rests and lowered, pointing toward the nomads and their camp. Fenwick told Bynar and Polim to go speak with their chief.

"He's asking them if the threat is real," Fenwick said quietly, passing along what he overheard. "They are telling him that the March, which they always attacked, is only a small part of the kingdom. The rest of the country is vast and wealthy. They confirm that the king assigned you—the warrior-mage—to put an end to their attacks. Both of them were surprised to learn I was also a warrior-mage. They had no idea until our little show. You know, I like that title, 'warrior-mage,' much better than Royal Assassin."

"I thought you were a Privy Advisor to His Majesty now," I whispered.

"Even that isn't as good as warrior-mage," Fenwick replied softly.

Albert overheard this exchange and barely controlled his snicker.

"Careful, Your Highness," I cautioned.

"Bynar is reaffirming that the threats His Highness just made are real," Fenwick continued. "Now he is mentioning the offer to trade livestock for wood and iron. That seems to be important. The chief is questioning him about it."

The chief ran out of questions. He was silent for a time, obviously pondering everything he just heard. Finally, he urged his horse forward slowly, drawing up to Prince Albert. The chief spit in the palm of his right hand and extended it to Albert.

Fenwick quickly asked Bynar, "Is this your custom?"

"Yes, to seal agreements," Bynar replied.

Fenwick passed this along to Albert. The prince spit in his own hand and clasped the chief's. They shook three times before the chief let go.

"It is agreed," the chief said. "Your men can put their spears away."

9

The first day after our arrival, the chief, whose name we learned was Kushedt, took us to a nearby village—one of the larger ones in their realm. It took all day to reach it. Albert, Fenwick, and I rode with Kushedt, Bynar, and Polim. We peppered them with questions about how they lived, their customs, their religion, and anything else that piqued our curiosity.

One thing we wanted to know immediately was how much power Kushedt exercised. Though he agreed to Prince Albert's decrees, we worried that his people might resist. Fenwick told us that Kushedt sent out riders to summon all the sub-chiefs for a meeting where Kushedt would share the news, and to return the captives.

"Changing the tradition of generations upon generations will not be welcomed," Kushedt admitted when we asked. "But when the alternative is the continued slaughter of our youth and a possible reprisal from your powerful king, it becomes easier to accept."

He turned to me. "Bynar tells me that you, warrior-mage, now command the border for your father and that you are steadfast in your determination to end our practice. He reports that your king shares this view. We have not encountered a warrior-mage in generations, but there are legends among us of what your type can do. It would be the height of foolishness for us to continue, especially since your mighty king supports you. Why did he not support your father?"

I explained how the success of my father and his predecessors in controlling the annual raids was responsible for the lack of regal attention. Kushedt understood immediately.

"If one of my more distant sub-chiefs had problems with his neighbors, I might not know of it unless he failed," he said. "Still, your father never inflicted upon us the kind of losses you have. You add to the legends we have of warrior-mages and their abilities."

I wanted to say something in my father's defense but held my tongue. If Kushedt wanted to think my success was supernatural, it served our purposes. As long as I remained in the March, my presence served as a strong deterrent to their resuming their old ways.

"Your gift of weaponry," Kushedt said to Albert, "will appease the disgruntled. You will excuse me for telling my people that the arms and the captives are an exchange of gifts between two people who wish to become more friendly with one another. I know that you gave us no choice, but you also offered the weaponry without conditions."

Albert nodded his agreement at this once Fenwick translated.

"Your agreement to trade livestock for iron and wood is also welcome," Kushedt added. "Bynar and Polim did well to extract that concession from you. We accept the warrior-mage as the arbiter of fair exchange."

I could see on Albert's face that he wanted to correct Kushedt's impression that Bynar and Polim brought forth the subject of trade. Just as quickly, he dismissed the thought. Allowing the chief to think his emissaries pressed for it only strengthened the chief's position with his people.

On the afternoon of the third day after our arrival, the last of the captives arrived, along with Kushedt's remaining sub-chiefs. Including Patsy, there were twenty-two women and three infants. I thought there would be more women and children, and asked Patsy if there had been other women who did not survive the ordeal, or children that the nomads were not returning to us."

"No, this is everyone. They were very specific in the women they took," Patsy replied. "All of us were between our late teens and early twenties. Our captors wanted us to bear them children."

"But I see only three children?" I said.

"What the men wanted and what their women here would accept were at odds," Patsy explained. "Their women supplied us with an herbal drink that they said would prevent pregnancy. The three of us did not receive it in time."

"How many of them will return to their husbands like you?" I asked.

"None of them," Patsy sighed. "Nine were unmarried. All of them watched as their husbands or parents were killed before their eyes. I was the only one whose husband survived."

"Are they apprehensive about returning to the March?" I asked.

"From speaking with a few, they have mixed emotions," Patsy said. "They are happy to be leaving here, where we are treated as slaves, but uncertain about what awaits them in the March. I would like to be optimistic and say that their extended families will help them, but I suspect that will not be the case for a handful."

"Patsy, I pledge to you now that my wife and I will ensure that no one is abandoned," I stated. "You met Lucy only briefly, but your husband may be able to tell you more about her and what she has done for the March already. She is the kindest, most generous person I have ever encountered."

Kushedt had erected a large pavilion to hold everyone for the meeting to be held that night. Albert, Fenwick, and I were present. Kushedt had arranged several sets of the armor for examination. Fenwick translated for us in a whisper as the proceedings began.

The gathering started on a sour note. Kushedt reminded his people of the losses we inflicted upon their forces the last two summers. He informed them that I was indeed a warrior-mage, and I had promised that future incursions would be met just as harshly. This provoked grumbling from several of the audience. The discontent began to swell.

"They don't believe him," Fenwick reported quietly. "I'm afraid we will need to show them."

I nodded and opened my connection to Bellona while accessing the stored energy in the diamond in my sword. Fenwick did the same. As before, the people saw us increase dramatically in size and stature. Fenwick added to this.

In an unnaturally deep and booming voice, he said in their language, "Do not doubt Kushedt, upon pain of death!"

As I returned to my normal state, I noticed that the grumbling ceased. All noise, in fact, stopped. Many members of the gathering had taken involuntary steps backward, mashing into those behind them. From that point, the meeting went better.

We departed the following morning. Kushedt, Bynar, Polim, and other high-ranking people accompanied us to the trailhead. Albert, Fenwick, and I allowed our long column to depart while we said our farewells. We then began riding up toward the pass, at the rear of our procession.

I thought about what we had seen. Unlike the Rhetian Empire to the west, there seemed to be no animosity toward us from the nomads. None of them knew when or why they first attacked the March, hundreds of years before. In their time, it was seen as a rite of passage for young men to learn to become warriors—a process that required completing two campaigning seasons. Until recently, only a dozen or two of their young men would die in each campaigning season. They considered it an acceptable price to pay for the experience the others received. The slaughter of their men in the last two seasons was unexpected and disturbed them greatly.

The rite of passage was important to them because every man in Kushedt's people considered himself a warrior. When tensions boiled over with one of the neighboring groups of nomads regarding grazing territory, which occurred every few years, all males would answer the call to arms. In those clashes, hundreds would die on both sides.

There were much smaller skirmishes with these same neighbors from time to time, but not on a predictable schedule. That was one reason attacking the March was attractive. Our towns were fixed in place. The military resources we brought to bear in the past were not overwhelming in scale. In terms of the scope of the conflict, it was manageable and predictable.

To be sure, some of the customs practiced by Kushedt's people were strange. Aquileia did not make slaves of captives. Burning dung for fuel was something we were happy to leave to them. Living in a hut made from sod held no appeal for us.

By the standards of Aquileia, they were poor. They had very few possessions. Yet, as a people, they appeared healthy and fit, and seemed content with life. Like us in Aquileia, they were proud of who they were.

There were other similarities. They worshipped the same Gods, though they called them by different names. Like our country folk, they accepted the presence of magic in the world. Those who dwelt in our larger cities pretended they were too sophisticated to believe in it.

"I rather like them," Albert said, interrupting my ruminations.

"Pardon me, Your Highness?" I asked, coming out of my reverie.

"I like them," Albert repeated. "I didn't think I would."

"Funny," I commented. "I was just about to come to the same conclusion."

"As allies, I don't think they could contribute much in time of need," he said, "but better to have friends than enemies. Do you think we can trust them not to attack?"

"As long as Kushedt is their leader," I answered. "I did not learn how he came to power, so don't know how long he will last."

"He took control roughly a dozen years ago," Albert said. "I asked him how. Apparently, their people suffered a humiliating defeat to one of the neighboring groups. The sub-chiefs forced out the leader at the time. It then became a political contest between a handful of the more powerful underlings. Kushedt possessed the largest following but by no means a majority. Through a combination of favors owed and promises made, he won over enough of his rivals to gain the support he needed."

"Will ending their raids on the March hurt his standing?" I asked.

"Your success the last two campaigns and the deaths of all those young men hurt his standing," Fenwick said. "He sent Bynar and Polim out of desperation because his situation was so precarious. From the savagery you displayed in battle, Kushedt genuinely did not expect them to return, though Bynar and Polim did not know that."

"These people must have thought I was a monster," I said.

"From their lore regarding 'warrior-mages,' that was understandable," Fenwick said. "Kushedt did not think they would have any success in convincing us to allow them to resume their annual attacks, but he needed to be seen by his people as doing something."

"So when they returned—alive, obviously—and with me, the king's son and heir, that was already helpful to him," Albert said. "The armor we brought—which gives them a significant advantage over their local rivals—solidified Kushedt's position as an effective leader. Opening up trade to obtain iron and wood in the future—and our skilled craftsmen who can make useful weapons and tools from it—puts Kushedt in an unassailable position for the time being."

"Huh," I grunted. "Funny how all the tumblers clicked into place."

As the day continued, we saw black clouds approaching from the east. By nightfall, a cold, hard rain was falling. The track became slippery as it grew narrower on our ascent to the pass.

The miserable weather continued all the next day. Albert, Fenwick, and I again trailed the rest of the column. Everyone in our party was soaking wet and chilled to the bone. It was getting late in the afternoon, and Albert was in the midst of grumbling about the weather when he suddenly fell silent. At the same time, there was a loud rumble accompanied by a whooshing noise. I looked over my shoulder to see if the noise was related to why Albert stopped speaking. The prince was no longer there. Neither was the portion of the trail on which he had been riding. I immediately reined Andy to a stop and called to Fenwick as I slid from the saddle.

"I think the trail gave out under Albert!" I shouted. "Get some rope!"

Fenwick spurred Davy forward, hollering ahead for the column to stop. I tiptoed as close to the edge as I dared and peered over. At least two hundred feet downslope, I could see Albert's horse, half-buried in debris on a small ledge, floundering with what I guessed were a couple of broken legs as he tried to free himself. There was no sign of Albert.

It was an anxious wait until Fenwick returned. He brought with him three of the officers. All of them carried coils of rope.

"Who is going to go down?" Fenwick asked.

The three officers and I all responded, near simultaneously, "I will."

"I will," I said again, as forcefully as I could.

The officers nodded. Fenwick was already busy with the rope, fashioning what turned out to be a crude harness. He assisted me in putting it between my legs and around my chest. When he finished, he looked around. Whatever he was seeking, he did not find. He then took the rope and looped it over the horn of his saddle.

"Right," he said. "Caz, we are going to lower you down. Face the slope, lean back against the harness, and stay on your feet. You three are going to pay out the line slowly. When we get near the end of this section, tie it to the next. One of you is good with knots?"

All three nodded.

"I'm going to move Davy up ahead just a little to make sure he has solid footing. I'll tell you when to start."

Fenwick climbed in the saddle and urged his horse forward. He went about twenty yards before he was satisfied. He waved at me to proceed.

I went to the washed-out edge and turned around. Following Fenwick's instruction, I leaned back into the harness. The three officers allowed the rope to play out just enough that I was now at an angle to the slope.

"Go ahead," I said.

They gradually let the rope out. I moved my feet downslope to maintain the same angle. It was an awkward feeling at first, like walking backward down a wall. I struggled in the beginning, trying to find the right pace to stay in harmony with the line and the slope.

"Hold on, milord!" one of the officers called down. "Adding more rope."

While I waited, I tried to see how much farther I needed to go. It was difficult to tell, but I guessed I was one-third of the way down. They called down again, asking if I were ready to resume, and I told them to continue.

It was easier this time to find the proper rate of movement. At least, it was until I stepped back, and my foot encountered nothing but air. My other foot slipped, and I flipped upright, dangling as the harness dug into my crotch.

"Hold!" I shouted.

In front of me was a large rock face. The drop from the edge of it was sheer, accounting for my stumble. I lifted my legs to plant my feet on the rock.

"I just went off a ledge," I called up. "I'm alright now. Go ahead—slowly!"

I skipped down the vertical drop until I felt the slope resume under my feet.

"I'm back on the slope," I yelled. "Let the rope out as before."

They stopped again to add another length of rope. My thoughts were as dark as the weather. Now that I was becoming more accustomed to the terror of what I was doing, I began to dread what I might find. Albert's horse was occasionally still trying to stand, and mewling in pain with every attempt. I heard nothing from Albert.

Some gravel landed on top of my head. I was just wondering what that meant when a cascade of mud and stones came down on top of me. Holding onto the rope with one hand, I put my other arm over my head for protection. Even so, I felt a large rock hit my scalp. The impact stunned me. My feet were swept from under, and I would have been cast down the side of the mountain if the harness had not held me.

Dangling in the harness, I was trying to recover my wits when I heard Fenwick call, "Caz?"

"I'm still here," I shouted.

"What happened?"

"Another mudslide."

Getting my feet back on the slope, I resumed my downward progress in the cold, pouring rain. Eventually, I reached a spot where the ground under my feet was loose and easily dislodged. A minute later, I was standing on a piece of relatively level terrain, though my feet sunk into the loose rocks and mud past my ankles. I shouted at the men to hold, and I turned around carefully.

Albert's horse was five yards to my left, looking at me with wide, frightened eyes. On seeing me, he attempted to rise again, and failed. I could see that both his forelegs were broken. The rope would not allow me to reach him, so I hollered for them to give me some slack.

I withdrew my sword and, as soon as I could move, I crossed quickly to the stricken animal. Panicked, he tried to lift himself up again. I took advantage of his posture and thrust my blade up through his lower jaw and into his brain to put him out of his misery.

Of Albert, there was no immediate sign. Sheathing my sword, I began to examine the mud and scree carefully. After what seemed like an eternity, I saw a gleam of metal. I quickly began scrabbling with my hands to clear away the rocks and dirt.

It was the prince's breastplate. When I recognized it, I attacked the pile of debris in a frenzy, hoping he might still be alive. Uncovering his head and seeing the unnatural angle of his neck, I knew the worst.

Continuing to dig his body out, I thought about Albert and how much he had changed and matured in the last few years. He had certainly shown me that he was a worthy heir to his father, and now he was gone. It took me a few moments to gather my composure.

"I found his body!" I called up, my voice cracking as I did.

"Majors and Minors!" I heard one of the officers gasp.

"He's dead, then?" Fenwick shouted.

"Aye."

"Put him in the harness and loop the rope under his arms several times," Fenwick instructed. "We'll pull him up, then send the line back down to you."

10

The death of the crown prince cast a pall over our entire company. With all of us already miserable due to the cold and rain, his demise sent everyone's emotions to low ebb. I ordered the soldiers to break apart a half-dozen of the now-empty wagons for firewood. If ever there was a time when we needed the light and warmth of a fire, this was that moment.

Albert's body was put in another of the empty wagons. The rain, which cursed us for so long, at least washed the grime from him. I sat in the mud and rain near one of the fires, my head in my hands. The medic came to attend me. There was a nasty cut in my scalp where the rock hit me. He told me he needed to stitch it together and asked if I wanted something to dull the pain.

"Just get on with it," I grumbled. "I've had stitches before."

He called someone over to bring a torch so he could see better. He washed the wound with water, gently trying to remove the dirt. When he finished cleaning, he poured alcohol in the cut, which stung like the blazes of the fires in the Seven Hells. The needle and thread didn't seem so bad after that.

The pain suited my mood. Part of my grief was for Albert, who had become my friend—at least as much as the crown prince can be friends with anyone. Another component was my understanding of the political turmoil that his death would generate. King Mark would need to find and name a successor. Every family who could claim even the slightest trace of blood relation would put forth candidates. Civil war was a distinct possibility.

There was no escaping the responsibility I felt to deliver the sad news to the king and queen personally. It put me in the most uncomfortable position. If you read my other stories, you know I killed Prince Wim, Albert's younger brother.

It was not by my design. Wim had engineered a plot that would completely discredit Albert in the eyes of his father, enabling Wim to leap over him in the succession. The structure of his scheme centered on making me the public scapegoat. I unraveled Wim's plans, trying to extricate myself from the snare in which he placed me. Facing ruin, Wim kidnapped my new love, now my wife, Lucy. When I went to free her, he and I fought a duel. I won.

Now, for being present at the death of the older brother, King Mark might make a connection where none existed and blame me. It would be as incorrect as it was understandable. Nevertheless, this was a duty I could not shirk.

Everyone left me alone in my misery. Fenwick asked if I wanted anything to eat, but I had no appetite. Eventually, I found my blankets and curled up under one of the wagons to sleep.

The sun returned in the morning but it did not brighten anyone's spirits. What should have been a triumphant return after traveling to a land that, as far as we knew, no one from Aquileia ever visited, was now a funeral cortège. Our journey down the mountain, across the desert, and to Easton was largely silent, with one exception.

You have returned, Shasha communicated to me as we left the desert.

"Yes."

You are sad. It pains me to feel. Was the journey not successful?

"The journey was a success, but—" I shared with her my memory of finding Albert's body with his neck askew.

Ah. I know him. He rode with you. I am sorry.

"Thank you."

I will go now. We will connect when your grief is less.

Nearing Easton, I saw that preparations for the Harvest Fair were well underway. The fair would begin in two days, and there were already a handful of canvas-covered wagons parked. I stayed with the group until they reached the spot where they would bivouac for the night. With the officers, I discussed the next morning's departure time and urged them to keep the soldiers from spreading news of Albert's demise. Then I rode to the manor. Fenwick did not join me. Though he was welcome, he must have felt I needed to be alone with my wife.

Clausen was manning the gate. He saw my sour expression and did not try to engage me. He merely opened the gate and allowed me through.

Riding to the rear of the manor, I saw Lucy waiting at the back entrance. Tom Collinwood came to take Andy's reins. I slid from the saddle and headed for my wife. From the look on her face, I could tell she knew what happened.

She embraced me, and I buried my face in the crook of her neck, holding her tight. She gently patted and rubbed my back, as one does to calm a frightened child. At length, I pushed myself away. I could see tears in her eyes, as she could see them in mine.

"You know," I said—not asking, merely confirming.

She nodded.

"Come inside," she urged. "Your bath should be ready. Then we can talk."

Climbing the stairs, I felt my weariness. The journey across the desert and mountains was difficult. Bearing the emotional burden of the prince's death made it even more draining.

Entering our bedroom, I began to strip off my clothes mechanically. The bath was waiting, and I eased myself in. Lucy joined me a minute later, sliding in behind me. She enfolded me in her embrace again.

I opened my mouth to say something, but she whispered, "Sh."

She began to wash me tenderly. In the past, this sort of care would make all my cares vanish. Now, however, it felt like a brief respite from the troubles I would face and the difficulties the kingdom would undergo.

She got up from the bath and came back with a pair of scissors. Asking me to dunk my head, she washed my wound carefully. Quickly and painlessly, she removed the stitches.

"Do I want to know how you're aware of Albert's death?" I asked while she tended to me.

"No," Lucy replied.

That told me it was something she had seen through her clairvoyance. Lucy only rarely admitted to knowing glimpses of future events. She had been taught by her grandmother not to share any information from her visions, and later she learned this was indeed sound advice. It would jeopardize the future to share her knowledge even with me, her husband. While I occasionally found her reticence frustrating, my exasperation was tempered by knowing she bore the greater burden.

"Is my father here? I did not see Aster," I asked.

"Yes," she replied. "He was out with Madame Hernandez, taking care of some things related to the fair."

"I need to tell him," I said. "And I must accompany the body to the capital. I will miss the fair."

"There will be another next year," Lucy reassured me.

"Good," I grunted. "I can only hope I will be able to help you prepare for it."

Lucy chuckled softly. "It was far easier going through it the second time," she said.

We finished the bath. I dressed in clean clothes. One of the girls had brought my saddlebags up, so I packed them for my journey to Aquileia.

When I arrived downstairs, I heard voices emanating from the study. My father was there, sitting close to Madame Hernandez on the sofa. Lucy occupied an armchair, but she stood when I entered.

"Sit, son," my father said expansively, "and tell me all about it. Would you like a glass of sherry?"

Madame Hernandez, bless her, knew something was wrong. She placed her hand on my father's arm, stopping him in mid-pour. He looked up quizzically.

"Our mission was a success, father, but all is not well," I said, then paused for a moment. "Albert suffered an accident. The trail gave way underneath him as we were approaching the pass on our return. He fell and broke his neck."

"Majors and Minors!" my father gasped.

"I will be leaving in the morning to accompany the body back to the castle."

"I must join you then," he stated.

I thought he should stay behind. The fair was beginning, and Lucy and I had been expecting guests. It was bad enough that I would be absent.

"I agree, father. I think you should," Lucy agreed as she slid onto my lap.

My protest died in my throat when I saw the determined set on her face. Lucy knew this was coming and was obviously prepared. I shook my head in wonderment at her strength.

"The armsmen all have their assignments," she said. "The constable knows what to expect. There should be no trouble they can't handle."

"Should I join you?" Madame Hernandez asked.

"I would appreciate your company, but this is a difficult circumstance," my father said. "There will be a far better time to introduce you to Their Majesties."

He resumed filling my glass with sherry. When he handed it to me, he said, "You have greater need of this than I would have imagined."

For the next hour, he pressed me on details of the trip and the agreement we reached with the nomads. That took until dinner was served. Over dinner, he wanted more specifics regarding Albert's death.

As the dishes were being cleared away, my father said, "Well, at least His Majesty does not need to worry about the Braintrees."

The Braintrees had been cousins of the king. They had long insisted they had a claim to the throne equal to his (and probably did) and seized every opportunity to stir up trouble for King Mark. When their behavior changed from vicious whisperings behind the king's back to actually fomenting rebellion, Mark needed to act. He did so decisively. The four most powerful members of the Braintree clan were arrested, along with the head of another family, the Morningstars. All were tried, found guilty of treason, and executed. They would have brought the kingdom to a civil war.

"There are surely others like them," I cautioned.

"Not really," my father replied. "In terms of blood ties, the closest kin need to trace back five generations or more to prove consanguinity. That is virtually meaningless. Mark will be able, within reason, to select the strongest candidate as his successor."

"Within reason?" Madame Hernandez asked.

"He will need to choose a member of the nobility," my father explained. "Otherwise, the aristocrats would never support his choice. Beyond that, he will aim for a man who has good relations with the more powerful families, and no significant enemies. If there is no one like that, he will seek a man who is respected by nearly everyone. In either case, he will look for a man who is currently childless."

"Why?" Lucy asked.

"Because the courts ruled many, many years ago that pre-existing children are not legitimate heirs," my father said. "Only children born after their father's ascension to the throne are counted in the line of succession."

"That's ridiculous," Madame Hernandez exclaimed.

"I agree," my father said, "but that ruling still stands."

"After he finds someone suitable, then what happens?" Madame Hernandez inquired.

"Mark will formally adopt him and name him the heir," my father said.

We retired to the study and continued asking my father about the political ramifications of Albert's passing. Since my father had been unable to follow the ebbs and flows of the realm's politics until recently, he warned us that his knowledge was limited. Still, he felt the king would weather this misfortune and emerge the stronger for it.

Having slept on the ground for nearly three weeks, I was eager to climb into a real bed. In addition, the emotional burden I was carrying had worn me down. The third time I yawned, Lucy rose from my lap and tugged my hand.

I would like to be able to tell you, dear reader, that my wife and I made passionate love that night. Sadly, that was not the case. I fell asleep almost as soon as I climbed under the covers, comforted by her loving embrace.

Morning came far too early for my liking. The sunrise also brought the necessity of leaving again. I was not looking forward to arriving in the city and facing the king. In addition, I felt guilty leaving the management of the Harvest Fair, and the entertainment of the half-dozen guests we expected, entirely on Lucy's shoulders.

Lucy, on the other hand, was chipper. I didn't know whether it was because she relished the challenge, or because she was looking forward to seeing our friends visit. She joined me for breakfast, then shooed me out the door with a hug, a kiss, and a warm smile.

My father and I met the troops, and we began the three-day journey to the capital. The weather was fair, and the leaves were at the peak of autumnal splendor. Fenwick and my father both tried to rally my spirits, but they were not successful. I was not morose—just quiet.

Before we reached the gates of the city, I instructed the officers to cover Albert's corpse. Word would spread quickly enough, but I did not wish to instigate a general panic. When we reached the guardhouse at the bridge leading to the castle, I instructed the guard to send a page to fetch the seneschal. I would meet him on the far side of the bridge.

My father, Fenwick, and I crossed over and waited. It took a few minutes before the seneschal appeared. He looked cross at our interruption of whatever he was doing. His day was about to become far worse.

"What in the Seven Hells do you mean, summoning me like that?" he demanded.

I stepped close to him—close enough to make anyone uncomfortable—and whispered in his ear, "Seneschal, in a wagon on the other side of the bridge, is the body of Prince Albert. If you would prefer, we can just bring it over the bridge. I thought it would be better to involve you as quickly as possible. Was I wrong?"

"Majors and Minors, Lord Oritur! I had no idea," he stammered quietly. "Please accept my apologies. What happened?"

"Returning over the eastern mountains, the trail gave way and slid out from under him," I explained. "He fell and broke his neck."

"We need to get the body over here," the seneschal said, thinking out loud, "with a minimum of fuss. Then I need to inform Their Majesties."

"I can do that if you like," Fenwick offered.

The seneschal looked at Fenwick like a man who just saved him from drowning.

"That would be quite helpful if you would," the seneschal replied. "Lord Oritur, if you could join me, we can instruct the soldiers to bring the wagon across."

"I'll go with you, Fenwick," my father said.

Fenwick nodded, and they headed into the castle. The seneschal joined me, and we walked back to where Albert's body was. The officer we spoke to made the decision to unhitch the mules and have a party of his men pull the wagon over since it might be a length of time before the wagon was empty again.

The seneschal and I followed the wagon. We had the men draw it close to the entrance, then sent them back. The two of us waited for Their Majesties to arrive.

Queen Liliana looked grief-stricken when I saw her. She was hanging on my father's arm. King Mark seemed furious. His reaction was the one I feared most. The king glared at the seneschal, who quickly scurried to his side. His Majesty growled angrily in the seneschal's ear, then put his arm around his wife, who was now leaning over the side of the wagon looking at the corpse.

"Your father, Mr. Fenwick, and you are to spend the night here in the castle," the seneschal instructed after returning to me. "I will arrange dinner for you, but you are to remain in your rooms until you are summoned."

"When will that be?" I asked.

"I cannot say."

As well as I slept three nights before in the tender arms of my wife, I spent that night poorly. My mind raced, flipping from worry to grief and back. When morning came, I was in a state of wakeful exhaustion. A page brought me some bread, and my father entered not long after.

"You look terrible," he commented.

"I didn't sleep."

"Why not?"

"Grief over a friend's sudden death … fear of the hangman's noose—"

"You need have no fear, son," he said. "Mark does not blame you at all. Grief, I can understand, though. His Majesty wants to see both of us when you are ready."

I had not been that hungry to start, and now what little appetite I possessed disappeared. Setting the bread aside, I rose. I smoothed out the wrinkles in my clothes as best I could.

"I'm ready now," I said.

My father led me to a small drawing room in the private chambers of the castle. The queen was informally attired. King Mark looked as though he slept in his clothes, if he slept at all,

"Sit," the king commanded.

"We've heard from Fenwick, who can lie as easily as he breathes, though we sensed nothing but truth from him," the king began once we sat down. "We've heard from Duncan, your father, who could not tell a lie to save his life. Now let us hear from you."

"Where would you like me to begin, Your Majesty?" I asked.

"Begin with what happened, then summarize the results of your mission up to that point," he instructed.

11

That is what I did. When recounting the success of our mission, I told him the thoughts Albert shared about the nomads. The king let me speak without interruption.

"And how do you feel about Albert's death?" he asked when I finished.

"I am greatly saddened, Your Majesty," I said, "both on a personal level and in thinking about the political turmoil this might cause. It is no secret that Albert and I were not friendly for many years. In the last three years, though, we established as much of a friendship as I believe the crown prince could enjoy with anyone. He demanded to be one of my seconds in the duel against Barrowton. Not long after, Albert was one of my bridesmen. I did not ask him in order to curry favor with him—I wanted his presence because of how I felt toward him. He changed a great deal in a fairly short period of time. With the troops, he showed the gift of command and shared their hardships without flinching. He proved—to me at least—that he was worthy of being your successor, and would be an admirable king."

The queen's eyes filled with tears at this. I heard her sniffle. The king showed nothing on his face, but there was a long pause before he spoke again.

"Thank you for that, Caz," he said in a strained voice. "Now, why are you worried about the political aspects?"

"You need to choose a successor," I said. "Many noble families will be presenting candidates. You run the risk of alienating most of them. What was a settled matter may now be the source of chaos."

"Your father thinks this is an opportunity," Mark said.

"I am not as politically experienced as either of you," I admitted. "He explained his views to me. I grasp his logic, but uncertainty still troubles me."

"It troubles us as well, lad," he agreed.

He paused for a moment.

"We will conduct a state funeral on the fifteenth of Gorman," he then said. "We request that you be one of the bearers of Albert's pallium."

"I would be honored."

"Thank you for bringing his body back to us," Queen Liliana said. "Fenwick told us it was difficult and dangerous to retrieve."

"I could do no less for my friend," I replied quietly.

Tears filled her eyes. Seeing that made my eyes water as well. The king nodded gravely, then made a slight motion of his hand. My father interpreted it, correctly, as dismissal. He took me by the elbow and gently tugged me toward the door.

The seneschal informed us later that my presence was no longer needed, but His Majesty requested that my father stay. He reminded us that we should return by the fourteenth to prepare for Albert's funeral. It was still early enough in the day that I decided to set out for Easton.

Given my lack of sleep, I will admit I dozed off in the saddle several times. Still, I wanted to be home with my wife. Being with her would calm my emotional turmoil.

On the third day, just after midday, I encountered my friends who had come to enjoy the Harvest Fair, now returning to the city. Linc Ellsworth and his wife Nellie, Quint and Siobhan Pompeo, and Ratty Hawkins with Inger Fairchild hailed me, and we stopped on the road. Quint was one of Prince Albert's oldest friends—the only one who made the same transition Albert did, from arrogant snob to responsible noble. They all knew about Albert's death.

"I nearly turned right around and headed for the castle when I heard," he said. "But Lucy convinced me a few days' delay would be better for all concerned."

"How was the fair?" I asked, wanting to shift the discussion to a lighter topic.

"Marvelous," Nellie replied. "I've never seen Linc eat so much."

"Fair food is my weakness," he confessed.

"Mine, too," I agreed. "Did the smelly fortune-teller return?"

"The mysterious Doctor Flamel?" Ratty clarified. "I didn't see him."

"How did Lucy bear up?" I asked.

"She seemed in her element," Siobhan answered. "I've known her longer than anyone except her family, and she handled everything with aplomb. Of course, by the time we arrived, the majority of the work of organizing the fair was done. As far as handling a houseful of guests, your staff is impressive—especially your cook. Even though Quint stuffed himself with naughty treats at the fair, he still managed to clean his plate every night."

"Just being polite, dear," he quipped with a smirk. She dug her elbow into his ribs for that.

"Again, I apologize for missing your visit," I said.

"You were where you needed to be," Ratty said. "All of us understood. Besides, we will see you again soon, though not for such a happy event."

On that note, we said our farewells and resumed our journeys. Seeing them and the good spirits they were in—despite the bad news about Albert—helped restore my mood. I reached Easton late in the afternoon.

Lucy greeted me with a warm embrace. Saying nothing, she slid my saddlebags from my shoulder, allowing them to drop to the hall floor. She led me to the study and pushed me down into an armchair. Then she climbed onto my lap and simply held me.

Being held so close restored my weary soul. Lucy understood far more about the supernatural than I did, and she once tried to explain to me why. I must admit I did not listen as attentively as I should. All I knew, from the time I was introduced to her by her cousin Freddy, was that being in her presence affected me. She filled me with love, and hope, and joy. I could never get enough of it.

Later, I shared with her the details of my meeting with the king and queen. She told me of the fair, and how much our guests enjoyed themselves. Everything had gone smoothly.

"Thanks to you, dear husband, the people of the March are feeling especially blessed this year," Lucy said. "It is natural to feel a little better about the world when one has a bit more money in his pocket. No one can remember a year like this, when prosperity was so general. It showed itself in small ways—

like a man I saw buying sweets for someone else's children, just because he saw them gazing longingly at what the vendor was offering. Hroth Martinelli shared with me that the Temple has been well-attended, and that worshippers are not coming because they have problems, but instead wish to show their gratitude to the Gods. People expressed their appreciation to me wherever I went. I only wish you were here to enjoy the accolades as well."

"The only praise I seek is from you," I said.

"Ugh," she groaned, teasing me. "Too sweet—you'll make me gag."

"Is Madame Hernandez still here?" I asked.

"Yes. She was helpful during your absence. It's clear that she misses your father, though. He will return soon, I hope?"

"I think so," I said. "King Mark wanted him to stay. For how long or for what reason, I do not know. I suspect it is to discuss the ramifications involved with finding a new successor. Father seems to have a keen grasp of kingdom politics, even though he has not been actively engaged in them for many years. I think Mark welcomes having a fresh perspective from someone with a more objective view."

"I'm sure it makes your father happy," Lucy said. "He and Mark were much closer in their youth. Getting married pulled them apart. Your father was then expected to take on a greater weight of responsibility. That kept him tied to the March and mired in his unhappy marriage."

"My grandfather raised me," I said. "And until recently, I considered him to be faultless in every way that my father was not. It was only after learning about his role in arranging my father's marriage that I understood what a huge mistake he made and how that influenced everything that followed. At first, I was disappointed that the man I always thought was perfect was just as flawed as anyone."

"And now?"

"We are all human," I said with a shrug. "Human beings have flaws—some more than others—except you, that is. You *are* perfection in human form."

Eight days later, we set out for the city with Madame Hernandez. Father wrote us, asking us to bring some of his clothes, as he would be staying in the capital after the ceremony. Other than the weather—the usual cold drizzle of early Gorman—our trip was uneventful.

We arrived at the house in the city as evening fell. After getting the ladies and our bags inside, I took the three horses to the Foaming Boar. Andy and Bella recognized where we were and neighed loudly when we stopped in the small yard behind the inn.

Jerry slid down the ladder from his loft and held out his arms. Both horses went to him, nuzzling his face as he embraced them. I shook my head in wonderment.

"You truly have a gift, Jerry," I said. "It has been years since Andy and Bella were under your daily care, and they still love you."

Jerry looked at me. His mouth twitched, but he held his tongue for a moment. Then he spoke.

"I was going to say something smart, Mr. Caz," he admitted. "But then I reckoned you meant what you said. So, I'll say thank you."

"That's awfully grown-up of you, Jerry," I said.

I extended my hand to him. He ducked under Bella's head to come shake it. When he drew close, I quickly reached up and rumpled his hair as I always used to. He gave me a hurt look, but I extended my hand again. He was more tentative in reaching out, but we clasped hands.

"You are turning into a fine young man, Jerry," I said. "But remember the boy inside you. Even though I am old and decrepit, I still like to let mine out to play every so often. Life is more fun that way."

When I returned to our house, I heard the squeaking from the pulleys of the hoist but did not see anyone. I hullo'd my greeting. My father's voice came down from above.

"Good. You're here," he said. "We're preparing baths. I'll stay up here and pull the buckets up if you'll draw the water."

Over the next half hour, I filled buckets from the well and helped Roberta pour the water once it was heated. For the last two buckets of hot water, my father told me I was on my own. I trudged up the stairs and pulled them up, then poured them in the tub in the lavatory connected to Lucy's and my bedroom. As I was carrying them from the hoist, I thought I heard giggling coming from the room my father was using.

"Are they...?" I asked Lucy.

"I believe they are," she laughed quietly.

After pouring the hot water in, and putting the buckets back in the hoist, I returned to our bedroom. Lucy was already stretched out in the bath. She crooked her finger at me and gave a giggle herself.

The next two days were bittersweet, though less sweet than bitter. Freddy and Greta returned to the city, along with his parents. Lucy's parents arrived as well and ended up staying with us. It was delightful to see everyone, but the circumstances that brought us to the city were awful.

Freddy was asked to join me as a bearer of Albert's pallium, or death shroud. Quint Pompeo would also share this duty, as would the king. I suppose I should have felt honored, but my sadness at Albert's untimely death washed away those feelings.

The body was placed in a coffin, and the coffin in an elegant black wagon. The four of us each held a corner of the pallium, suspending it over the coffin. Once the wagon with Albert's body crossed the bridge from the castle, the four of us mounted our horses and continued holding the shroud aloft as we proceeded out of the city.

An enormous procession of mourners followed us. Every nobleman who held land granted to him by the king was in the entourage. The streets were lined with people, and bunting of black crepe was everywhere. What was eerie was the absence of noise, considering the number of people. The crowd was so quiet, we could hear the occasional dog barking or baby crying as we passed.

The burial grounds were outside the city walls. We headed for them at a slow and stately pace. The grave was prepared when we arrived. My last duty was when we carefully draped the pallium over the coffin before it was lowered into the ground.

Riding back into the city, Freddy, Quint, and I followed the royal carriage. The king joined his wife inside it for the journey back to the castle, his horse trotting behind. On the return, the people on the streets called out their blessings for the king and queen, asking all the heavenly beings to comfort and aid them.

Reaching the guardhouse at the bridge to the castle, the royal carriage continued on. The rest of us did not. Our sad duty for the day was finished.

That evening, we dined at Freddy's for the simple reason he had a bigger table that would seat all of us. Freddy's and Lucy's parents joined us, Madame Hernandez and my father, and Greta's parents were also included. The conversation quickly turned to politics.

Freddy's father, David, was the Duke of Manton. Lucy's father, Noel, was the Duke of Gulick and David's brother. My father was Earl of the March. The two brothers had known my father since boyhood, and they held similar views. Like my father, they felt this was an opportunity for the king to strengthen his position. All of them remarked that it was a blessing from the Gods that the Braintree faction was no longer an issue.

"Seven Hells!" David exclaimed. "If they were still above ground, we'd already be at war!"

"I don't know about that," my father cautioned. "They were always more noise than action. However, they would have done their absolute best to make Mark's life miserable."

Their discussion turned to people they believed might be candidates. They agreed that the best candidate would have demonstrated military or economic prowess and be recognized as a critical thinker who was not hamstrung by tradition. Various names floated out, but one or the other of them gave a reason why the person was ultimately unsuitable.

This might sound like a painfully dry conversation to you, dear reader, but I assure you it was not. The exchanges were lively, witty, and occasionally vulgar. I would have thought Madame Hernandez would be bored, but she was as engaged as any of us. Apparently, being around my father had advanced her political awareness.

The guttering of the candles reminded us it was late, and we said our farewells. All of us were leaving in the morning except my father and Madame Hernandez. He avoided answering the question as to why.

Saying goodbye to Freddy and Greta was emotional. They were our best friends, and we had shared a couple of thrilling adventures together. Now, with them in Manton and us in the March, the opportunities to see one another were few.

"We hardly had the chance to chat with Freddy and Greta," I complained as Lucy and I lay in bed. "I want to know how they are doing."

"Greta and I trade letters," Lucy said. "They are settling into their new life, preparing to take over for Uncle David and Aunt Susannah. Freddy does everything from adjudicating property disputes to helping deliver calves and foals in difficult births. You should write to him and stay in touch. Now that you have forged what we hope is a lasting peace with the nomads, your life will be similar. Do you think you will be able to cope with the lack of excitement?"

Though Lucy said this in a teasing tone, there was an element of gravity to what she asked. It was a question I occasionally pondered. Whenever I began to think about it, however, some new crisis or opportunity popped up that needed my full attention.

"I've thought about it," I confessed. "There have certainly been times when I wished for our lives to be calmer. Being a country nobleman will be less exciting, I'm sure. However, I'm equally certain that there is nothing I cannot do if I have you with me."

"You can be awfully sweet sometimes. You must want something," she teased.

"Only to fall asleep with you in my arms, and wake up with you still there," I said, punctuating this with a quick peck of her lips.

12

Other than three days of cold rain, there was nothing remarkable about our journey back to Easton. My father and Madame Hernandez returned five days later. When I quizzed him about what he had been doing, he was vague and provided no detail.

"His Majesty asked several of us to stay," he said.

"What did you discuss?"

"The future."

"Your future? The future of the kingdom? Possible successors?"

"Yes."

"If I keep asking questions, will you provide more specifics?" I asked.

With a sly smile, he replied, "Probably not. I did bring this back for you."

He handed me a sheaf of papers and what turned out to be a large map rolled into a tube. Looking at the documents, I recognized Graham Throckmorton's handwriting. I unrolled the map and spread it out and saw how he referenced unclaimed plots of land in Port Charles to the documents.

"What is it?" my father asked.

"You remember that we discussed establishing minimum bids for the parcels coming up for auction in Port Charles in order to discourage land speculators?"

"Now that you mention it."

"I engaged my solicitor to learn what he could about land prices in Aurora since it is the closest basis of comparison," I said. "This is the result of his research."

"Interesting," my father commented, leaning over to look more closely at the map. "What does he say?"

"I haven't had the chance to read it," I chided. "We can review it together if you'd like."

The two of us repaired to the study. My father placed the map on his desk, weighing it down at the corners. I sat opposite, and handed over the pages of the letter as I finished reading them. When I surrendered the last of them, I waited for him to finish his perusal.

"What do you think?" I asked.

"I think I'm glad you'll be paying the bill for this," my father teased. "This information, scanty though it is, probably took him days to dig up."

Land does not often change hands in Aquileia. It is one of the reasons I wasted no time when buying our house in the city, even though the building had suffered decades of neglect. Landowners held onto real estate for generations, and good properties were rarely sold.

Throckmorton's research of Aurora went back nearly a hundred years and provided only a few examples. Nonetheless, I was convinced he did the best he could. In his letter, he proposed some strategies that I thought were a solid starting point.

He did his best to estimate the value of the unclaimed parcels in Port Charles based on the limited information he found. My father was now comparing them to the map. I went around the desk to look over his shoulder. He moved aside to give me a better view.

"We will need to study this carefully," my father said, "but I will say that your solicitor is a clever man. The only thing I would change right away is the minimums he has devised for the parcels that have frontage of the harbor. I would increase those a bit, but we have more than two weeks before the auction. Plenty of time."

The auction, when it took place, was a busy affair. I thought we might see a dozen interested people. Instead, more than fifty were crowded into the reception room of the manor. Among them were Ratty Hawkins and Julienne Traval.

"Why didn't you ask to stay with us?" I asked Ratty.

"I thought Julienne was, and we are competitors, you know," he replied.

"Nonsense," I snorted. "We're all friends."

"Sometimes—most of the time," he said, "but not for this. Once the bidding is over, we can be cordial again. Not until."

When I asked Julienne why she wasn't staying with us, she provided a similar answer. I shook my head as I walked away. The two of them stayed as far away from one another as they could in the crowd.

My father entered and the room grew quiet as people noticed his arrival. He walked to a spot in front of the map of Port Charles that we had tacked to the wall. I would be acting as the scribe and took my seat at the desk, which we moved into the room. Father cleared his throat and opened the auction.

"Thank you all for coming," he began. "I've never conducted an auction like this, so please be patient as I feel my way through it. Have you all seen the list of the minimum acceptable bids for the different parcels?"

"There weren't enough copies for everyone," someone complained from the crowd.

"I apologize," my father said. "We did not expect so many people. If you have a copy, please allow your neighbors to take a look at the list."

"But I've made notes on mine," someone else said.

"Then keep it to yourself. Are there copies without notes?"

Several were raised in the air.

"Those of you without a copy of the list, please see those people," he instructed.

"While that is taking place, let me explain how I plan to proceed," he continued. "Beginning with the parcels that have frontage on the harbor, I will read down the list one at a time. If you plan to bid on that property, raise your hand. We will then conduct the bidding between the interested parties. If you are the only one interested in a particular parcel, there will be no bidding, provided you meet the minimum price listed. All bids must be settled by three o'clock tomorrow afternoon by furnishing a bank draft. Should anyone not meet that requirement, the property will be offered to the next highest bidder for the amount of their last bid. Does everyone understand?"

"Will a letter of credit be sufficient?"

"A letter of credit can be converted into a bank draft by any of the established banking houses in Easton," my father replied.

My father then pointed to the map, saying, "We will begin with the first parcel, located at the southwest of the harbor mouth. Are there any bids?"

It was not until he reached the fifth parcel that someone raised his hand. No one else did. My father beckoned the man forward to me. With no other bidders, he would pay the minimum price we established. As I wrote down his information, I silently thanked Fenwick and Julienne for the idea of establishing floor prices. Otherwise, the property might have sold for far less.

The next property went unclaimed. After that, Julienne Traval raised her hand. As she did, she watched Ratty Hawkins to see if he would bid against her. He caught her glance and responded with the slightest shake of his head. She gave an almost imperceptible nod in return.

Julienne claimed the next three properties. Together they would add to the land they already controlled where their warehouse was located. With these additional parcels, they could expand their facilities.

The next five parcels went to the same man. After that, as we neared the mouth of the river, we began to have multiple bidders. My father called out new prices, raising the amount by a hundred ducats each time. When someone wished to drop out, he lowered his hand.

We reached the river and jumped over. Those who had been unsuccessful in obtaining the parcels on the other side continued to bid until each had what he wanted. There were then three lots that went unclaimed. Finally, Ratty raised his hand. As Julienne did to him, he gave her a quick look. Again, there seemed to be a silent agreement not to interfere with the other. Ratty bought five lots in all.

When my father reached the end of the properties with harbor frontage, he called for a break. Rose, Gladys, and Hazel appeared, bringing pitchers of water and cider that they placed on a sideboard, along with glasses. Ratty and Julienne both departed, as did the others who successfully bid on harbor front land. Roughly three dozen were remaining when my father returned to the map.

"I have no wish to waste anyone's time," he said. "There is a long list of properties still, but I would imagine most of you have a specific piece in mind. I will start on my left and ask for lot numbers. If no one else expresses interest, it will be yours for the floor price. Does that meet your agreement?"

Mumbles of affirmation and nods greeted his proposal. He called on the man to his left, who stated two lot numbers. My father repeated them so everyone could hear. No one else raised a hand, so my father waved the man over to me. The next person mentioned three parcels, all along the west bank of the river. Four others raised their hands as my father repeated the information.

"We will come back to those. Next?"

This process moved things along quickly. Twenty-six people claimed forty-one different lots. All of them departed after giving me their information. Twelve men were left, and they were interested in fourteen pieces of riverfront property. Three were on the west bank and the others on the east.

It did not take my father long to conduct the bidding. In less than a half hour, all fourteen properties were sold to eight different men. Four left empty-handed. After they provided me with their names, my father walked them to the door and thanked them for coming.

"Well, Caz," he said when he returned, "what's the total?"

"Twenty-seven thousand, three hundred ducats, sir," I replied.

"Our share of that will cover the cost of the plantation house and all the improvements Mr. Balboa wants to make to the property," he grinned, rubbing his hands together.

"I thought the money from the road contracts was earmarked for that," I said.

"If the king had not been so generous with the terms of escheatment, I would have used that money for the farmstead," he said. "Instead, it will sit in the March's account and help us restore our financial health."

He disappeared for a moment, then returned with a small piece of graphite.

"Read off the list of the properties that were claimed today," he asked.

Lucy and Madame Hernandez came in while we were doing this. I would give him the number of a parcel and he would shade it lightly with the graphite. In that way, we could see what remained available.

"It does not seem that the auction was very successful," Lucy said, eyeing the map where only about a fifth of the lots were shaded.

"On the contrary, my dear," my father smiled. "Our portion of the proceeds will come to over eighteen thousand ducats."

"But most of the land remains unsold," Madame Hernandez pointed out.

"Nearly all of the more valuable lots were purchased," he explained, "and some at prices higher than we guessed. In all honesty, I did not expect there to be as many people as showed up."

"What will happen to the rest of the land?"

"It will remain for sale at the prices we set for almost a year," he said. "At that point, it will become the crown's responsibility."

I spent the rest of the day documenting all the sales and preparing the information the king's magistrate would need to issue new deeds. A number of the purchasers delivered their bank drafts, including Ratty and Julienne. I offered them lodging for the night, but both declined.

The next three weeks were spent with my father, reviewing the accounts for the March. Unlike how Lucy and I handled affairs when I first returned, the account for the March was separate from my father's personal finances. Unfortunately, to keep the March solvent, my father had spent nearly his entire life's savings.

He showed me the effect of my late stepmother's profligate spending. The account for the March showed a balance of nearly a hundred thousand ducats when my grandfather died. From that point, the balance began to dwindle. It was impossible to tell from the account books what happened. Veronica was supposed to be managing them but did not.

"These balances came from the bank," my father explained. "I have no idea where she was spending the money, and shame on me for not paying attention and for not confronting her when I discovered what a mess it was. I just found reasons not to be here and hid from the problem."

"Then let's skip over this mess and pick up the thread from when you took over again," I suggested.

That is what we did. It was dull work, but important—even critical. If my father stepped aside and turned the March over to me, I needed to know everything about managing the territory. He and I went item by item. I took copious notes. When we finished, I reviewed the books again, checking against what I had written in my notes. Even so, I needed to ask more questions.

While I was immersed in this, Lucy was planning the dinner we would host at the Winter Solstice. We were inviting the mayors and head men and women of our largest fifteen towns. Last year, my father held this gathering for the first time since my grandfather died.

"Sadly, you should not invite any of them to stay here," my father suggested.

"Why not?" I asked. "Not that I am close enough to any of them to ask them to stay in my home."

"Well, you might be in the future," he said. "But if you invite one, you risk angering everyone else you did not include."

"That makes sense," Lucy said.

"Also, serve dinner promptly," he advised. "If you delay, some will have too much to drink. As soon as dinner is finished, act as though you expect them to leave. Otherwise, you may have some stay far too long."

"What time is the solstice this year?" I asked,

"The actual moment of the solstice will not happen until the middle of the night," Lucy said. "No reasonable-minded guest would expect to stay that long."

"You will need to make that clear, my dear," my father cautioned. "I will help you word the invitations."

It fell to me to copy out the invitations, during a break from examining the account books. I did not mind. In fact, I considered it a welcome respite. Plus, I was happy to help with the preparations in whatever manner I could.

Madame Hernandez also proved to be of great assistance, from what I observed and Lucy's later comments. Though I wanted to help to atone for my absence from the Harvest Fair, there was little for me to do once the invitations were sent.

A week before the holiday, my father and Madame Hernandez departed for the city. They were invited to the king's annual gathering. My father was looking forward to it. He had not attended since the first year after he was married. Apparently, Veronica had proven to be so unpleasant that he was not asked again.

The day before they left, my father pulled me aside and asked me to meet him at the stable. Puzzled, I threw on my cloak and joined him. He actually pulled me behind the building. I was beginning to question his sanity.

"Caz, I wanted to speak with you where no one could overhear," he said. "I apologize for dragging you out like this."

"I'm guessing it is important to you," I said with a shrug.

"It is. I plan to ask Madame Hernandez to marry me while we are in the city—possibly even at the king's gathering—and I wanted you to know," he said."

I had not been expecting this, but it made good sense.

"You have clearly introduced her to the king and queen, and they must approve," I commented.

Nodding, he said, "My other friends met her when we stayed over after the funeral. They like her, too."

"Is she comfortable in that setting?" I asked.

"Surprisingly so," he replied.

"It's kind of you to give me advance notice, father, but you don't need my blessing," I said.

"Do you have any objection?" he asked earnestly.

"No," I said, shaking my head and laughing. "I like her, and the two of you make each other happy. Does Lucy know?"

"I haven't told her, but you know Lucy…"

I laughed again, even harder. We had not shared with my father the full extent of Lucy's abilities. He had noticed, however, that Lucy was never surprised by anything.

"Congratulations!" I said and embraced him.

My action startled him slightly. From what I remembered as a boy, and what I observed since, our family was not typically prone to display our emotions. Still, it felt like the right thing to do.

13

Our solstice celebration was a success. The guests behaved, though I understand they continued the revel at the Tawny Lion in town, where things grew more boisterous. Everyone was effusive in praising us for the positive changes that had taken place since our arrival. It was deeply gratifying.

I opened the dinner, requesting that everyone ask the Gods' blessings for Prince Albert's soul. After a long moment of silence, I took the opportunity to share with them the results of our visit across the mountains. When I finished, they all stood and applauded.

The dinner Laurie cooked was wonderful. We managed to shoo our guests out the door shortly after we finished eating. Then Lucy and I retired upstairs for our own celebration.

The third day after the solstice, Lucy and I were sitting in the study in front of a cozy fire. She was in my lap, and we were both reading books. I was absent-mindedly twirling a lock of her golden hair around my finger when we heard a loud knock at the door.

I heard the clatter of Toby's paws as he and his master Theo went to answer the knocking. Lucy gave a deep sigh. She pulled herself from my lap gracefully. I looked at her, puzzled by her reaction.

"It's Fenwick," she said in a gloomy tone.

Sure enough, a moment later, a snow-encrusted Fenwick appeared in the doorway. Toby was clinging to his lower right leg, demanding attention. While

Fenwick bent down to give the dog a scratch, Theo took Fenwick's snowy cloak from his shoulders.

"Apologies, Your Loveliness, for my unannounced intrusion," he said, bowing to Lucy. "Stir your stumps, lazybones," he said to me. "We have a boat to catch."

"Who is this '*we*' of whom you speak, varlet?" I demanded crossly.

"The '*we*' could refer to the royal '*we*' who commanded me to come to collect you," he said. "It also means the '*we*' of you and me—not Her Loveliness, sadly.

"What sort of boat?" I snapped.

"A riverboat to start, then we sail away, over the ocean blue," he said.

"I'll get some ginger oil and licorice," Lucy said.

Her face appeared troubled, which scared me. She was usually excellent at hiding her knowledge of the future, but something about this disturbed her. I was glad she remembered the ginger oil and licorice. I was prone to seasickness, and sailing in winter weather did not promise a smooth voyage.

"Come with me while I pack and tell me more," I snorted as I headed for the stairs. "Including why you are rushing me out of here. How can we even travel on the river? Isn't there ice?"

"There is some ice," Fenwick admitted, "but thin enough that the boat smashes through it easily."

I waited for him to follow me into our bedroom, then slammed the door behind him.

"You seem angry, Caz. Is it something I said?" Fenwick joked.

"Fenwick," I growled, low in my throat, grabbing his shirt with my left hand and jabbing my finger into his chest with the right. "For whatever reason, Lucy looked like her heart would break when you knocked on the door. She knew it was you before you came in, and I suspect she knows where you are taking me. She's worried, which makes me terrified."

"We need to go inside the Rhetian Empire," he said with a gulp.

I took a moment to absorb the news, closing my eyes and taking a deep breath.

"Oh, that's fine, then. I thought you were going to tell me we needed to visit each of the Seven Hells," I said sarcastically. "The Rhetian Empire? What could be easier?"

"His Majesty just received some reports that mention the Rhetians might be staging large quantities of supplies in their forts close to the border," Fenwick explained. "In addition, they have added a great number of skirmishers in the last month. They've pushed the Rangers back from the normal frontier about two leagues. His Majesty is concerned they have decided to mount an invasion in the spring. The timing of it, given the news of Prince Albert's death, makes sense."

"This is ridiculous," I sputtered while trying to keep my voice down. "There is no way either of us could pass for Rhetian."

"Who said anything about that?" Fenwick protested. "I will be Ako Bharwani, an esteemed trader from Nagah. You will be Sabu, my servant."

"We don't look like Nagahny either," I said.

"Don't worry, Sabu. Walnut juice and cutting most of our hair off will get us close enough," Fenwick said soothingly. "I'll need to use some hair dye, but yours is dark enough as is."

"Cutting my hair?" I protested. "Lucy likes my hair."

"Perhaps that is why she is so disturbed," Fenwick remarked. "The Nagahny wear their hair extremely close-cropped—something to do with the heat in Nagah, I think."

"That's not funny. And why do I always have to play the servant?" I complained, stuffing clothing in my bags.

"Don't pack too much," Fenwick cautioned. "You only need clothes for a few days. Bebo has your Sabu outfits on the boat."

"Bebo? The pirate from Scaramanga?" I asked.

"He's not a pirate," Fenwick replied. "He's an … opportunist. We were lucky he was in Aquileia when this came up. Otherwise, things would be more complicated. And to answer your question, you get to play the servant because you speak neither Nagahny nor Rhetian, where I am fluent in both. I can even speak Rhetian with a Nagahny accent. Now that I think of it, it might be best if Sabu were dumb—unable to speak because of some childhood trauma."

"Now you're being mean," I said.

"Now I'm being smart," he retorted. "One word out of your Aquileian mouth and we are both dead."

"What about my sword?"

"Sabu would not carry one," Fenwick admitted. "I'm sorry. Leave it behind. Bebo can give you a dagger. You should leave your ring, too. A servant would not possess such a piece of jewelry. I did not bring mine."

Lucy appeared, holding a small bottle of ginger oil and some licorice wrapped in waxed paper. She handed them to me. Her face was more composed, but I could tell she was still troubled.

"He's taking me to Rhetia," I groused, hoping a display of childish grumpiness might cheer her even a little. "We're going to be disguised as Nagahny, which means I need to cut off all my hair. He's making me act as his servant again."

"You'll use walnut juice to stain your skin?" she asked Fenwick, disregarding most of my outburst. "Have someone else apply it, or it will get on your palms. Stained palms will give you away. You'll need to cover yourselves head to toe, except for your palms and the bottoms of your feet."

"Thank you for the advice," Fenwick said.

"You'll need lemon juice to remove the stain once you return," she said without emotion.

I went to the lavatory to fetch my toiletries. After adding them to my bag, I closed it. I handed it to Fenwick.

"Please take this downstairs for me," I instructed firmly. "I will join you soon."

Fenwick understood I wanted a moment alone with Lucy. When he left, I shut the door. I turned to Lucy, whose eyes were downcast.

"I often think how difficult it must be for you to keep silent when you have seen a glimpse of the future," I said, clasping her shoulders gently. "You have been so strong for the entire time I've known you, but tonight you seem frightened."

"I'm scared because I do not know what will happen," she said as tears welled in her eyes. "I've experienced visions showing me two different outcomes. The hinge point for both was Fenwick's arrival tonight. I'm sorry to be reacting this way—it's the last thing you need as you set off. It's just—the two visions are so opposite."

"Then I will be careful and put my trust in the wisdom of the Gods that the better of the two is what will come to pass," I said as I embraced her. "Regardless, I love you with my entire soul. That must count for something—if not in this world, then the next."

Lucy flung her arms around my neck and buried her face in my collar. I tried to comfort her as she sobbed. Seeing her so distraught forced tears from my eyes. It was some minutes before we composed ourselves. Leaning back, she wiped her eyes with her sleeve, pushed herself up on her toes, and gave me a passionate kiss.

"That's so you have more reason to come back," she mumbled.

I could think of nothing else to say. After embracing her again, I walked out the door of our bedroom. She did not follow. I looked back before she disappeared from view. Lucy was fighting to wear a hopeful smile, but I saw fresh tears on her cheeks.

Fenwick was waiting downstairs with my bag and was holding my cloak. He helped me put it on, then headed for the front door. I picked up my bag and started to follow, then stopped.

"Do I need my horse?" I asked.

"No. I borrowed this one. She's a draft animal, actually. No saddle or stirrups. We'll ride double to Commerford. It's not that far," he explained.

It was snowing heavily. I gave Fenwick a leg up so he could get on the huge animal's back. He brought the horse to the front of the veranda, and I was able to use its height to climb on behind him while he held my bag. The horse did not seem to mind carrying two full-grown men. He would never win any races, but strength he seemed to have in abundance.

We reached the landing at Commerford nearly four hours later. As soon as we climbed aboard, the sailors cast off the lines and pushed us into the river. That took me by surprise.

"We're going in the dark?" I asked, somewhat alarmed.

"The tide won't wait for us," Fenwick said.

"Seems dangerous to me. You never told me why we are in such a hurry," I pointed out.

"Don't worry about the danger. That's what the boatmen are for. The king is paying a substantial amount to cover any possible damages. As far as the rush—the sooner we leave, the sooner we reach Rhetia," he said. "The quicker we get there, the faster we can escape once we see if the reports are accurate. I'm not particularly thrilled about this assignment myself, Caz. I was planning on celebrating the solstice quietly with Julienne, not spending the holiday on a small ship in a wintry sea. Given a choice... Oh, Seven Hells! You know I don't have a choice in matters like this. That aside, I do understand why it's important. I wish there was someone else who could go in our places, but there isn't."

The journey to Port Charles on a riverboat, with the Pheas swollen, rushing between icy banks, would have frightened me to death if I could have seen anything. The Gods alone knew how the boatmen did. Even so, there were frantic calls to "fend off" that occurred often enough that I knew we were taking substantial risks.

Sleep was impossible, with the occasional sudden lurch of the boat and accompanying shouting, plus the worried lowing of the two oxen on the deck who had pulled the boat upstream against the strong current. There was no cabin—no shelter of any kind. I sat on the deck, out of the way, and let the snow pile up on my cloak. My thoughts were of the darkest sort. I wanted to be angry—at Fenwick, at the king—but, like Fenwick, I understood the importance of our task and why Fenwick and I were the only ones the king could have chosen for this mission.

If Fenwick and I were able to confirm the reports, Aquileia would have enough time to mobilize our forces to meet a spring offensive from the Rhetians. You might wonder why the king would not do so regardless, but I understood his problem. A general mobilization would disrupt every territory in the realm—well, every territory but the March, where we drafted and exercised our militia every year up to now because of the nomads. The other duchies and counties might draft a militia annually, but only to conduct some perfunctory drills over a few days at a time when the men could easily be spared from their fields or their trades.

Summoning the militias to face a *possible* threat, and then having the threat fail to materialize, would cost the king an enormous amount of political capital, similar to the boy crying, "Wolf!" in the old fable. The only worse alternative would be not to summon the militias and have the Rhetians invade. The king, and the kingdom, might not recover from that.

The utter darkness began to fade to murky gloom. With the snow still falling thick and fast, there was no sunrise to mark the beginning of the day. Even with the additional light, I could hardly see the banks of the river as we sped along. Occasionally, we passed under a bridge. I had no idea where we were.

"When should we arrive in Port Charles?" I asked Fenwick.

"A few hours after nightfall, I hope," he replied. "The tide starts to ebb just before midnight. We need to be aboard Bebo's ship by then, or we will need to use the hard way to leave port."

"The hard way?"

"Rowing the anchor ahead of the ship, dropping it, then winching the ship forward," Fenwick explained.

"Oh! Warping," I said brightly.

"Yes, warping. If we arrive on time, however, Bebo's men can row us out of the harbor—much easier and faster."

With the greater light, the boatmen needed to shout less, and the boat suffered fewer sudden jerks to one side or the other. I fell asleep for a time but almost wished I didn't. Waking, I was stiff and cold. I was also ravenously hungry.

"Is there anything to eat?" I asked.

Fenwick tossed me a leather pouch. I opened it to find some jerky and dried fruit. Pulling out a strip of the dried meat, I began to gnaw on it. My jaw was tired by the time I finished one piece. The dried fruit was much easier to chew and tasted better.

When I finished eating, I asked, "What's the plan?"

"Well, as I told you, I will be Ako Bharwani, a trader from Nagah," Fenwick said.

"Why Nagah?"

"Because Bebo has a hold full of merchandise from there," Fenwick said.

"And he's going to give it to you?"

"Majors and Minors, no!" Fenwick snorted. "We bought every scrap of it—paid the going rate, though I doubt Bebo obtained it legally."

"Meaning he stole it or took it from someone by force."

"I tend not to ask those sorts of questions," Fenwick said.

"And in exchange, he is taking us to Rhetia?"

"No, that's extra."

"I hope you don't plan to pay him until he comes back and collects us," I said.

"Not exactly," Fenwick replied.

"What does that mean?" I demanded.

"He is not coming back for us," Fenwick said.

I stared at Fenwick in disbelief. "Say that again, slowly. I want to make sure I understand."

"He is not coming back for us."

"Then how in the Seven Hells do we get home?"

"Either we make our way north and east to the border, or we steal a boat and sail away," Fenwick answered glibly, as though what he proposed would be simply done.

I began to laugh. It was not a joyous, happy form of mirth. I was hysterical, like a madman who has lost his final grasp of sanity.

"He can't linger," Fenwick tried to explain. "It will be difficult enough landing us without being caught. If he stays nearby, he will surely be apprehended."

"Tell me more," I pleaded. "I want to learn how much worse this will get."

"I don't think I care for your attitude," Fenwick sniffed. "I did the best I could with the time and resources available."

"Go on. Tell me what your plan is."

"Bebo will land us just north of Sagun," Fenwick explained.

"With this Nagahny merchandise," I added. "What do we use to carry it? My back?"

"No, there is a wagon, and these two oxen," Fenwick said.

"Oh, ho! We're going to land on a hostile shore and somehow transport a wagon, two oxen, and a bunch of trinkets to dry land without being caught. That will be a marvelous trick. I can hardly wait to see it."

"We'll be using a raft and landing at night," Fenwick stated calmly, as though I were stupid. "That is another reason for our haste. By the time we reach the Rhetian coast, high tide should still fall before daybreak, giving us enough time to reach the coast road and Bebo enough time to sail away."

"And then?"

"And then we travel along, selling our wares, until we get close enough to see what is happening with the Rhetian fortresses in the foothills," he said.

"How far is it from one of the border forts to the nearest town large enough to attract a traveling peddler?" I asked.

"A day's ride," Fenwick responded casually.

"On horseback," I said. "Two days for an ox-drawn wagon. Three days on foot."

"So, maybe we *borrow* a couple of horses," Fenwick shrugged.

"And this is the best you could dream up?" I asked.

"As if you could do better," Fenwick snorted.

"I could hardly do worse than this half-assed collection of ridiculousness," I snapped. "Do we have a map, at least?"

14

It was dark when we reached Port Charles, but no longer snowing. Fenwick pointed out to me the change in the boat's movement as we neared the harbor. We were no longer rushing along. Our pace was more placid.

"We're nearing the mouth of the river," he said. "Do you miss your friends, the leeches? I know they were quite attached to you."

When my father and I first learned of a farmstead the family owned on the west side of the river, I went to investigate. There was no bridge, so I needed to swim across. By the time I reached the other side, I was covered in leeches. That was bad enough, but then I needed to swim back. Fenwick had shown up unexpectedly and helped me remove the disgusting things the second time they covered me. I just growled at him.

A few minutes later, we were tying up to the wharf at the Traval warehouse. A voice called out of the darkness, and Fenwick answered. Seconds later, a torch flared into life. Others followed, and I could now see a rope ladder hanging down. Following Fenwick, I climbed up with my bag over my shoulder and could now see the mast of the small ship we would now board.

The men on the wharf quickly rigged a small crane and lowered a large sling to the riverboat. In minutes, I heard the anxious lowing of an ox and saw it lifted into the air. They swung the crane around with the animal still suspended and lowered it into Bebo's ship.

"C'mon, Caz. No time to dawdle," Fenwick said, as he headed to a different rope ladder.

Bebo's ship was not much bigger than the riverboat, but it did offer shelter from the elements. There was a section of the deck in the stern that was raised. Below that were quarters for the crew.

I went below to drop my bag and looked around. It was certainly not luxurious. There was a small table, currently folded and stowed against the bulkhead, some chests that I guessed were also used as seats, and a number of serpentins hanging from hooks, swaying slightly with the rocking of the vessel.

When I went back on the main deck, I saw a wagon lashed to the deck just forward of the mast. I could hear the second ox protesting its flight from the riverboat to our ship. The sailors put the two animals in a makeshift pen toward the bow, forward of the wagon. Sternward from the mast, I noticed what looked like sections of planking stacked on top of one another.

Once the sailors judged the oxen to be secure, the men cast off from the wharf, pushing us away with two long poles. They quickly stowed the poles and broke out long slender oars. Fitting them into oarlocks, they waited patiently for instruction. Bebo called out in Scaramanga, and they began to row.

Without the snow, there was the light of the moon, just past full, by which to steer. I could see buoys marking the edge of the channel that had been dredged. Bebo aimed us just beside them as he began to chatter with Fenwick.

"He says our timing was good," Fenwick reported. "The tide started going out roughly a half-hour before we arrived. We should not have any problems clearing the harbor. He suggests we turn in for the night."

That sounded like a good idea to me, having been awake for most of a day and a half. I went back into the small cabin. Rummaging through my bag, I found the ginger oil Lucy gave me. I rubbed some on my upper lip, then grabbed a blanket and my cloak. Wrapping myself in them like a cocoon, I carefully arranged myself in a serpentin. Sleep claimed me quickly.

Oddly, it was the bellowing of the oxen that woke me after too brief a sleep and not the pitching of the ship. Even so, I was glad I had my ginger oil. The winter seas were rough, and Bebo's ship was not large. We were being tossed around as though we were sport for the Gods. The oxen, at the bow, suffered wave after wave crashing over them and were clearly unhappy.

The motion and the darkness combined to make me queasy. The ginger oil helped me through it. When day began to break, and I could see the horizon, I started to feel better.

Fenwick saw me and pulled me below. We sat on one of the chests and Fenwick showed me a map of the part of the Rhetian Empire where we would be. The border and the mountains were clearly marked, as were six of the border forts in this area. Fenwick pointed to where Bebo would land us.

"He showed me one of his charts, and this is clearly the best spot," Fenwick said. "The water is deep enough that he can pull in close, and there is a beach of sorts. Everywhere else where he can pull in close, there is a steep rise. In addition, the coast road is only a few yards from the beach."

"How close can he get?" I asked.

"Roughly fifty yards, he reckons," Fenwick replied.

"Do oxen swim?"

"How else did you think they would reach the shore?"

"You mentioned a raft."

"The raft is for the wagon and the merchandise," Fenwick said. "You and I, and a couple of Bebo's men, will row ashore, trailing ropes. The ropes will be fastened to the oxen. Bebo will lower the oxen into the water, and we will use the ropes to guide them to us. Bebo's men will return to the ship with the rope, which they will attach to the raft."

"I did not see a raft."

"They will make it from the planking you saw on deck. After they lash the planking on top of the boats, it will serve as a raft. They will load the wagon on that, and we will use the oxen to pull it ashore," Fenwick explained.

"I hope this works," I said skeptically.

"Bebo thinks it will."

"Has he ever done something like this before?" I asked.

"That's a good question."

Later that day, Bebo cut our hair off. We both were left with stubble. Fenwick stripped down and dyed his remaining hair black. When he washed off the excess hair dye, two of Bebo's men had me strip also, then began to rub walnut juice all over us, from our scalps to the tops of our feet and everything in between, including our eyelids and our most personal areas. By the time they finished, both of us were shivering from the cold.

I then put on my Sabu clothing. The tunic and pantaloons were made from some type of flaxen homespun material. It might have been quite comfortable in the warmth of Nagah, but in this winter weather, they would do me no good. There were also low shoes, instead of my customary boots. Before I had the chance to complain, Fenwick handed me a pair of woolen leggings and an animal skin vest such as they wear in Rhetia. He added to that woolen mittens that went to my elbows and a thick scarf.

"We'll explain we traded for them," he said.

His clothing, though from finer cloth, was just as thin as mine, and he put on leggings as well. Instead of a vest, though, he wore a full coat of markedly better quality than mine.

Looking at Fenwick, I grudgingly admitted that we might pass for Nagahny, particularly to people who were not familiar with them. Our Nagahny clothing was visible, though largely covered by the Rhetian items we wore for warmth. The one area where we failed was our eyes. Mine are blue, and Fenwick's are gray. Most Nagahny had brown eyes.

Six days later, Bebo's men began bringing things up from the hold and putting them in the wagon. There were bolts of cloth, small kegs full of colored glass beads, a great number of what seemed to be ax handles and either spears or shafts for other implements, like hoes, and a varied miscellany of unusually shaped cooking instruments.

"The mopani wood you see is the prize," Fenwick explained. "Very durable. That will probably be our biggest selling item."

When they finished loading the wagon, they covered it with a canvas tarp. They tied the tarp down on top of the goods tightly. I presumed that was to keep anything from shifting position once the wagon was put on the raft and started bobbing up and down.

We dressed in our mish-mash of clothing and waited. I caught sight of the land just before sunset. We continued to sail closer under the light of a waning quarter moon. Bebo's men swung the small rowboats out. Fenwick and I were directed to one. Two large coils of sturdy rope and the oxen's yoke went in the other.

They rowed us ashore with little difficulty. We took hold of the two ropes and looked for something around to which we could bend them to help us if an ox decided to go astray. There was nothing useful.

The men rowed back. My rope twitched first. Then we heard the lowing complaint of an ox as it was hoisted in the air. When the sound changed, I reckoned the ox was in the water, and I quickly ran up the slope of the beach to take in the slack of the rope. Thank all the heavenly beings, the ox did not fight me. He responded to the tug on the rope, and I was able to gather it in hand over hand. In a few minutes, he climbed up onto the beach.

While I was bringing my ox to dry land, Fenwick's was dropped into the sea. This one was less amenable to the persuasion of the rope. I saw Fenwick staggering with the rope around his waist, straining with all his strength to pull the frightened animal in the proper direction. Finally, wide-eyed and snorting with fear, the second ox stood on the rocky shingle.

We allowed Fenwick's animal to calm down before we put the two of them under the yoke and attached the ropes to it. It was quite some time before we felt movement from the lines. Apparently, rather than try to fashion the raft in the rolling sea, they hoisted the boats back onto the ship and then fastened the sections of plank. They then hoisted the wagon aboard and lashed it to the planks. Once they finished, they lifted the entire assemblage into the air and lowered it to the waves.

The slack from both ropes was hauled in by the sailors. A minute later, we felt three sharp tugs, the signal to begin towing the raft ashore. The team of oxen had no difficulty with the load, and the two boats under the planking scraped onto the shingle soon after.

Two of the sailors had come along. One busied himself in untying the wagon from its moorings. The other extended two planks at the width of the wagon's wheels from the platform to the shingle. With Fenwick pulling and them pushing, the wagon glided onto the beach. Before it could roll back into the water, one of the sailors thrust a piece of wood under one of the rear wheels to stop it.

He climbed back aboard the improvised raft. His partner tugged on the rope attached to the stern, and they were pulled back to the ship. I led the pair of oxen to the wagon, and we attached their yoke to the traces.

Fenwick climbed onto the seat and said, "Go ahead, Sabu. Take us to the road."

I slapped the ox nearest me on the haunch, and he started forward. His companion matched his movement, and we began to rumble up from the beach. At the top of the slope, we reached some tall grass. The land was blessedly flat, and we reached the road in a few minutes.

I marveled to myself at how smoothly we were able to get from the ship to the beach. The optimist in me hoped this was a sign of how our mission would progress. The realist part of my psyche wondered if we had just used up all of our allotted portion of good fortune.

When we reached the road, we turned north. Fenwick allowed me to climb up next to him. The oxen plodded along through the night. We thought we would reach the first town sometime in the morning.

My hodgepodge of clothing kept most of me warm, except my ankles and upper arms. Fenwick was obviously not suffering at all. He fell asleep within a mile.

We reached the first town about an hour after the sun rose. We drove to the small square at its center. Fenwick instructed me to remove the tarp and display our wares. I was just finishing when a man in some sort of uniform strode up and barked harshly at Fenwick.

I continued folding the tarp until Fenwick clapped his hands and gestured for me to stop. I did and looked at him questioningly. He gestured for me to cover the wagon again. The man in the uniform had his arms crossed and a smug look on his face. I began to wrestle the tarp back on the wagon. Fenwick got down and came to help.

"He is a town constable. It's their holy day," he whispered very softly. "No one is allowed to conduct any business. We also need to attend their religious observance with them, or we will be thrown in jail as infidels. I tried to explain we were Nagahny, but the law requires everyone to attend. We will need to move to the next town after we finish attending their ceremony."

By the time we finished with the tarp, other people were arriving in the square, heading to the large building on the square with a forbidding appearance. The constable led us into the building. I hoped we would be placed in the rear, but he took us to the first row of seats.

As we walked down the long central aisle, I noted that newcomers knelt and bowed their heads for a lengthy period before sitting. I also saw that there were cushions for their knees. There were no cushions in the front rank.

The constable gestured for us to sit. I went to my knees on the stone floor and bent my head as I observed the others do. Fenwick was clever enough to do the same.

While I was in a prayerful posture, I silently worded pleas to our Gods. First, as I had been taught, I asked that Their will be done. Then, I voiced my hope that it was their will to keep us safe, to return me to my wife and homeland, and for us to obtain the knowledge we sought. Finally, I apologized for where I was, praying to them from the building of a false god. When I finished, I sat on the hard wooden bench.

From our location, I expected them to make a spectacle of us. I decided my safest choice was to expand my muteness into overall simple-mindedness. Fenwick spoke the language. I did not. I would let the burden fall on his shoulders.

Suddenly, the faint whispers of the people behind us fell silent. A door opened to the right, and a man in black robes strode out. From the moment the door opened, he began to glare at us. He climbed atop a speaking platform with a lectern, still staring angrily. He raised his arm and pointed at us, and he began shouting.

Fenwick immediately went to his knees again. I continued to sit, open-mouthed and slack-jawed, until Fenwick hissed at me and pulled me forward. From my knees, I kept the same witless look on my face, looking goggle-eyed at the priest as he continued to shout at us. Fenwick reached over and bent my head forward and down.

Fenwick began responding verbally to some of the priest's ranting. I guessed the man was asking questions about who we were. As this went on, I slowly started to lift my head to look at the priest, maintaining my stupefied expression. Fenwick noticed and shoved my head down again.

I sensed the priest was no longer shouting at us but was instead bellowing to the crowd. Fenwick later confirmed that the man lectured the gathering about the evils of non-belief, using the two of us as examples. He focused on me, equating my muteness and apparent lack of intelligence as punishment from their one true god for being an infidel, with Fenwick's sentence being the responsibility to take care of me.

The ceremony lasted hours. Fenwick and I were required to spend the entirety of it on our knees. The pain from kneeling on the stone floor finally subsided into blissful numbness. Since I could not understand a word of what the man was saying, I amused myself by thinking of magical punishments I would ask Lucy to inflict upon Fenwick for dragging me here.

Finally, the priest stopped his ranting and began reciting some passages. The audience answered as one, mumbling whatever the standard and expected responses were. This went on for quite a bit. When this part of the ceremony ended, the priest again began shouting at the two of us. When he finished, he strode back to the door from which he entered and departed.

Fenwick and I stayed on our knees, though we could hear the rest of the gathering getting up and leaving. The constable eventually returned and told Fenwick he could rise. We stood up, our knees trembling from kneeling so long, and stumbled outside. No one else remained in the building or even in the square by then.

Our wagon seemed undisturbed, and the oxen were waiting patiently. The constable walked us to the wagon and watched as we headed out of town. Being the simpleton, I turned and gawked at him as we drove away.

"We have no chance of making the next town before dark," Fenwick said. "And the animals need to eat. We will stop and let them graze along the way and spend the night in the open."

I cursed Fenwick for my aching knees. I then asked him to relate what he heard during the service. Much of it I shared with you in the paragraphs above, but that was not all the priest said.

"The priest also mentioned that the infidels of Aquileia were already feeling the might of their god's wrath, as evidenced by Albert's death. He then said that even greater vengeance would be visited upon Aquileia in the months to come," Fenwick related. "I think we will find what we seek."

15

We spent a cold night huddled underneath the wagon. Fortunately, Fenwick had a number of blankets in the merchandise, and we used all of them to stay warm. Dinner was jerky and dried fruit. We did not dare start a fire for fear of drawing attention to ourselves.

"We'll reach the next town tomorrow," he said as we gnawed on the jerky. "Depending on how early we start, we may have enough of the day left to sell some of our wares."

"Or we could press on," I suggested.

"I have no desire to be in this country any longer than necessary," Fenwick said, "but that is a bad idea. We are presenting ourselves as a traveling merchant and his helper. If we don't stop to try to sell something, that immediately draws suspicion. Do you remember how quickly that constable was on us? We will face that level of scrutiny everywhere. It will be safer for us to play our parts."

"That will drag us out another eight days, by my reckoning," I countered. "Eight more days for someone to figure out we are not from Nagah."

"If you show people what they expect to see, they don't look too closely," Fenwick said. "Let's just play our parts for now."

"Have you come up with a better idea of how we leave the wagon behind and get close to the nearest fort?" I asked.

"No," Fenwick frowned. "We won't get close with the wagon. A patrol will stop us and turn us around, if they don't do worse. Therefore, we must ditch the wagon. Then the question is whether we are safer on foot or stealing horses. Horse thieves draw a lot of attention, so I'm inclined to suggest we go on foot.

The problem is the wagon and the oxen. If they are found, they will begin searching for us. We will be on foot, and they will be mounted. I don't like any of our options too much right now. There is still time before we need to decide. I hope a better idea comes to one of us."

Something in what Fenwick said struck me, but when I tried to grasp the thought, it vanished. I did not try to chase it down. Experience has taught me that it's better not to dwell on it. Stray ideas like these return in their own time, if they come back at all, and don't respond to pressure.

We arrived in the next town in the late morning. As before, we reached the central square, and I uncovered the wagon. Again, before I finished, a constable appeared.

The man seemed less hostile than the previous constable we met. I kept fussing in the back of the wagon, trying to look busy and uninterested. The discussion reached a point where Fenwick and the constable went back and forth over something. At last, it sounded as though Fenwick admitted defeat. I saw him reach into his money pouch and withdraw some coins.

"He tried to tell me we needed a vendor's permit to sell anything," Fenwick told me in a whisper. "When I asked where the magistrate was in order to obtain one, the conversation got interesting. He tried to tell me the magistrate was not in town today. Then he changed his mind and said that he had not been entirely honest, but it was to spare my feelings since the magistrate hated foreign infidels and would not grant us a permit. I pleaded with him, asking him to be our go-between to obtain permission."

"Let me guess," I said. "He expressed reluctance to be involved since it might affect his reputation. You begged him. He finally relented, then told you how much the permit would cost, and asked for an equal sum for the risk he was taking."

"You've run into this before?" Fenwick asked.

"Before you and I met," I said, nodding. "I occasionally walked on the shady side of the street to help retrieve what my clients had lost."

Fenwick laughed. "After that, it was merely a question of setting the price for his services since the fee for the permit was non-negotiable. Of course, you and I both know that no permit is required. We will see variations on this theme in every town we visit."

"It's nice to know that Rhetian constables are so similar to the ones in Aquileia, in spite of their horrible religion," I said.

"They're the same in Scaramouche, Mooresa, Nagah, and everywhere else I've been," Fenwick added with a smile.

Townspeople walked by us two and three times, staring at the strange-looking foreigners. A couple of women were the first to come to view our wares. They admired the bolts of brightly colored cloth and the glass beads but did not touch them, let alone buy anything. I wondered why, then realized that none of the people in Rhetia wore colorful clothing. Reviewing my memory of the two women, and the women we saw in the first town, I realized I had seen none of them wearing jewelry either.

Other women stopped by later and displayed the same behavior. None of them wore jewelry of any kind, and their clothes were drab. We did not sell anything until near the end of the day, when a man who had walked by the wagon repeatedly came over. He pointed at the ax handles and wooden shafts and asked Fenwick a question.

Though I could not understand what he was saying, I could tell that Fenwick was immersed in his role as a traveling merchant. I heard the word "mopani" and figured Fenwick was extolling the many virtues of this wood from Nagah. It was also easy to tell when they started to haggle over the price. Eventually, the man fished some coins out of a pouch and walked away with one of the wooden shafts.

"I told you those would be our biggest sellers," Fenwick said smugly later that evening.

"We sold one wooden shaft," I snorted. "Not a particularly profitable day."

Our experience in the next three towns was similar. We still had nearly all the merchandise that we started with. In each town, we sold one or two pieces of mopani wood. The only success we enjoyed was being clever enough not to be caught in a town on their holy day.

The night before we reached the last town, closest to the nearest fort, the idea that had escaped me before returned as I was falling asleep. I woke up and prodded Fenwick. He grumbled unintelligibly at me. I poked him again.

"What do you want?" he snarled.

"I know how we're going to get to the fort," I said excitedly.

"What?"

"I know how we're going to get to the fort," I repeated.

"I heard you the first time," Fenwick grumbled. "What's your brilliant idea?"

"We head to the fort in the wagon," I said. "Perhaps we are intercepted by a patrol. Perhaps not. If we reach the fort, we ask if we can sell our goods. They'll probably turn us away, but we will have approached close enough to see what we came to find."

"And what if a patrol stops us—which is more likely?" Fenwick asked.

"We take their horses and uniforms," I said triumphantly.

"Um, Caz, you mean kill them, don't you?" Fenwick clarified.

"I suppose," I admitted. "I certainly expect them to resist."

"And killing them doesn't bother you?" he asked.

"I don't like the idea of murdering people for profit," I said. "No offense intended. You were very skilled at it. But war is different. A state of war has existed between the Kingdom of Aquileia and the Rhetian Empire for centuries. A patrol that stops us will be made up of soldiers."

"So were the nomads you ambushed six months ago," Fenwick pointed out. "And I distinctly recall you feeling disturbed because they were so young."

"It did disturb me," I said. "I probably would still have done it, though. They were coming to attack, and they outnumbered us. I was determined to stop them. In this case, it is the same as when I encountered Rhetians when I was in the Rangers. They were the enemy. Given the opportunity, they would kill me without hesitation."

"How many people do you expect would be in a Rhetian patrol?" Fenwick asked.

"Four to six men," I answered. "Of course, there's always a possibility we run into a whole troop. Then we can only try to talk our way out of it."

"And if we can't?"

"Then we're in trouble," I said. "But our chances of making it back alive from this were never very good, were they?"

"If we were two ordinary people, I would agree with that," Fenwick said. "But for us, I thought we had an even chance."

"I don't consider a coin flip to be very good odds, my friend. I like things a bit more in my favor."

"Yet your idea seems risky," Fenwick stated.

"It's no worse than the alternatives, and might even be better," I said.

"How?"

"On foot, the only way to get close enough to see inside the fort is at night when you know they will have regular patrols," I said. "If we steal horses, we would still need to make the approach at night on foot with the same risk—plus with the countryside roused looking for horse thieves. If we follow my plan, we might be able to bluff our way to the very gates during daylight. Should a patrol intercept us, we take their horses and uniforms. In a Rhetian uniform, we should be able to ride close enough to see what we need to."

"What if someone questions us?" he asked.

"Then you tell them something believable so they don't ride out after us right away," I said. "Other than that, they won't know anything is wrong until the patrol doesn't check in, which should give us a lead of a few hours. The only way my idea is worse than yours is if we encounter a whole troop, and they drag us in for questioning."

"Let me sleep on it," Fenwick said. "I'll let you know what I think in the morning."

When we arose, Fenwick admitted no other ideas came to him. He was willing to try my suggestion. We entered the last town that morning, bribed the constable, and set out our wares. As before, a few women came and looked but did not buy. We sold two staffs—and still had over half the supply we set out with originally.

At the end of the day, we left town the way we entered. We waited until the middle of the night, then crossed through it again, heading to the nearest fort. A couple of dogs barked, but not for long enough to raise any alarm. We continued on the road all day. With every plodding step toward the fort, we grew more anxious.

At the end of the day, we pulled well off the road. We had not seen much traffic the entire time we had been in the country, but we still did not want to risk someone riding along at night and seeing our wagon. Having been awake the entire night before, I was able to sleep soundly, swaddled in blankets under the wagon. Only my nose was exposed to the chilly air.

At first light, we set out for the fort. We encountered no one on the road. Our good fortune in no way lessened my apprehension. The oxen continued to plod forward until we were within a couple of furlongs of the walls. For a moment, I allowed myself to think we might reach the gate.

No sooner did I have that thought than a group of twelve armored men burst out at the gallop. They reined in just short of us, lances leveled. One of them barked at us.

Fenwick responded. I could tell he was trying to convince them we were traveling merchants who thought the soldiers might be interested in our merchandise. It probably didn't matter what he said. The soldiers had their orders—to bring us in for questioning.

Fenwick acquiesced to their demands and set the oxen in motion. Surrounded by the soldiers, we plodded into the fort. Before they commanded us to halt, I saw what we had been sent to find. The fort was packed with supplies—stacks of barrels lined the interior walls. I imagined the storehouses were full of bags of grain. There were also soldiers. The place was full of them, almost all looking at us curiously.

When we climbed down from the wagon, they searched us. They found my dagger—it wasn't hidden—took Fenwick's sword (not his good one, he was carrying a cheap blade suitable for a peddler) and were very excited to seize his money pouch. They prodded us inside and down some steps.

Keys were produced, and a man unlocked a heavy wooden door. A dimly lit corridor was revealed. There were six cells, three on each side. We were taken to the last on the right. The door was unlocked, and we were shoved inside roughly. As I was recovering my balance, I heard the door shut and the lock click.

There was a small window that allowed some of the afternoon light in— just enough that we could see what was in the cell. Two cots, covered with straw, each with two blankets—one to sleep on, one to cover oneself. There were two buckets. One held a ladle, so I knew what the other was for. I sat down on one of the cots heavily.

After the door at the end of the corridor shut, a voice called out in Aquileian, "Welcome to one of the Seven Hells!"

I opened my mouth to answer, but Fenwick slapped his hand over it. He shook his head vigorously. I gave him a puzzled look.

"No sabe dis talk good," Fenwick replied. "Who dere?"

"We are Ah-kwi-lay-an," the voice said slow and loud, as though speaking to an idiot.

I almost laughed out loud. Fenwick stopped me by glaring at me. We could hear other voices muttering in the background.

"How much?" Fenwick answered.

"How much? Do you mean how many?" questioned the voice.

"How many you?" Fenwick asked.

"Eight," came the answer, after more muttering.

"Ate ah-kwi-lay-ah? Udders?" Fenwick asked.

"There are eight of us," the voice said, again speaking loud and slow. "We are all from Aquileia. We are soldiers."

"Ah-kwi-lay-ah," Fenwick repeated. "No udders?"

"There aren't any others," the voice replied, sounding more exasperated. "There are six cells. Two men are in each cell. We occupy four cells. You are in the fifth. The sixth is empty."

"Sure dat?" Fenwick asked.

"Yes, we're sure."

"No retchin scum?" Fenwick asked.

"What?"

"No retchin scum?"

"He means 'No Rhetian scum,' I think," I heard from one of them.

"Sisi. No retchin scum," Fenwick said.

"No. Just Aquileians."

"Sabe," Fenwick stated.

"It's not unusual to have someone listening in," Fenwick whispered to me. "The men we can hear muttering are probably all Aquileian, but there's the cell across from us."

I looked at Fenwick crossly. He wasn't thinking. He and I could both determine if there were men in that cell.

I searched within myself for the place or thing that doesn't really exist in the physical world that is my connection to Bellona. Finding it, I withdrew a tiny tendril of her energy. Using that, I expanded my senses.

There was no one in the cell across from us. I sensed no danger from the other four cells. I closed my connection to the Goddess.

"There's no one across from us," I reported in a whisper. "And I sense no threat from the others."

"I still prefer to wait before we reveal ourselves," Fenwick said. "They will probably take us for questioning. Remember, you are mute. It means you can't talk, but you can make other sounds. They will probably be rather physical, so if it hurts, you can react. Just don't say any words."

"What about you?" I asked.

"I'm going to stick to the story that I am Ako Bharwani from Nagah," Fenwick said. "It will take more than a beating to get me to change my tune."

Almost as if they heard Fenwick's faint whisper, we could hear the lock in the door at the end of the corridor. We heard the door open, the footfalls coming closer. Our lock scraped, then our door was thrust open violently.

Two men charged into the cell with short clubs. They swung at our heads, and when we ducked and tried to cover with our arms, they flung us on the floor. With a knee in the small of my back, my arms were seized and bound behind me. When that was complete, two other men lifted me by the armpits and began dragging me out of the cell.

I scrabbled to get my feet underneath me. Once I did, the two men started shoving me from behind, keeping me off balance, jabbing their clubs into my kidneys. Leaving the cells, we reached the stairway, where I was shoved down and then dragged up the stairs.

They took me to a room with a chair and a desk on one side and a short stool in the middle. After plunking me down on the stool, the two men started trying to knock me to the floor, hitting me with fists that I saw were encased in leather gloves.

I decided to let them knock me off. That was a bad idea. They then began kicking me. Curling into a ball, I tried to squirm toward the wall so they could only kick one side. Guessing my intent, they picked me up and put me back on the stool.

No one was there to ask questions. I reckoned that would come later, after the two men felt I was in the proper state of mind to answer honestly. They didn't know that I'd been beaten before, by professionals. These two were enthusiastic amateurs. That's not to say it didn't hurt. It did—a lot. They forced the appropriate noises out of me in response. But I knew they couldn't break me right away.

16

E ventually, a man entered the room and sat at the desk. He wore the wispy mustache I remember Rhetian officers affected. He spoke to me in Rhetian. I shook my head, indicating I did not understand. He tried heavily accented Aquileian, and I gave him the same response.

He spoke to the two men. They grabbed me under the arms again and began dragging me out. When we reached the stairs, they threw me down. That hurt in places different from the beating they gave me. They untied my wrists before tossing me back into the cell.

Once back in the cell, I stretched out on the cot. It was probably infested with bugs, but I didn't care. I cataloged my bumps and bruises, assessing if they did any serious damage. They stayed away from my head, for which I was thankful.

Fenwick arrived back in the cell later. He looked like I felt—banged up but not seriously injured. Like me, he lay down for a few minutes. When he sat up, he beckoned me over.

"I have good news and bad news," he cracked. "The good news is I think I convinced them you're mute. The bad news is that they might keep beating you just for the fun of it."

"Thanks," I whispered sarcastically.

"Since there is no one lurking to overhear us, can we give up the ruse and talk to the others?" I asked.

"In a minute," he cautioned. "If they are Aquileian soldiers, they are from the Rangers, correct?"

I nodded.

"Are Rangers generally observant?"

"It is what separates a good one from his peers," I said. "Why?"

"I think I can get us out of these cells," Fenwick explained. "But that's only a first step. Getting out of the fort will require knowing where we can lay hands on some weapons and, ideally, horses. Rather than bumble around in the dark, it would be helpful if one or two of them know more about the layout of the fort than what we saw on the way in."

"I know where the stables are," I said. "They're not quite directly opposite the door they took us in."

"Where is the armory?" Fenwick asked.

"I have no idea."

Fenwick shook his head. "I'm getting ahead of myself. It would be best if all of us were armed once we are out of the fort, but we need to get out first. There is simply no chance we can fight our way out—too many soldiers. We need to sneak out or bluff our way to freedom. I need to think."

"Use Bellona," I said.

"What?"

"Use Bellona," I repeated. "When I visited Her Temple, they instructed me that, as she is the Goddess of war, she can help you with battlefield strategy. I know she guided me in our fights with the nomads. There is no possibility I would have been as successful without her help."

"I don't remember learning that," Fenwick replied thoughtfully. "It's worth trying."

He lay down on the cot again and closed his eyes. I returned to my cot and did the same. I reached within and found my connection to Bellona. Pulling the smallest tendril of her energy from it, I tried to think about our current circumstances.

I did not make much progress in developing useful ideas before we heard the sound of the door at the end of the corridor open. Darkness had descended outside, and it seemed it was now feeding time for the prisoners. I heard the scrape of something on the floor and comments in Rhetian from the guards. I quickly closed my link with Bellona.

"Eat quickly, friend," came a voice from one of the other cells. "If you make them wait to get the plate back, they come in and give you a beating."

Two tins were shoved under the door. In the dim light of the torch outside that came through the small opening in the door, dinner was an unappetizing looking, and worse smelling, sort of ragoût. They provided no utensils, so I began eating with my hands. As bad as it looked and smelled, it tasted even more foul. Nevertheless, I forced myself to eat it quickly. I saw Fenwick doing the same, with an ugly grimace on his face as he choked it down.

He waited until we heard the guards leave the corridor before saying out loud, "Majors and Minors! That was worse than the beating!"

"Hey!" came a voice from one of the other cells. "Are you the same guy as before?"

"Yes," Fenwick called back. "Sorry for the play-acting. I didn't know if they might be listening."

"You in the Rangers? Whose unit?" another voice asked.

"Not a Ranger," Fenwick replied. "Something other. Aquileian though, and my colleague served in the Rangers a few years back. Are all of you healthy?"

"A little banged up," one called, "but nothing serious. We've only been here a few days."

"Captured?"

"We were coming back from patrol and ran into twice our numbers," one explained. "We gave better 'n we got, but still lost six men, including our sergeant."

"Did any of you notice where the armory is?" Fenwick asked.

"Aye," came a different voice. "Next to the stable, further side."

"How many guards are outside the door at night?" Fenwick asked. "And when do they change?"

"Just the one. He'll arrive soon—we can hear him yapping with the guys he relieves," someone said. "He's all alone until two come for him, just before sunup."

"Anything else you can think of about the fort?" Fenwick asked.

"Well, it seems full up, from what we saw when we arrived," said one.

"Any idea how many sentries they post at night?"

"Sorry, no," came the answer, after we heard them mumbling between themselves. "If it helps, Chet thinks a bunch of 'em are recent conscripts."

"What gave you that idea, Chet?" Fenwick asked.

"Some of 'em looked sloppy, if you know what I mean," he said. "Like they weren't used to the uniform, and their posture was sort of relaxed-like—unsoldierly."

"That's good information," Fenwick said. "Thanks."

"What are you going to do?"

"I'm still figuring that out," Fenwick replied. "I've got some ideas, though. Just be patient. I'll let you know soon."

Fenwick arranged himself on his cot and closed his eyes.

"Well," he said when he sat up a short time later, "I have an idea of what to do. It's risky, and I have no confidence we will be able to pull it off, but it's the best I've come up with."

"Tell me."

"Getting out of these cells and overcoming the guard outside should not be a problem," he began.

"Oh? How are you going to open these doors?" I asked.

"I palmed my lockpicks when they apprehended us and hid them in my shoe," Fenwick explained. "It hurt to walk on them until they put us in here."

"Why haven't you mentioned it?" I demanded quietly.

"As I said, getting out of the cells is only a small part of the solution," he reminded me. "I did not want to raise your hopes in vain. Anyway, after we take care of the guard outside the door, we need to try to get in the armory and the stable. If we can accomplish that without being detected, then our chances improve."

"Are we just going to make a run for it?" I asked.

"I hope we can avoid that."

"How?"

"Well, I hope the Rhetian army is like any other—that they assign the worst duties to the newest soldiers," Fenwick said.

"That's human nature, I think," I commented.

"From what the others told me, the midnight watch probably runs from eight o'clock until four o'clock in the morning. There is no clock, so that is my guess. If the recent conscripts are on duty, by one or two o'clock in the morning, I'm hoping they will be asleep at their posts."

"That is a serious infraction!" I cautioned. "In the Rangers, you can be hanged for falling asleep at your post."

"But does it happen?" Fenwick asked. "Particularly with new men?"

"Well, yes, but—"

"The Rangers are also an elite unit of professional soldiers, living in the open, on the front lines," Fenwick remarked. "Here, we have conscripts, in an enclosed fortress, leagues away from the enemy. I guess I'm saying that I'm willing to bet our lives that most of them, if not all of them, will be asleep. Even if they are not, I doubt they will be at their most alert."

"I'll concede the point," I said.

"When we get out of the cells," Fenwick continued, "I'll go take care of the guards at the gate. You take the other men to the stable and the armory. Get everyone a sword, including one for me, and bows if they have them. Take enough horses for all of us. I am tempted to try to take all the horses, but I'm afraid it will cause too much commotion. Don't waste time trying to saddle them in the dark. Then we leave as quietly as possible. If all goes well, we will have another two hours before they discover we are gone."

"And you think this will work?" I asked.

"I haven't the faintest idea whether we will be successful," Fenwick replied. "This is just the best I have been able to figure."

"When do you want to tell the others?"

"Maybe now. Hold on," he told me.

"Men," Fenwick called out, "do the guards ever visit after dinner?"

"No," came a chorus of voices.

"Good. That's what I hoped," he responded.

Fenwick stuck his hand into the straw on his cot and pulled out a group of three skeleton keys, and some implements attached to a metal ring. On the inside of the door, the lock mechanism was covered by a blank plate with no hole for a key. One of his tools was a metal rod with an end similar to a chisel. Fenwick shoved the flattened portion under the plate and began working it around the edge, prying the plate up as he did. In less than a minute, the plate popped off. Fenwick then stuck his finger in the hole, feeling around. He withdrew his finger, inserted the first tool, and rotated it. With a click, the bolt withdrew, and the door began to open.

He went to the cell next door. After warning them to remain quiet, he inserted one of the skeleton keys and twisted it. The door swung open. Within a minute, all ten of us were in the corridor. The men, all clad in tattered Ranger uniforms, adhered to our admonition to be silent.

"I'm glad you told us you were Aquileian," one said, "because you sure don't look it."

"Thanks, I think," I replied. "We were trying to pass for Nagahny."

"What?"

"People from Nagah, on the southern continent," Fenwick explained.

"Which of you was in the Rangers?" another asked.

"I was," I said. "I made captain, then realized later that I didn't have the money or the influence to go further."

It was obvious that learning of my former rank removed all their hesitancy. Fenwick went over the plan with them. They nodded their heads and whispered between themselves, determining which of them would go to the armory and which would get the horses.

"When we get outside the fort, I want you men to make your way to the border," I said. "After you put some distance underneath your feet, travel at night and stay hidden during the day."

"Where are you going?" one asked.

"We're going to try to steal a boat and sail home," I said. "By splitting up, one or the other of us should make it back to safety. We need to let people know the Rhetians are preparing to invade."

"Go rest now," Fenwick said. "We will collect you later, when it is time to move."

We spent the next few hours watching the progress of the stars through our tiny window. At last, Fenwick and I reckoned it was time. We collected the others and went to the door at the end of the corridor. This had a keyhole, so

Fenwick inserted one of his skeleton keys and carefully and quietly opened the door.

The guard was asleep in a chair. Fenwick clamped his hand over the guard's mouth. The next instant, he wrenched the guard's head around, breaking his neck.

"Do we want the uniform?" I asked.

Fenwick shook his head. "It won't do any good. Let's keep moving."

We headed upstairs and reached the door to the courtyard. It was unlocked, and Fenwick opened it slowly. He peered out as the door swung open. Seeing nothing alarming, he stepped outside and headed for the gate.

The rest of us quietly crossed the courtyard, heading for the stable and the armory. Three men were to gather weapons while the rest of us collected horses. Entering from the small side door, we saw there was a guard in the stable, his head down on a table. One of the Rangers had grabbed a bridle from the table and quickly wrapped it around the guard's neck. He made some quiet choking noises as he died. From the armory next door, we heard the thump of a body falling to the ground and knew they dispatched the guard there.

The five of us in the stable each grabbed two bridles and quickly put them on the nearest animals. As quietly as we could, we opened the stalls and let them out. We then removed the cross bar holding the main stable doors shut. Slowly, to avoid making noise, we swung them in and brought the horses out. Using the mounting block just outside, we clambered onto our mounts.

The three from the armory appeared and gave us each a sword. I took one for Fenwick. We guided our horses to the gate, where Fenwick was waiting. He vaulted onto the horse I was leading for him. Once he had the reins, I handed him the sword.

We proceeded outside. The ten of us rode together at a canter until we could no longer see the fort. When we reached the first crossroad where the road to the fort turned either north or south, I reined in and stopped.

"I think this is where we should part ways, men," I said. "By the way, my name is Casimir FitzDuncan, Lord Oritur. My companion is Fenwick, Privy Advisor to His Majesty. If you make it back and we don't, please tell someone you saw us."

"Likewise, milord," said one.

The eight men gave us their names and thanked us for freeing them.

"Thank us when we see you in Aquileia," Fenwick said.

"May all the blessings of the Gods, Major and Minor, be with you on your journey," said one.

"And with you as well," I replied.

The eight of them turned to the north. Fenwick and I continued to the east on what was no more than an overgrown path. We rode in silence, alternating our pace between trotting and walking in order to get the most out of the horses, while putting as much distance as possible between us and the fort.

"You know that getting out of the fort was only part of the challenges we face," I said to Fenwick.

"I'm aware," he replied. "Still, well begun is half done."

"Maybe a third, in our case," I said. "Do you have any idea where we are?"

"Rhetia," he quipped.

"Thanks," I snorted sarcastically. "How far away from the coast where we might find a boat?"

"If we ride all day and all night and find a spot where we can lay low the next day, we should reach the coast that next night sometime," Fenwick said. "It will be something small—five or six houses. Near where Bebo put us ashore is the last big town on this section of coast."

"Why is that?"

"I don't really know," Fenwick admitted, "but from looking around, this reminds me of the area just on the other side of the river from Oritur, when we went with the nomads."

"The grass is even thinner here," I remarked. "Probably not much rain and not very good grazing land."

"Not good for crops, not suited for livestock—that's probably as good an explanation as any," Fenwick stated.

As the gray of false dawn appeared in the sky, Fenwick said, "The change of watch probably just happened. We'll need to keep our eyes open for a dust cloud behind us."

"You realize the reason I split us up was so the Rangers would draw the pursuit," I said.

"Everyone understood the reason, Caz," he said. "The men certainly did. They accepted it. They're soldiers. Plus, we gave them a fighting chance. They know their odds aren't good, but they also understand ours aren't much better. If you had not suggested it, I would have."

"Well, I hope they make it," I said, feeling guilty.

"I hope *we* make it," Fenwick retorted. "Seven Hells! There is dust behind us."

"Should we pick up the pace?" I asked.

Fenwick shook his head. "No. To get this close this quickly, they've exhausted their mounts," he said. "They don't even know if anyone went this way, unless they have an expert tracker. I doubt anyone like that would be so far from the front. If we speed up, we'll create our own dust. Then they'll know someone is up ahead. Their horses will be completely spent soon, and they'll have a long walk back to the fort."

A part of me wanted to panic, but I realized Fenwick was correct. As the sky grew lighter, I turned every so often to see their progress. At first, the plume of dust seemed to be growing nearer. Suddenly, it disappeared entirely.

"See?" Fenwick said. "Their horses are blown, and they never caught sight of us."

17

We continued riding through the day and into the night, keeping to a walk to conserve the animals. The first stream we reached, we stopped to let the horses drink. Fenwick and I had no food, so we tried to fill our bellies with water as well.

In spite of the chilly air, and the pain I still felt from my beating, I slept for stretches as we rode. I knew Fenwick did as well. When his horse stopped at another stream to drink, Fenwick nearly slid off his back, grabbing handfuls of mane to stay on. When darkness fell, my fatigue began to get the better of me.

"Fenwick, I don't want to stop, but I need sleep," I said. "It's probably not a good idea for us both to leave everything to the horses. We should take turns. Can you stay awake for as long as you can? When you're about to collapse, wake me, and I'll take over for a bit."

"I'll do my best," he said. "But you probably won't get much of a rest."

"Something is better than nothing," I replied.

I leaned forward and placed my head on the horse's neck, grabbing a handful of his mane in my fist as a precaution against falling off. Within a handful of strides, I was unconscious. Fenwick's voice woke me what seemed like an instant later.

"Caz, I need you to wake up," he pleaded, probably not for the first time, judging by his tone.

"I'm awake," I said. "I'll take over."

We switched back and forth through the night. When morning came, we were still both exhausted. In examining the landscape, there was no suitable spot where we could get out of sight. We rode for another hour past dawn, hoping to find something, but all we saw was thin grass on a featureless plain.

Fenwick reined in. "Nothing we can do," he said. "Might as well stop right here.

He slid off his horse, holding onto the reins. I did the same and sat on the ground. I looped the end of the reins around my ankle to keep my horse from wandering off. Then I stretched out on the ground.

I woke from time to time, when the horse tugged on the reins, but fell asleep again quickly. The last time I woke was because I was hungry and thirsty, and I needed to relieve myself. The sun was low in the sky, so I felt we'd rested long enough.

I kicked Fenwick on the sole of his foot as I went to urinate. He woke with a jump but made no noise. When he saw what I was doing, he stood up to do the same.

"It's late enough," I figure," he said. "I think we'll reach the coast in a few hours."

"Then what?"

"Then we choose north or south, and head in that direction until we find a boat," Fenwick said.

"I vote north," I said. "It's closer to home."

"It probably won't make any difference," Fenwick said.

"Then north it is," I stated.

We climbed back on our horses and set out. An hour or so after the sunset, I thought I heard the sound of the surf. I stopped and listened. The sound came from the left.

"Fenwick," I hissed. "Listen."

Fenwick turned his horse and headed for what we heard. There was a quarter moon, waxing, and we could see in the dim light. Fenwick stopped again and cursed.

"What's wrong?" I whispered.

"Nothing is wrong," he replied. "We're just on a peninsula. Look over there—can you see the line of the surf?"

I could see it once he pointed it out. It glowed faintly, slightly brighter than just reflected moonlight. I followed the line of it with my eyes.

"If we work our way back to the top of this inlet, we will probably find a small settlement," Fenwick said. "I cursed because we overshot and probably wasted an hour or more."

We headed to the left to reach the head of the inlet. It did not take an hour to reach it—maybe half that time. We saw a group of four small huts. As we drew closer, I spied our salvation—boats.

Two of them were obviously fishing boats. They were resting on logs, well above the high tide line. There were another two, rowboats, that were closer to the water, resting upside down.

Looking at the fishing boats, I realized there was no way Fenwick and I, even with the help of the horses, would be able to drag them into the water without making a commotion that would wake everyone. That left the rowboats. They were about the same size as the boats Bebo had on his ship.

Fenwick slid off his horse and handed me the reins. He approached the nearer of the smaller boats and got down on his knees. Bent over, he was feeling around underneath. He stood up, brushed the sand from his knees, and returned.

"It has four oars, and a small mast and sail," he said. "If the Gods are with us, it could be enough to get us to Aquileia. I don't mean Newcastle, which is the nearest port—I mean just past the mountains and the border."

"How long?"

"Three, four days maybe," he answered. "But if a storm comes up, or the wind blows ill…"

"What other choices do we have?" I asked, after thinking about it for a minute.

"We can ride to the next settlement to see if we find something better," he said.

"We probably wouldn't," I said with a sigh. "What do you think our chances are of waking these nice people up, and asking them politely to deliver us back to Newcastle?"

"If I still had the money I was carrying as Ako Bharwani, they might do it," he said. "Of course, they might just take the money and then dump us over the side in the middle of the ocean. Since all we have is a promise that they will be rewarded later, they would probably prefer to slit our throats right away."

"I was afraid that would be your answer," I sighed, as I slid from my horse. "Might as well get started."

We went to the boat and tipped it over, right side up. Underneath it were laying the four oars, a small mast and sail, a rudder, and another board of some sort. Fenwick and I dragged the boat to the water line. I held it there while he went to retrieve the other items. The last things he brought were the rudder and the strange board.

"What is that?" I asked, as he placed them in the boat.

"A centerboard," he said. "It goes through that slot in the middle. It helps when you're trying to sail upwind."

"If you say so," I replied. "You realize I know nothing about sailing."

"I think I figured that out on the first day of the trip to Scaramouche," he joked.

Fenwick put the oars in their locks. He had me climb in and sit facing him on the bench in the part of the boat that was already floating.

"Take the oars," he advised. "I'm going to shove us out while you pull on them to get us off the beach. Keep rowing until I tell you to stop. That won't be for a while."

Fenwick strained and pushed the boat into the water. I pulled on my oars clumsily, almost completely missing the water with the left one. The second time, I adjusted my angle, and both bit into the water. Fenwick clambered in and took the other pair of oars.

"Watch what I do, and mimic my movements," he said. "If we pull our oars at the same time, we'll make good progress. If you get out of rhythm, we'll go nowhere."

I did my best to row in unison with him. Within a few minutes, we opened up a decent gap to the shore. I was fairly pleased with our success. Fenwick tucked the ends of his oars inside the boat and put the rudder in place. He then slid the centerboard into its slot in the middle of the boat.

"Stop rowing for a minute," he said. "Stow your oars the way I did. I need your help with the mast."

Getting the mast upright in a tippy small boat was a challenge like none other I had ever faced. I must have fallen half a dozen times, though not out of the boat, thank all the heavenly beings. Landing on the benches and the oars and the side of the boat added new bruises to the ones I received in my beating. Finally, we seated the bottom of the mast in the small box that held it. Fenwick unfurled the sail and angled it to catch the slight breeze that was blowing.

I stayed out of his way. That was the best contribution I could make. I quickly decided I liked sailing much better than rowing. That brief spell of pleasant thoughts ended as soon as we reached the open sea when we left the inlet. The waves seemed higher than the length of the boat. I wanted to huddle on the bottom of the boat and cling to the bench.

"Grab your oars and heave, damme!" Fenwick shrieked at me.

I did the best I could, though half the time I was pitched one way or the other, and my oar missed the water. Fenwick kept shouting, though I could scarcely hear him. He was clinging to the rudder with his left hand and to the line attached to the sail with his right. I noticed his knuckles were white from the strain.

Suddenly, the violence dropped by at least half. The swells were still large, but not as high, and there was more time in between when they hit us. It was still unpleasant, but not terrifying.

"Stow the oars, Caz," Fenwick said.

"What in the Seven Hells was that?" I demanded.

"Chop," he said. "Happens at the mouths of inlets at certain times. We made it through. Now we're in the open ocean. See that thing that looks like a bucket?"

"Yes," I said, spying something tied to the bench that looked like a bucket with a notch missing from the top.

"Use that to collect that water that washed into the boat and toss it over the side," he said. "It's called bailing."

It was hard for me, after a few minutes of bailing, to decide whether I disliked bailing or rowing more. Rowing hurt my arms and back and was already producing blisters on my hands. Bailing hurt a different part of my back and my knees, not to mention all the places where I banged into things when the boat tossed me around.

Eventually, I threw most of the water out. I set the bucket down and sat on my bench. All my clothes were wet, and the breeze was cold. The sun was up now but seemed to give no warmth. I had another awful thought.

"Fenwick, do we have any water?" I asked.

"Uh, no."

"Food?"

"No, again."

"Are you cold?" I asked.

"I don't think I've ever been so thoroughly chilled," he replied.

"We won't make it," I said flatly. "We need to get back to shore. Not where we came from, but somewhere we can dry out, warm up, and get some water and something to eat."

"There's a problem with that plan," Fenwick said. "The wind is from the west—the direction we need to go. Even with the centerboard, this kind of boat can't sail very close to the wind. We need to sail at a shallow angle toward shore and zigzag back and forth, shaving off a little east-west distance on each leg."

"I don't care," I said. "We don't have a choice."

Fenwick turned the boat and adjusted the sail. Unfortunately, by turning in that direction, the ocean swells began crashing into our boat. I got down on my knees and started bailing, but for every bucket of water I threw over the side, two more came in.

"This isn't going to work, Fenwick. The boat will sink before we get halfway," I groused. "Turn us back around, so at least I can stop bailing."

We turned and ran before the wind again, as we were before—a "broad reach," I remembered the sailing master calling it on our trip to rescue Julienne Traval from Rhetian pirates. I continued bailing. It hurt my back and knees, but it kept me warm in a way—at least until I stopped. Then I was wet, cold, tired, thirsty, and hungry. All those conditions were vying for preeminence.

"Do you remember the pirates?" I asked, suddenly breaking my morose silence.

"The ones who took Julienne?"

"Exactly," I said.

"What about them?"

"We can't reach shore. Thirst or hunger will kill us before we make it to Aquileia," I said. "But aren't the Persimmon Islands somewhere around here?"

"Caz, they are tiny little islands in the middle of a great big ocean," Fenwick sneered. "We have almost no chance of finding them."

"Aloysius," I said, using his given name, which he detests, "almost no chance is still a chance. Isn't it better to have some hope, than to have none?"

He had no answer for that. We continued on our course, bobbing up and down in the tiny boat. I began to pray silently. First, I addressed all the Gods and Goddesses, asking for their blessing for Lucy and Julienne if the Gods' will was for Fenwick and me to die. I thanked them for the amazing life I lived so far. While not all of it had been pleasant, it molded me into the man I was, and prepared me for the last few years, in which I was blessed with more good fortune than I could ever have deserved.

When I finished that lengthy meditation, I started another entreaty, addressed to Njörun, the Goddess of Good Fortune. As you may recall from my other tales, my primary bond with the supernatural was with Bellona, the Goddess of War. I had two lesser ties—to Eir, the Goddess of Health, and to Njörun. I had learned to make use of my connections to Bellona and Eir, but did not know of a way to access Njörun. My understanding was that she attended to you according to her own devices, and her power could not be summoned or controlled.

I thanked Njörun for having been so generous to me, as clearly she was. Considering how much assistance she had already given me in my life, I acknowledged I had no right to ask for anything more. I suggested, however, that all her gifts to me would go for nothing, if I were to die now—freezing, starving, thirsty, in this boat that was so ridiculously small compared to the vastness of the ocean. Finally, I apologized if my request was rather cheeky, but as miserable as I was, I was having a difficult time thinking properly.

"Have you been sleeping the last few minutes?" Fenwick asked when I opened my eyes.

"That would be impossible," I retorted. "I've been praying, if you must know."

"I hope you did a good job," Fenwick said. "Though if you made the Gods angry, it would be hard to tell. How much more could they punish us without killing us?"

"We could still be in Rhetia," I said, "in the cell, with that horrible food."

"True," he agreed. "At least we'll die as free men. That's a blessing, I suppose."

There was nothing more to say. We sat silent, our own thoughts weighing us down. I noticed I stopped shivering, and my teeth were no longer chattering. While the respite was welcome, I suspected it was not a good thing. Looking at Fenwick, his lips were quite blueish.

From the angle of the sun, I guessed it was near midday. We set off in the middle of the night. I wondered if either of us would still be alive when the sun set. It was at this point that my misery deepened. The seasickness to which I was prone returned.

I began to retch. There was nothing in my stomach to bring up, but the spasms still wracked me. It was agonizing, and I felt as though what little energy my body still possessed was being expelled. I curled up in the bottom of the boat, rolled into a ball of abject wretchedness.

My consciousness faded in and out. When my guts clenched and tormented me, I would wake. After the spell passed, I drifted away. Fenwick later told me I spent hours in that state.

At some point, Fenwick started singing bawdy songs. I suppose it was to keep himself company since I was huddled in the bottom of the boat. In my intermittent moments of lucidity, I thought Fenwick was drunk, from his slurred speech and the confusion he displayed regarding the lyrics from time to time.

"Cazsh, ya magnifishent bashterd, wake up!" Fenwick cried, kicking me repeatedly. "Wake up, wake up, wake up," he continued in a sing-song as he jabbed his foot into my ribs. "Wake up, wake up, wake up."

I rolled away to escape his kicks. That, of course, made my guts churn again. When the spasms passed, I struggled to get back on my bench.

"Turn around, turn around, turn around," Fenwick said with the giddy excitement of a little boy, or someone who has downed three bottles of wine and is halfway through the fourth.

I turned to look forward. All I saw at first was the side of one of the swells. When we reached the top of it though, land appeared about a half-mile away.

"Majorsh and Minorsh!" I exclaimed, finding my lips and mouth not working properly.

18

We reached the land and stumbled out of the boat. I had a difficult time standing. I remember crawling away from the water. Fenwick was staggering ahead of me.

The next thing I remember is heat. The right side of my face and my body were uncomfortably hot. I turned my head to look and stared right into the flames of a fire less than two feet away. Rolling away, I looked and saw Fenwick sitting cross-legged, not far away.

"There you are," he said. "Just like you to leave me to do all the work. That's why I need to set the balance square by making you the servant on our adventures."

The left side of me was still cold and wet. I struggled to a sitting position, rotating to expose the chilled part of me to the fire. Trying to make sense of the situation, I was now facing a smirking Fenwick. As wrung out as I was, I could not imagine how he would have been able to gather wood and start a fire.

"How?" was all I could think to ask.

"Other people have been here," he said, guessing what I wanted to know. "I think they come regularly for the sheep. There was a stack of wood already gathered and waiting. All I needed to do was find some tinder and strike a spark. Thank all the heavenly beings, because even something that simple was nearly beyond me. I finally managed to do it and was able to get some of the wood to catch before I collapsed. When I woke, I was half-warm, as I imagine you feel now. After I roasted my other side, I looked around a little more. I found water."

"Gimme," I muttered eagerly.

Fenwick stood and picked up a wooden bucket. He handed it to me carefully. It was half full.

"Rainwater, I reckon," he said. "Tastes sweet, though."

I was having a difficult time lifting the bucket. My arms did not seem to want to obey me properly. Fenwick saw and took over. He lifted it to my mouth and tilted it slowly.

He was right. It did taste sweet, especially after all the seawater I'd been unable to keep out of my mouth while we pitched about in the boat. I was gulping greedily when he pulled it away.

"That's enough for now," he said. "You'll hurt yourself otherwise. Plus, that's all we have until we find something tomorrow."

"Thank you," I said.

He was right, of course. The water hitting my completely emptied stomach suddenly made me feel as though I had swallowed a cobblestone. It took several minutes for the pain to subside. When it did, with my left side now warming up, I started to feel almost human again—a starving human.

I looked around, not that I could see much beyond the light the fire cast. In the sky, I found the moon, now waxing gibbous and about to set. That meant it was close to midnight.

"We should probably sleep," I suggested.

"I agree," Fenwick said. "I was just waiting for you to revive."

He stretched out on his side, facing the fire. I did the same, lying on my right side since it was dry. I put my arm up as a pillow and closed my eyes.

During the night, I sensed the growing chill when the fire died down and woke. On shaky legs, I stood and looked for the wood Fenwick mentioned. When I found it, I took an armful. I fed the fire with half and left the other half for later. Fenwick must have risen later because when I opened my eyes in the morning light, the wood I'd brought was gone, and the fire was again down to coals. I grabbed some more wood from the dwindling pile, fed the fire, and sat staring as the flames rose. Fenwick woke when he felt the renewed heat.

"Now what?" I asked.

"We need to find water and food, and make sure the boat is secure," Fenwick suggested.

"The boat is closest. Let's tackle that first," I said.

We retraced our steps to the beach—only a few yards through some underbrush. We found there was a path nearby, but we had not seen it when we stumbled ashore in the dark. When we reached the sand, the boat was gone. I walked up and down the beach, then out in the water, hoping to see it. I was disappointed in that desire.

"Perhaps it washed ashore elsewhere," I suggested, even though I knew in my heart it was gone for good.

"Perhaps," Fenwick said with a sardonic grin.

His expression told me he knew we would not find the boat. I realized that we were trapped on the island until the owners of the sheep came. That would probably not happen for several months, when they came to check on spring lambs. Of course, they would be Rhetians. Even if we managed to overcome them, or convince them to deliver us to Aquileia, we would arrive too late to inform the king of the impending invasion.

"Let's go look for water," Fenwick suggested as he headed back through the brush. "And maybe we'll find something to eat."

"Besides sheep?" I said.

"Haven't seen any yet," he replied. "I hope we do."

I took the bucket, and we tramped off, following a path. We came across a three-sided hut where Fenwick found the bucket and the supply of wood. There was enough wood to last for a few days. We would need to gather more. There were three other buckets, all full of rainwater.

We made our way out of the wind-blown, somewhat stunted trees and onto a huge grassy area. The landscape rose and fell in gentle curves. Sure enough, we could see sheep grazing in the distance. The path we followed grew less noticeable the further away from the trees we walked. We continued regardless.

About half a mile from the trees, we found a spring trickling from the side of a small hill. Fenwick bent down and cupped his hand. He tasted it and nodded.

"Freshwater," he said.

That was one of our needs met. The sheep would provide us something to eat. I hoped we might find some vegetables, too. From my time in the Rangers, I knew certain types of cabbages could still be found at this time of year. Though strong in taste, they would keep us in good health while we waited for someone to come.

We continued in the general direction we started. There was a small hill, slightly taller than the rest. Fenwick headed for it.

From the top, we could see enough to ascertain that we were indeed on an island. It was bigger than Manaway Island, from which we rescued Julienne Traval. There were three sheep on the far side of the hill. Fenwick walked down to them. They stared at him placidly. He walked to the far side of where they were standing.

"Hie! Hie! Hie!" he shouted, waving his arms.

The sheep looked at him stupidly. Fenwick pulled his Rhetian sword from his waist and smacked the nearest one on the butt. The sheep jolted and began trotting away from Fenwick. He then spanked the other two. Together, we guided the sheep back toward where we spent the night. We left the two in the open but drove the one into the trees.

I strongly suspect, dear reader, that you would rather not hear about our butchering of the animal. It was never something I enjoyed, so I will skip it. I will just say that in a short time, Fenwick and I were roasting hunks of meat on sticks over the fire. As hungry as we were, it was difficult waiting for them to cook.

When we satisfied our hunger, Fenwick suggested going on another walk, this time around the perimeter of the island. This was even more fruitful. We found another hut, but this was fully enclosed. Inside were four rope cots with sheepskin throws covering the ropes, woolen blankets, a clay fireplace, and two small kettles. This was clearly where we would stay until the next visitors to the island arrived.

Over the next few days, we explored the rest of the island. There was no sign of our boat. We found no other structures. I did find some of the cabbages I remembered, and we added them to our diet. I was about to go in search of more when my sight changed.

Lucy was lying in bed in the manor house. It was clearly during the day. The scene was more colorful than what I would normally see, as was usual with the visions Shasha shared with me. Lucy was obviously distressed. Her hair was unkempt, her features were drawn as though she had lost an unhealthy amount of weight, and there were dark circles below her eyes. She was staring into space.

Within myself, I found the reddish-brown mote that was my link to Shasha.

The owl is concerned for your mate.

"You saw this?"

No, the owl shared this with me.

"You and the owl can share thoughts like this? Pictures? What you have seen?"

Of course. I sensed Shasha's disdainful tone. *Humans cannot?*

"We communicate with words that describe what we see and think and feel."

So cumbersome. Our way is simpler, better.

"When is this? When did the owl see this?"

Not long. The owl feels her heartache. She believes you dead.

"I'm not dead."

Clearly.

My mind raced, thinking not only how I could show Lucy I was alive, but also provide a clue where we were. I thought of very specific images. First, I remembered the view Fenwick and I had from the hill that showed we were on an island. Then, I remembered what a persimmon fruit was, since these were the Persimmon Islands. Finally, I remembered Julienne Traval's face.

"Can you share those images with the owl?"

The view, the fruit, and a woman?

"Yes. They will tell my mate where we are, I hope. Unless you can share words with the owl."

Not words. Things you have seen.

"One more then."

I remembered looking at the nautical chart that showed the Persimmon Islands.

I will share with the owl.

"Thank you, Shasha. We trapped are on this island with no boat."

Island? Boat?

"An island is some land surrounded by water. A boat floats on the water and carries humans." I tried to send her a remembered sight of both.

I have seen boats. Not islands.

"Please share with the owl." I thought of the view from the hill, a persimmon, Julienne Traval, and the chart again.

This will make your mate happy?

"Yes. It may also make her very excited."

I will share.

"Thank you, Shasha."

"Why are you grinning like a fool?" Fenwick asked me when he returned to the hut a bit later.

"Because I think I just got word to Lucy where we are," I said.

"How?"

"Through the sparrowhawk," I answered. "She contacted me because Lucy's owl was worried about Lucy. Then the sparrowhawk showed me Lucy through the owl's eyes—what the owl saw. I didn't know they could do that."

"Communicate?" Fenwick asked.

"No. I've known that my sparrowhawk and Chauncey are able to communicate, but I thought it was through speech—that Shasha could understand owl sounds and Chauncey could interpret her squawks," I said. "But I was wrong. They share thoughts the way Shasha and I do. It's not speech, even though my brain converts it into that for me."

"You've tried to explain that before. I guess I'll understand if I find my own familiar," Fenwick said.

"Anyway, I realized they could send visual images of things they had seen to one another. I asked if Shasha could do the same and pass along things I saw to Chauncey. She confirmed they she could," I explained.

"What scenes did you use?" Fenwick inquired.

I told him, and he nodded. "The persimmon was clever," he commented. "So, now what?"

"Lucy is clever enough to figure it out. She'll remember we traveled here, to the Persimmon Islands, to get Julienne back from the pirates. Plus, Chauncey will inform her that the images came from me, so she will know we are alive," I said. "She will probably ride to the city and organize someone to come get us."

"Either Julienne or the queen," Fenwick mused.

"Or both," I suggested.

"Is there a way you can check?"

"I'll ask."

I reopened my connection with Shasha. As soon as she responded, I could see the world through her eyes at the same time I observed through my own. It was a bit confusing when the sparrowhawk and I first bonded, and it used to give me cracking great headaches, but I've learned better how to manage it.

Shasha was watching Lucy from high above. My wife was riding Bella and had nearly reached the west gate of Easton. She was clearly riding to the capital.

"Thank you, Shasha."

I terminated our link.

"Lucy is currently leaving Easton, through the west gate. She should arrive in Aquileia in three days," I informed him.

"Three days," Fenwick muttered, "then eight days of sailing, more or less. A couple of days to get a ship ready… We should expect to see a ship in roughly two weeks. That's good. I'll probably be sick of mutton and cabbages by then. I know I'll be sick of you."

We started counting the days. Beginning on the eleventh day, we started throwing rotted wood onto our fire from time to time to produce plenty of smoke. We also climbed the tallest hill several times a day to see if we might spot the masts of a ship.

The morning of the thirteenth day, Fenwick came running down from the hill shouting. I could not understand his words from so far away, but I knew what he was trying to say. Before I forgot, I went to my knees and thanked Njörun and then all the Gods for our tremendous good fortune.

A sleek ship bearing the Traval & Company colors hove into view later that morning. Fenwick and I stood on the beach and watched as they dropped anchor. Lucy and Julienne were on the deck, jumping up and down, and waving their arms. Fenwick and I started to do the same. We might have looked like fools, but I could not express my happiness and excitement any other way.

They lowered a boat, and six trained sailors pulled it smoothly to the beach. Almost as soon as it touched the sand, Fenwick and I waded into the water to help turn it around. I clambered in first while Fenwick gave one last push, then I hauled him aboard.

Realizing I was about to see Lucy for the first time in a month, I suddenly became self-conscious. Fenwick looked a mess. His skin was still quite brown. He had a scraggly beard, which looked ridiculous with his closely shorn hair. His Ako Bharwani clothes were in tatters. He had a Rhetian sword stuck through his belt. From tip to toe, he looked like the worst sort of pirate. I knew my appearance was every bit as disreputable.

19

As awful as we looked and probably smelled, it did not matter to Lucy or Julienne. As soon as I climbed over the side of the ship, Lucy launched herself into me, knocking me down onto coils of tar-covered rope. She fell on top of me and was showering kisses all over my face.

Fenwick and Julienne were still upright, but only because Julienne had mashed Fenwick into the ship's railing. He was bent over backward while she pelted him with pecks of her lips. I was worried they might topple overboard. Julienne must have had the same thought because she suddenly pulled Fenwick away from the side.

"My goodness!" Fenwick said. "Perhaps I should go away more often."

"Don't you dare!" Julienne growled.

I began to laugh. Lucy leaned up and poked me hard in the chest.

"It's not funny!" she barked.

That, of course, made it even more hilarious. Lucy's anger evaporated and she began to laugh. Fenwick and Julienne overheard our exchange and joined in.

Lucy dragged me back to one of the small cabins. She demanded I strip, then disappeared briefly. She returned with a bucket of hot water and proceeded to wash me as thoroughly as possible, given the circumstances. She complained because the walnut juice Fenwick and I put on our skin darkened our coloring and made it difficult to tell dirt from dye.

Of course, in order not to soak her clothing while washing me, she needed to remove it, which made the experience more fun for both of us. When she finished cleaning my body, she proceeded to shave my accumulated beard. She finished by daubing some ginger oil on my upper lip to help me stave off seasickness.

"I miss your hair," she lamented, rubbing the fuzz on my head as I dressed in my own clothing, which Lucy thought to bring.

"It will grow back."

"I missed you," she added. "I did not know whether you would come back. I had two different visions, both similar. In one, I learned you were dead. In the other, you were alive. Both of them involved Chauncey."

"He was quite concerned about you," I said. "He's the reason Shasha contacted me. She showed me how Chauncey saw you lying in bed."

"I know. I was miserable—heartsick. Please tell me you two found what you were looking for," she stated. "I would hate to have endured that torture for no good purpose."

"We did," I said. "The Rhetians are preparing for an invasion."

"You'll be going to war, then," she said sadly after a moment.

I had not been thinking in those terms. She was right, though. Like every other territory, the Earl of the March was oath-bound to supply troops to the king in time of need. In our case, that meant the armsmen and the militia—over seven hundred soldiers. My father would lead them unless he stepped aside. Even if he did not, I would join him. It was unthinkable to do otherwise.

"The foreknowledge Fenwick and I gained will give us a chance to prepare. They will not catch us by surprise. As far as it concerns me, the men of the March are more experienced than any other soldiers in the kingdom and better trained than any except the Castle Shield. We will acquit ourselves well," I said.

"But war is uncertain," Lucy said softly but firmly. "Even the most valiant warrior can fall to a stray arrow. Do not be over-confident."

"Must we talk of it now?" I asked. "All of that is waiting for us when we return to Aquileia. After the difficulties I have just been through, I simply wish to wallow in my wife's arms for as long as you can stand me."

We sailed into Aquileia in the middle of the night six days later. There were no hackneys at that hour, but Julienne roused one of the security guards in their warehouse and had him drive us all in a wagon. We headed straight to the castle. Julienne decided to stay with Lucy, and they went to our house after dropping us off. Though we would be waking the king in the middle of the night, we agreed he would be upset if we didn't, considering the news we carried. Our arrival caused a quiet commotion.

A soldier ran across the bridge to wake a page. Then the page roused the seneschal. The seneschal interrupted the king's slumber, then came to collect us.

The sleepy page arrived first to escort us across the bridge. We waited in the cold until the seneschal appeared. He seemed perplexed as he approached us, rubbing his head.

"Majors and Minors!" he muttered. "When he first woke, I was worried the king would slice my balls off. As soon as I told him it was the two of you, his entire demeanor changed. Come with me. He is eager to see you."

We followed the seneschal into a part of the castle where I had never been— the private chambers of the royal family. One of the first things I noticed was that the rugs on the floor were sumptuously soft—it felt like my feet had sunk in an inch. We reached a door, and the seneschal knocked.

"Enter!"

The seneschal opened the door and stood aside. Fenwick and I went in. Candles were burning brightly in what I guessed was an anteroom connected to the king's bedroom. Both Mark and Liliana were there, in richly embroidered dressing gowns.

"Your Majesty," Fenwick said, "we have just returned from our assignment. We saw only one of the Rhetian fortresses, but our view was from the inside. It is my opinion, and Lord Oritur's, that the Rhetians are preparing for an invasion in the spring."

"Well, there it is," the king sighed. "You say you saw the inside of the fort? How on earth did you accomplish that?"

"We were captured, Your Majesty," Fenwick replied.

"And yet here you are. How?"

"Do you wish me to be brief, Your Majesty, or tell the full tale?" Fenwick inquired.

"Be brief for now," he said. "It *is* the middle of the night, and we imagine the two of you are quite tired. Please attend us for lunch and share the complete version."

Fenwick told the most bare-bones version of our escape. As far as our rescue from the island, he mentioned a passing Traval ship saw the smoke from our fire. That much was certainly true, but it was nowhere near the whole truth.

"Fascinating," the king remarked as he stood, offering his arm to the queen.

His rising indicated our discussion was over for now. The two of us bowed and waited for the king and queen to leave. When the door closed behind them, we left the room, finding the seneschal waiting. Within minutes, we were back across the bridge at the guardhouse.

"We require a ride to his home," Fenwick stated authoritatively to the guard. "You will prepare two horses for our use, and a man to accompany us to return them. We do not wish to waste time."

To my surprise, the man obeyed without question. In ten minutes, Fenwick and I were on horseback, riding to my house. When we arrived, we handed the reins of our horses to the soldier who accompanied us.

In the morning, I woke to the sound of laughter rising from the ground floor. Throwing on a dressing gown, I went to see what was the cause of the mirth. Lucy, Julienne, and our housekeeper, Roberta, were in the kitchen, preparing breakfast. Lucy danced over and gave me a quick peck. As she did, Julienne headed for the door to do the same for Fenwick, who was not far behind me.

"It was pleasant to wake to the sound of ladies laughing," I said.

"We were talking about a chore we need to do this morning," Julienne said, her eyes twinkling.

"Yes. We must go to the market and buy every lemon we can lay our hands on. They will be expensive at this time of year," Lucy added, suppressing a grin.

"And why is this humorous?" Fenwick asked. "I thought you enjoyed my new appearance?"

"It was fine when we first saw you, but now you and Caz are—splotchy," Julienne answered.

"Splotchy?" I inquired. "Is that a word?"

"Yes, splotchy," Lucy confirmed. "The two of you look like little boys who were playing in mud puddles. We were laughing, wondering what the king thought when you saw him."

"Well, he didn't laugh and point fingers," Fenwick said, pretending to be hurt.

I had not considered it until now, but looking at Fenwick, his appearance was ... splotchy. My skin was likely just as mottled. Thinking of Lucy's "little boys" comment, I started to laugh.

"You, too?" Fenwick said with mock indignation.

That only made it funnier. Fenwick's façade soon cracked, and he joined in as well. Starting the day with a laugh was something I think we all needed.

The ladies went to the market not long after and returned with a small sack. They emptied the contents on the kitchen table. There were eleven lemons.

"That's every single one there was in the market," Lucy advised. "Now you men get busy drawing water. We're going to bathe and get the salt crust off all of us, and Julienne and I will try to get at least your faces and scalps back to their normal state. I don't know if we will have enough lemon juice for anything more."

An hour later, we were all clean and dressed. As Lucy thought, there was just enough juice to remove the walnut stain from our heads and necks. The rest of us was still ... splotchy.

As Andy, my horse, was back in Easton, Fenwick agreed we would share a hackney for our lunch meeting with the king. We found one idle in the market square nearby, gave him instructions, then clambered in. When we arrived at the guardhouse, we were ushered across the bridge immediately.

The seneschal met us and led us to a small dining room where we found Their Majesties. They were already seated. Fenwick and I bowed our greetings. The king gestured Fenwick to his right, and I took the chair to the queen's left.

"You look less ridiculous today," she whispered to me.

The king pretended not to hear her. Lunch was served and we ate. When our places were cleared, the king picked up a folded piece of paper. He tapped it on the table idly a few times.

"We just received a report from the Rangers," he said. "Eight of their men just returned after escaping from a Rhetian fortress. They confirm the preparations you reported. Your names are mentioned as being instrumental in their escape."

"Thank all the heavenly beings," I muttered.

"Wonderful news," Fenwick commented, "and part of the more complete version of our journey."

"Well, don't leave us hanging, man. Get on with it!" the king said with a smile.

Fenwick commenced sharing every detail of our adventure. The king and queen listened avidly. We reached the point where we split away from the eight Rangers.

"You did this so they would draw the pursuit?" the king asked.

"Yes," I said. "We did not discuss it with them, but they were experienced enough soldiers to comprehend that. Their fate has been on my conscience. I am delighted to hear they reached our lines. Their story is probably even more interesting than ours."

Fenwick's narrative continued from this point. He came to a stop with us on the island, just before I communicated with my familiar. Fenwick gave me a pointed look.

"Your Majesty, I am aware that the supernatural troubles you," I said. "Last night, Fenwick mentioned a passing Traval ship saw our smoke and rescued us. That is true. But there is a reason the ship was there. Do you wish to hear more?"

"The important part of the narrative is complete," the king said. "The Traval ship collected you and brought you here. If Her Majesty wishes to know more about it, you may tell her later."

"Thank you, Your Majesty," I said.

"We issued the call to arms this morning," the king said. "Couriers are riding now to deliver the summonses to the nobles. Today is the third of Porri. We instructed the nobles to assemble with all their forces at Reedsford in the western March no later than the spring equinox at the end of Goa. That gives them nearly two months to comply. Do you think the Rhetians will move before then?"

"From what I remember of the region from my time in the Rangers, I will say no, Your Majesty. The passes will be snow-covered for several weeks. There are no roads through the border mountains that are suitable for moving large numbers of men and materials," I said. "The last full-scale invasion was more than a hundred years ago, and whatever routes they cleared at that time have grown back. They will need to cut new paths. Though they have probably begun that work already, the earliest I would expect an attack would be the end of the next month, Einmann, or early in Harpa."

"That was our thinking as well," the king confirmed. Turning to me, he added, "You know that your father expressed his desire to step aside and turn the care of the eastern March over to you. This move by the Rhetians will prevent that from happening. We want you, and Fenwick, in the main with me. While your soldiers will also be in the main, we desire your presence in the group of our closest advisors. Though you are correct that the supernatural makes us uneasy, Albert and the queen have both testified to the usefulness of your abilities. We would be foolish not to avail ourselves of every advantage."

"I will be honored, Your Majesty," I replied.

Fenwick echoed my sentiment. The king rose, signifying the luncheon was over. Fenwick and I scrambled to our feet and bowed to him before he departed. Queen Liliana stayed.

"Tell me, Caz, how the Traval ship knew where to find you?" she asked.

I described how Shasha and Chauncey were able to communicate, and my misunderstanding of how that occurred. She listened attentively. When I finished, she nodded her head.

"My familiar did not communicate with any others," she said. "I wonder if the reason the sparrowhawk and owl can share thoughts is because they are both birds or because they are both familiars."

"Another reason might be affinities," I suggested. "The owl and I have the same affinities, while Lucy and the sparrowhawk are identical."

"Interesting," the queen mused. "This is certainly not common. I've never heard of two gifted people being able to communicate—even in such a limited fashion—through their familiars. I will need to do some research to see if this has ever been documented before. You may be right in thinking that affinities play a role. It may also be related to the strength of your bond with Lucy."

"Well, we are married—"

"That is not what I am talking about, Caz," she said. "I will ask Lucy to tell you more about what I mean. I would do so myself, but sadly, I have another appointment now."

She stood, and Fenwick and I rose and bowed to her as she left. The seneschal appeared to escort us out. On the other side of the bridge, one of the soldiers summoned a hackney for us, and we returned to my house. Fenwick then took his leave while I stayed with Lucy.

"Your father postponed the annual visits to the towns, waiting for you," Lucy said after I summarized our meeting with the king and queen. "Like me, he had nearly given up hope that you would come back. I was able to let him know you survived, so he is, I'm sure, eager to get started."

"He will not be happy when I share the news with him," I said.

"You said the king already sent the summonses," she reminded me. "He will know the day before you get back. Duncan has been a man of duty his entire life. He will be proud the king wants you at his side."

"I fear the people will be disappointed," I commented. "After finally hearing that we convinced the nomads to cease their raiding, to learn that the militia will fight on the other side of the kingdom will not be welcome news."

"Your people will not blame you or your father," she said. "In fact, your success will give them confidence that the Rhetians cannot prevail. You have earned their goodwill. They are not so fickle as to turn against you now."

20

My journey home via post-coach was long and uncomfortable. When I finally arrived, my father was surprisingly eager to see me when I found him in the study with Madame Hernandez. I had not seen him since he informed me he planned to ask Madame Hernandez to marry him. Though I worried that he would be upset since his plan of stepping aside would be delayed by the war, it did not seem to trouble him. On the contrary, the upcoming conflict with the Rhetians seemed to have given him new energy.

"I just returned from a meeting with the smiths," he said, rubbing his hands together. "We must arm the militia with halberds, and the only ones we still possessed in the armory were only good for serving as models for new weapons. Between now and when we depart for the west, we need at least eight hundred of them."

"Do the smiths have enough iron?" I asked.

"That was the purpose of the meeting," my father answered. "The smiths in Easton do not, nor do they have the capability of crafting that many in the time available. They will be sharing the work with the other smiths throughout the March. It should not present any difficulties since they all know one another. Many of them are related by blood or marriage."

"How much will this cost?" I inquired.

"Less than two thousand ducats," my father said. "Of course, if you had not restored the March to solvency, we would have had a problem paying for them."

"When do we begin our meetings?" I asked, brushing his comment aside.

"I will send out letters tomorrow," he said. "We will leave the following day for Quinn's Ford, then work our way south as we did last year. Now, tell me about your journey."

When I reached that part of my narrative, Madame Hernandez said, "Lucy was despondent until you managed to communicate with her. She neither ate nor slept. Your father and I were quite worried about her. Then, suddenly, she bolted out of bed and began packing her things in a frenzy. She hardly took the time to tell us where she was going and why."

"Madame—" I began.

She laid her hand on top of mine gently, saying, "Please call me Ariana, Caz, or Ari. It seems we will be related at some point in the future."

"Ari, I do not know you as well as I would like," I admitted. "It seems whenever we have the opportunity to spend time together, I am called away. I am delighted that he asked you to marry him and that you obviously accepted. Now, about Lucy and what happened. Has my father explained that—"

"That Lucy is a witch? And that you are also, in your way? Yes, he has," she said calmly.

"It does not trouble you?"

"Hardly," she said with a laugh. "I knew about Lucy before your father told me—from the feast day of Freyja. Her appearance that day reminded me of a story my mother told me when I was a little girl. I was thrilled to be able to witness something like that with my own eyes. When Duncan told me of your gifts, I was not shocked. And how could it trouble me? In Mooresa, where I was born, skilled witches are held in esteem."

"How do you feel about the prospect of war? Duncan must answer the king's summons. He has no choice," I said.

"I would prefer he stays out of harm's way, of course," she said. "But he has an obligation to the king. We discussed this for many hours when the summons arrived. He must do what he must do. It helps me to accept it when I see he secretly relishes the opportunity. He is not good at hiding his feelings."

My father looked chagrined to learn that he did not fool her. Ariana smiled at him in forgiveness. He blushed scarlet. Their interaction made me chuckle.

"What's so funny?" he asked.

"You are," I replied. "It's not that it's funny. When I see you and Ariana like this, it makes me happy."

She patted my hand.

"Ari, I'm curious—how do the people of Mooresa feel about the Rhetians?" I asked.

"We do not like them," she answered, "but there is not the same enmity between us. Of course, only Aquileia shares a border with them. For those of us on the southern continent, we only need worry about the occasional raid by one of their pirates, or how rude and unpleasant they are to do business with. They keep sending priests who try to convert people to their strange religion, but people try to avoid them if they can. Why are they choosing to invade now, I wonder?"

"Prince Albert mentioned to me that he felt we were overdue—that it had been far too long since their last attempt," I said. "The prince's death plays a part in the timing, I'm sure. I believe the Rhetians feel it is an opportunity to splinter the kingdom and cause dissension in the ranks of the nobility. It won't happen the way they hope, though."

"We discussed this," she stated. "I remember now."

The clacking of paws on the wood floor of the hallway warned us of Theo's approach. His dog, Toby, bounded into the room and headed immediately to Ariana. He placed his head in her lap and looked at her pleadingly, begging for a scratch behind the ears.

"Dinner is ready," Theo intoned.

I waited for Theo to leave and remove himself from earshot. "Ariana, does Theo like you?"

"I don't know about that," she said. "He's quite pleasant as far as I know but not inappropriately so. Why do you ask?"

"Theo can barely tolerate most people," I said. "Some, like me, he actively dislikes. Until just now, I could identify only two people for whom he has any degree of fondness. Lucy is one, and Theo has liked her from the first moment. Fenwick is the other, and I believe Theo only likes Fenwick because the dog Toby likes Fenwick. Toby is clearly fond of you, so that would make you the third person in the world that Theo likes."

"I find it difficult to believe that Theo dislikes you," she protested. "You are his employer, are you not?"

"He accepts my existence only because he knows Lucy loves me. Theo was previously employed by Lucy's cousin, Lord Rawlinsford—a good friend of mine since our school days. I often would come to Freddy's for breakfast. On nearly every occasion, Theo would try to hide something disgusting in my breakfast—rat droppings, pill bugs, floor sweepings, and, once, a dead mouse. After the first time, I never failed to check. Sometimes Theo would put the tainted serving in front of Freddy because we would occasionally trade plates to try to trick Theo. He would be embarrassed if Freddy ended up with the serving he prepared for me, but never—ever—apologized to me. There are a dozen other ways Theo would insult and belittle me, but I won't go into them now."

"That's impossible," she stated firmly. "Theo is one of the sweetest people I know."

"Because Toby likes you," I said.

"Then why do you have him here?" Ariana asked.

"Lucy and my friend Freddy are cousins—it's how we met," I explained. "Freddy tried for a couple of years to get rid of Theo, but the family refused to allow it. When Lucy and I married, the family decided to send him here. And, in spite of his strange personality, he manages the household extremely well. He adores Lucy, so she directs him, and I stay out of the way."

My father and I departed Easton and rode to Quinn's Ford for the first of our annual town meetings. These meetings all followed the same format. We would meet briefly with the mayor, or head man or woman. He or she would introduce us to the assembled townspeople. We would give a brief summary of the year, then invite questions. The last order of business was administering the oath of service to the men who were drafted into the militia for the year.

Those who drew militia duty last year were especially fortunate. In addition to drawing militia pay, they were also hired to clear the old, overgrown roads between the different communities of the March and the old landings on the Pheas River. The crown paid for their labor. In effect, they were paid twice for the same job.

In addition, the opening of the Pheas River and Port Charles provided a market for farmers to sell surplus production. Given advance notice, most increased their sowing by a conservative amount. Every sack they filled found a buyer.

At the beginning of summer, we ambushed the nomads as they arrived for their annual raids. For the first time in memory, there were no nomad attacks on any town in the March. The agreement we reached recently with the nomads meant there would be no raids in the future.

The result of this created a jolly mood for the meeting. It was hard to find anyone who did not enjoy a prosperous year. Unlike the previous year, when I was largely unknown to everyone, this year they welcomed me with warm embraces, and especially asked after "Lady Lucy," as my wife was now known.

I allowed my father to present the summary of all the positive developments since our last visit. He had worked and struggled his entire adult life to defend the March. It was only proper that he be allowed to engage in delivering the good news.

When he finished, I took on the much less welcome task of informing everyone about the impending invasion from Rhetia. Not only would the militia be needed, they would be sent to the far side of the kingdom to fight a foe of long-standing. I could see the mix of emotions play across the people's faces. Disappointment that the militia would not have a year off. Worry about a war, and one so far from home. Anger at the Rhetians and their undying hatred of everyone who refused to accept their crackpot religion.

The questions we received were almost all about the mustering and deployment of the militia. There were a small handful seeking advice about putting additional land to use. In every meeting, someone would ask if I thought we would win the war. Though it would be difficult and bloody, I firmly believed we would, and told them that.

Our militia were selected by lot from the population of service-eligible men. They must be able-bodied and between the ages of eighteen and forty. The term of service was one year. Once a man served three years, his obligation was fulfilled.

The swearing-in of the year's militia was marked by anxious looks from parents or wives, and sometimes tears. The men being sworn in, however, held their heads high and their backs straight and proud. Our success in the last two seasons against the nomads gave them confidence.

At every stop, after the swearing-in ceremony, I called for volunteers.

"We will face the army of the Rhetian Empire," I reminded them. "Their hatred of us knows no limits. It is likely to be a desperate struggle. Anyone who was not chosen in the draft may join us, and it will count as one of your years of service. Anyone who has already met his service requirement may elect to join us as well. We will welcome their wisdom and experience."

By the time we completed our visits, there were only five days remaining until the militia was due to muster outside of Easton. My father was a whirlwind. Every night while we were visiting the communities, he had been writing letters issuing instructions to different people and groups.

Upon our return, he ordered the armsmen to gather all the materials he bought to support the militia when they were working on the roads last summer—portable shelters, wagons, cooking implements, and the like. They also collected their own equipment from Bannock Hill, Quinn's Ford, and Clearview. We took delivery of a hundred mules from Bruce Kinchen, who was, according to my father, the least dishonest of the horse and draft animal traders. Williamson sold us two hundred cattle. The halberds arrived.

I did my best to support my father, but I must admit he did most of the work. He possessed a real gift for organization and planning. I learned a tremendous amount from him during these few days.

On the fallow field where the Harvest Fair was held a few months before, a small town of canvas shelters sprang up. I was gratified to learn that a hundred and eighty-three men volunteered to join us, swelling our numbers to just short of one thousand soldiers. My father divided the militia into different units and chose the men who would command them.

One thing he did caused some grumbling. He spread the men from each town across several different units. The men wanted to serve with their friends and neighbors and groused. He addressed the matter on the first day of training.

"I've heard some of you complaining that you would rather fight alongside your neighbors," he said, "and I understand your discomfort at being separated. There is, however, a reason why I split you up. We are heading to war, men. And though I know we will be the most experienced fighting force in the entire kingdom, there will be casualties. If the unthinkable were to happen, and one of our units suffers severe losses, think of how devastated the people of your community would be if you and all your neighbors fell. That would only compound the tragedy."

The faces in the crowd changed expression as they began to understand what my father said. None of them enjoyed the reminder that some men would not be coming home. They were still uncomfortable being placed with a group of strangers, but they realized my father did this for a good reason.

"I hope that by the time we reach the western March, the men in your units will no longer be strangers—that you will by then have become brothers in arms," my father continued, "as we all will be."

We started training. During the first few days, we covered the organizational structure, basic commands, and camp discipline and hygiene. The last three days were devoted to learning how to use the halberds my father procured.

The night before halberd training was to start, five men showed up at the manor. My father invited them to dine with us, where I learned they were retired weapons masters who had spent their entire careers with the Castle Shield. They would teach the militia the basics of how to wield the halberd and would travel with us all the way to the western March. Training would continue every evening when the day's travel was finished.

They also delivered a letter from King Mark addressed to me. When we set out with the militia, His Majesty wished for me to ride ahead to join him at the castle. The militia would need six days of marching to reach the capital. On horseback, I would cover the same distance in three.

Halberds are fearsome weapons. Imagine a stout spear with a bladed tip. At the base of the blade, there is an ax on one side, and opposite that, a pick with a downward curve ending in a barbed point. The wooden shaft is six feet in length, and the metal blade and ax at the end then add another foot. The halberd can be used to thrust, to slice, to chop, and to drag cavalry from their horses.

We began halberd training the next day. I took part and quickly found similarities to some of the basic fencing moves, in terms of thrusts, lunges, and counters. Of course, with a weapon of that length and weight, two hands were needed. In addition to me, there were others who quickly mastered the rudiments, and the weapons masters spread us among the men to speed their progress.

On the last day before we broke camp to begin our trek across the kingdom, I returned to the manor early to pack for the trip. When I rode behind the house to the stable, I saw a dozen of Lucy's students loading a wagon with items from the workshop I had built for her. Lucy was directing them.

I wondered what their purpose was. Lucy and I had not discussed anything like this. Granted, between the community visits and the mustering and training of the militia, I had not been available. I sauntered over to see what they were putting in the wagon.

"Hello, dear," Lucy said, rising on her toes to kiss me.

"Hello. What's all this, then?"

"Every army needs healers," she said, "and I have been teaching them for most of the past year. This is every one of my students who could be spared from home."

Every army does need healers, and Lucy's initiative made perfect sense. It was just that we had not talked about it. I selfishly felt slightly put out to be surprised like this. Before I grew too grumpy, I realized my father must have known. It was one of the myriad details—one I did not see or did not understand—among all the other items. Then the next logical thing occurred to me.

"You're planning on joining us, too," I said.

"Of course, silly," Lucy replied, smacking me on the shoulder.

Oh, dear reader, the conflict that raged between my head and my heart in those moments. Lucy's skill as a healer had already saved me from dying more than once. We would need someone like her with us. But she was my life and the other part of my soul. The last place I wanted her to be was anywhere near danger. And yet, I knew her presence would steady me. So many opposing thoughts fought for preeminence and strove to make their way from my brain to my tongue.

What came out of my mouth was, "Oh."

Madame Hernandez would stay behind for now. When the spring equinox arrived, she would guide Mr. Balboa in recruiting tenant farmers for the jute plantation outside of Port Charles. Though war had reared its ugly head, we did not wish to sacrifice any of the progress we made elsewhere.

21

Lucy joined me the next day as we set out for the capital under a bright blue sky and blustery breezes. We rode with my father and the soldiers for a short time as the militia began their journey. Much to my embarrassment, the men began to sing a bawdy song about our exploits against the nomads, full of scatological humor. Imagine my surprise when my father and Lucy joined the chorus, singing lustily:

> Under Oritur's steely gaze,
> They shit their pants and ran for days.
> Then the men whom Oritur led
> caught the stinkers and left them dead.
> We piled their bodies in a heap
> Then lit a fire and went to sleep.
> Just bones were left in the morning,
> They sit there still as a warning.

My father and Lucy laughed uproariously at my awkward expression when the song ended.

"Why didn't you sing?" my father asked. "Don't you know the words?"

"No," I admitted. "I never heard it before. How do you know about it?"

"It's very popular," Lucy said with a twinkle in her eye. "Everyone in the March knows it. You need to get out more."

"Just don't tell Fenwick," I asked.

"He's the one who taught it to us," my father said.

"Majors and Minors!" I grumbled.

Three days later, Lucy and I arrived in Aquileia. We rode directly to the castle. At the guardhouse, soldiers took our horses and our baggage, including my helmet and armor. A page escorted us across the bridge immediately. The seneschal came out within minutes and took us inside.

"You will, of course, spend the night here as guests of Their Majesties. Baths are being prepared—"

"Only one is necessary," Lucy said. "We like to share."

The seneschal's cheeks turned flaming red at this. It took him a moment to regain his composure. He cleared his throat and resumed as he led us to the chambers we would be occupying.

"Any clothing that is soiled," he said, "please give to a page, and it will be washed and ready for you in the morning. A page will come to collect you when it is time for dinner."

He delivered us to our rooms. The next few minutes were like a well-choreographed dance. Servants filled the bathtub in the lavatory attached to the room. Others delivered our saddlebags. Then suddenly, we were left alone.

"Shall we?" Lucy asked over her shoulder as she started undressing while walking to the lavatory and the waiting bath.

We saw Fenwick at dinner, and were introduced to Lord Houlsin, the Count of Wickburn, and his wife, and Lord and Lady Chafter. Both Houlsin and Chafter appeared to be the same age as His Majesty and were large-framed men with florid complexions. Their wives both wore expressions of hauteur and disdain. I soon determined their displeasure was directed at me after overhearing one of them mutter the phrase, "jumped-up bastard."

During dinner, the two men tried to monopolize the conversation. They considered themselves military experts, despite never having led any troops in battle. I wondered why they were present.

"The Count and Lord Chafter both arrived with their soldiers today," Fenwick said. "Lord Houlsin commands a force of some twenty-two hundred foot soldiers, while Lord Chafter is nearly his equal, with nineteen hundred and fifty-two men under arms. Their forebears—your great-great-great-grandfathers?"

The two men nodded.

"Their several times great-grandfathers were instrumental in beating back the last invasion by the Rhetian Empire," Fenwick added.

"His Majesty will review our troops in the morning," Chafter said. "You should join us. You might learn a thing or two."

Lucy dug her nails into my thigh below the tablecloth, warning me to behave. Fenwick's eyes danced with mischief. I took a brief moment to compose myself before answering.

"That is quite gracious of you to invite me, Lord Chafter," I replied sincerely, though my throat wanted to shape my tone into the most bitter sarcasm. "I shall look forward to it."

I patted Lucy's hand and smiled innocently back at Fenwick. Fenwick was not finished in trying to provoke me, though. Later, he complimented both Houlsin and Chafter on the seeming breadth and depth of their military acumen.

"How did you both come to possess such great command of battlefield tactics and strategy?" Fenwick asked. "Each of you seems to be a veritable compendium of martial expertise."

"Well, part of it is hereditary," Chafter drawled. "Lord Houlsin and I could hardly avoid it, being heirs to families who have historically been indispensable in the defense of Aquileia."

"In addition," Houlsin added, "I possess the most comprehensive library of military tracts in Aquileia, and Chafter's is nearly the equal of mine. We have absorbed the thoughts of the greatest military minds of history, like Manat, Rollair, and Gilliver."

"Don't forget Fagles," Chafter added.

"Quite right," Houlsin acknowledged, "we mustn't forget Fagles. His treatise on the Battle of Jardell is essential."

Fenwick looked over at me and wiggled his eyebrows just the tiniest bit, trying to incite me to respond. Lucy gave me a look advising me to stay quiet. The only response I would have been able to generate would be to laugh out loud, so it was easy to avoid trouble.

I glanced over at the king and queen. The king was seemingly unaware of the ridiculousness of these two men. Queen Liliana, though, was alert to the subtle byplay between Fenwick and me. I don't think she quite understood the basis of it, as her attention was being taken up with the Countess of Wickburn and Lady Chafter.

Thankfully, the dinner did not last forever. It just seemed as though it did. Fenwick followed us to our chambers.

"You were very naughty, Fenwick," Lucy chided him.

"Me? What did I do?" he protested with mock innocence.

"Oh, don't pretend you weren't trying to provoke my husband," she said, "by flattering those two blowhards."

"Fine," Fenwick sighed. "Maybe I was—just a little—but that was the most fun I've had in ages!"

"Answer me this, Aloysius," I demanded. "Does the king really give credence to those two?"

"Having met them for the first time when you did, I can't say," Fenwick replied. "However, their soldiers will make up roughly a tenth of our army. His Majesty certainly cannot afford to alienate them. The king is also acutely aware of his own lack of military experience. Outside of you and your father, none of the nobility can claim any. Your father's record is not stellar, as the only thing some of the rest of the nobility knows about him is the near-ruin of his territory without any understanding of that particular situation. Your own success is the cause of some jealousy, aggravated by feelings about your lineage. Therefore, people like Houlsin and Chafter attribute your successful ambush last year to the involvement of the Castle Shield."

"That's absurd!" Lucy sputtered.

"That's human nature," Fenwick countered.

"I thought we were past that," she said.

"The majority of the nobility are," Fenwick explained. "The more involved and aware families have come around. But there are those like Houlsin and Chafter who stay in their fiefdoms and only listen to rumors spread by other close-minded people like themselves."

"Well, tomorrow's review of the soldiers will certainly be interesting," I remarked.

"I can hardly wait!" Fenwick said gleefully.

In the morning when I woke, I found my armor outside the door of our chambers. Someone polished it during the night. It was spotless.

Lucy and I found our way to breakfast and encountered the same group we dined with the evening before, absent the king and queen. Houlsin and Chafter were wearing breastplates. I viewed their effort to appear more martial as comical. Their wives refused to acknowledge me and did not speak to Lucy. Of course, they ignored Fenwick as well, so they were even-handed in their snobbery.

The seneschal appeared when we were nearly finished eating, informing us the king would be along presently. We did not wait long before he arrived. Our horses were waiting for us on this side of the bridge, and we climbed into the saddles. On the other side of the bridge, we were surrounded by a troop of the Castle Shield. The women did not join us, though I could tell Lucy wished to.

During the ride to the north gate of the city, Houlsin and Chafter boxed the king in on either side. I was content to trail slightly behind with Fenwick, listening to the two of them discussing possible strategies for upcoming battles, when we had not even seen the lay of the land. It was beyond preposterous.

Leaving from the north gate, we arrived quickly at the place where the troops were encamped. There were two groups, one dressed in bright red uniforms, the other, slightly smaller in number, in a bilious green. I saw only a handful of portable canvas shelters in either camp. From the numbers, I guessed only officers were provided shelter. Common soldiers were exposed to the elements. It rained in the night, and the temperature in the month of Goa, before the spring equinox, was still frigid—sometimes brutally so.

Both groups of soldiers seemed to be searching for their weapons in a leisurely manner and assembling into ranks slowly until I heard someone yell, "Ten lashes for the last man in line!"

I did not know from which camp that order came, but both groups responded. The soldiers reacted as though they were stung by bees. The ranks began to fill quickly, with soldiers standing straight, weapons on their shoulders.

From a distance of fifty yards or more, it was an impressive sight. Houlsin and Chafter seemed reluctant to approach more closely as they both reined in.

Andy and I, and Fenwick upon Davy, walked closer. The king hesitated, then followed us, which dragged Houlsin and Chafter along.

I looked at Houlsin's soldiers first. As I drew closer, I could see the red uniforms were threadbare, the embroidered frogging on the front frayed. Buttons were missing. From a distance, their uniforms presented a formidable appearance. When you could see the eyes and expressions of the soldiers, those told a different story, one of dispirited men. Quite a few had red noses, with snot running from them, along with the watery eyes of a head cold.

Their weapons were a motley assortment. Some carried simple pikes. A few had halberds. I saw glaives and a couple of pole-mounted cleavers. None of them appeared new.

Chafter's men were no better equipped and displayed the same low morale as Houlsin's soldiers. The uniforms were just as tired, their weapons just as ancient. The same percentage of them appeared to be suffering from head colds.

While the men of the March would not present as colorful an appearance, each man had a jerkin of thick boiled leather and an undershirt of quilted padding that would provide at least some protection from enemy blows. We did not flog our men. Our soldiers slept in portable shelters, protected from the elements. We provided them not only with new weapons but also effective training in how to use them.

I knew which group I would rather have with me in battle, and it was not the poor, sad men in front of me. My lips remained sealed, though I longed to expose Houlsin and Chafter's stupidity and cruelty. I wanted to ask them, in front of the king, how often they thrashed their soldiers, why so few had portable shelters, how old their weapons were, and anything else that would expose them for the sadistic imbeciles they were. Instead, I remembered that these soldiers were nearly ten percent of the forces we could expect, and I should not do anything that might cause Houlsin or Chafter to leave in a snit. Fenwick was not so well-disciplined.

On the ride back, I heard him ask Chafter, "How often do you flog your soldiers?"

"As often as they deserve," Chafter answered casually. "Rollair and Fagles both agree that the only way to motivate commoners like these is by applying the lash frequently."

I nudged Andy next to Fenwick and gave him a cross look. Fenwick grimaced in acknowledgment and held his tongue the rest of the way back to the castle. I overheard Houlsin and Chafter saying that they were planning on spending the night in the castle again. Fenwick gave me a sly look that I hoped meant he would try to find some way of excusing us from another night of their company.

While I did not enjoy my morning outing, I was sure Lucy spent her time pleasantly. When we returned to the castle, I was informed that she and the queen had been in private since we left. Lucy and Liliana were friends and enjoyed one another's company immensely. Lucy's residence in Easton prevented them from seeing each other as often as they would have liked.

Fenwick disappeared once we returned. I trudged back up to our assigned chambers. While I waited for Lucy, I tried to think of how I could influence Houlsin and Chafter to change their ways and salvage those soldiers in the month or so before the enemy came out of the mountains and into the western March.

I did not know how long I needed to wait for Lucy. Leaving our chambers, I found a page wandering along a corridor. I pulled the boy aside.

"Please find the seneschal," I asked. "I would like to visit the library and read the accounts of the last time the Rhetian Empire invaded."

It took more than a quarter-hour for the seneschal to find me. He guided me to the library. As far as the material I sought, he could only give the most general directions.

"I think it's in those shelves over there," he said while pointing. "His Majesty would know better, but he is in a meeting with the Chancellor of the Exchequer, and I will not interrupt him."

They say you should never judge a book by its cover, but that is what I did. In the general direction the seneschal pointed, I scanned the shelves. I selected the tome that looked most like what I thought a chronicle would resemble.

It was an account of the last war with the Rhetians, one hundred and ninety-one years ago, written by an unknown author. I found a chair in the light of a window and sat down. In no time at all, I immersed myself in the narrative.

The Rhetians invaded without warning, spilling over the mountains and occupying the western March. King Robert the Steadfast quickly gathered an army. He halted their further advance and pushed them back to the western side of the Tumid River (which flows into the port of Aurora). The Rhetians made several attempts to break through the king's lines, but the Aquileian forces had fortified their position with entrenchment and ramparts.

According to the chronicle, it was true that the Count of Wickburn and Lord Chafter's soldiers turned back the last serious Rhetian attack, but there was more to the story. The war had dragged on for more than a year. The Rhetians had sixty thousand men, but not enough to break through the Aquileian fortifications, and the Aquileians, with just under thirty thousand soldiers, did not possess enough strength to force the Rhetians out. The bloodiest battles were for control of the port of Aurora. We managed to hold it.

At the beginning of the second year of the conflict, the Duke of Manton (Lucy and Freddy's ancestor), with the assistance of Malcolm Barry (my ancestor!), took a small group of volunteers by sea and landed at the foot of the border mountains on the Rhetian side. From there, they worked their way across to the Rhetian supply route.

This small and daring group of Aquileians played havoc with the Rhetians' supply line. Despite the best efforts of the Rhetians, the Aquileians continued to attack again and again. The author estimated that the raiders destroyed half of everything the Rhetians tried to send to feed and clothe their army. The attack where Lord Chafter and the Count of Wickburn made their reputation was mounted by desperate, starving troops. Yes, Lord Houlsin and Lord Chafter did hold the line, but the author attributes the outcome more to the strength of the fortifications and the hunger-induced weakness of the Rhetian soldiers than to other factors.

I was so engrossed in the book I did not notice when the king entered the room. He waited for me to look up. When I did not, he cleared his throat, breaking my rapt concentration. Seeing who it was, I jumped to my feet, dropping the book on the floor. The king laughed at my startled reaction.

"It's a thrilling tale, isn't it?" he commented as I scrambled to pick the book from the floor. "Read it dozens of times as a boy. Just a few days ago, we found ourselves looking at it again."

"Then you understand—"

"That Houlsin and Chafter are full of crap?"

"Your words, not mine, Majesty."

"Then we should have used more offensive ones," he said. "But they also delivered a great number of men to our cause. We wouldn't call them soldiers at this point, but we need to start with men and then make them into soldiers."

"I will admit, Your Majesty, I was trying to think of a way—"

"That will not be your responsibility, Caz," he said. "Come. We must talk."

22

As I followed the king, it struck me that he used my name, Caz (short for Casimir), for the first time. In the past, His Majesty addressed me as "Lord Oritur" and before that, "FitzDuncan." I wondered what, if any, the reason could be.

I realized I was thinking much too hard about something that probably wasn't important. If Lucy knew what I was doing, she would laugh at me and tell me to stop before I hurt myself. As I mentioned, Lucy helps steady me.

The king took me to his office and shut the door. I waited for him to sit behind the desk before I occupied the chair facing him. King Mark rubbed his hands over his face, then looked at me with a faint smile.

"Do you remember our first meeting in this room?" he asked.

I could never forget it. It was after I killed his son, Wim, in a duel. Though Wim created the entire mess with his malicious scheme, I doubted then whether I would leave this room as a free man, or even alive.

"Yes, Your Majesty," I replied soberly.

"Good," he grunted. "Did you find it interesting that your family and your wife's ancestors played such a critical role in the last war?"

"It was something I did not know," I admitted. "I will admit I was proud to learn of it."

"Our three families have enjoyed an unusual friendship that goes back even farther in history," he said. "Now, for the reason we wished to speak with you … We realize you would desire more information, but what do you think will happen in the war to come?"

"Whew," I sighed.

"Here is what we believe will occur," the king said, not waiting for my answer. "From the reports we have received, the Rhetians will probably deliver an army of nearly one hundred thousand—a far greater number than you read in the chronicle of the last war. If we were unprepared, they would penetrate deep into Aquileia before we could stop them. They would gain control of the port of Aurora, which eliminate their supply vulnerability."

"But they will not find us unprepared, Your Majesty," I protested.

"Not completely," he said. "Sure, they are worried that you and the Rangers who escaped from the fort may have managed to warn us, but we do not believe that will deter them. They also know that we will, at most, muster forty-five thousand to oppose them. With a better than two-to-one advantage, their confidence will still be high. From the reports we received that you and Fenwick confirmed, they have, we are certain, been preparing for this invasion for quite some time. You will guide us in making sure we deploy our limited numbers in such a way as to deny them the success they seek. We want you by our side as much as possible. There is another reason we desire this. Can you guess it?"

"No," I answered, after trying to think of what it could be.

"In addition to guiding our actions in war, we hope to provide you with an understanding of political realities. You have demonstrated good instincts. Now we will train you."

"I will look forward to starting," I said.

"Caz, it has already begun," he replied. "And you passed the first test by the way you handled yourself with Houlsin and Chafter in spite of my ordering Fenwick to coax them into saying something provocative this morning."

"That was by your design?"

The king merely smiled in response, then added, "We depart for Reedsford in the morning. You will ride with us, as will Houlsin and Chafter. They will remain by our side so that we can avail ourselves of their vast stores of martial knowledge."

I had never heard His Majesty use sarcasm before. It confused me briefly. He stood, and our brief conversation was over. Once again, I tried to puzzle out the king's intentions. I returned to the chambers assigned to us and found Lucy waiting.

We discussed her time with the queen. Lucy claimed their conversation was more social than regarding any particular topics of importance. She did have some news to share.

"Lily is jealous of me, and wishes she could accompany us west," Lucy said. "Mark has expressly forbidden it, so she will be stuck here in the castle."

"We leave tomorrow, I'm told," I said.

"I know. I will be staying until your father arrives and will join our people for the journey to Reedsford," she said.

One small consolation for my impending separation from my wife was that we were not forced to dine with Houlsin and Chafter that evening. Instead, we joined Fenwick and Julienne Traval at an inn within walking distance of the castle. The dinner was as good as anything the king and queen might have served, and the company was far more pleasant.

In the morning, Fenwick and I joined the king's party. Houlsin and Chafter were there, looking extraordinarily pleased to be included. I learned later that their soldiers were staying behind. The Castle Shield would accompany us, as would a group made up of most of Houlsin and Chafter's officers. We did expect to meet other friendly forces along the way, though, answering the king's summons.

"The king has taken half the sergeants from the Castle Shield," Fenwick whispered to me later. "They are staying behind to take care of Houlsin and Chafter's soldiers. Those poor lads need shelters, proper clothing, weapons, and decent leadership. Once they are properly equipped and regain their health, they will come to join us."

"How did the king convince them to leave the soldiers behind?" I whispered back.

"He convinced them that he needed their advice desperately and that they would do far greater service to him by staying at his side. Rather than commanding just their soldiers, they would help the king command the entire force," Fenwick replied.

"And their officers?"

"The ones coming with us are all relatives," Fenwick answered. "The king suggested that they would be used to communicate the grand strategies they develop to the rest of the army. The others who are staying with the soldiers are those we judged to actually know how to lead—Houlsin's and Chafter's oldest sons among them, actually. They are completely unlike their fathers."

"How long does the king believe he can maintain this ruse?" I asked.

"Until the rest of the army assembles, when it would become nearly impossible for Houlsin and Chafter to withdraw without destroying their reputations. By that time, His Majesty hopes we will have won over the hearts and minds of the men so that they would not follow Houlsin and Chafter even if they did depart and will instead stay with the sons. He will soften the blow by informing Houlsin and Chafter that, as far as the history books will be concerned, they will be described as his trusted military advisers—unless they choose otherwise."

When His Majesty mentioned he would begin educating me in the nuances of the political world, I had not expected such an example so soon. His way of neutralizing these two idiots played precisely to their weaknesses. In order to do this, he needed to know both of them well enough to understand how to take advantage of them.

As we rode, I pondered the task of learning about the different nobles. I wondered what his aims would have been for Albert. He would not have expected his son to know Houlsin and Chafter well enough to circumvent them the way he had. No—he would need Albert to know about the next generation in both families.

That thought improved my outlook considerably. I was already acquainted with more than half of those in my generation. Some of them, like Freddy, I knew well.

Why the king singled me out for this was a puzzlement that I chewed on next. I suspected that my father had become something of an informal advisor to the king. It would explain his lengthy stays in the capital, for which he provided me no explanation. Perhaps King Mark wished for me to serve in the same role for whomever he appointed as his successor?

I decided that must be the reason. Then I turned my mind to which member of my generation the king would select. Suddenly, I understood the king might have already given me a strong hint when he mentioned the long-standing relationship between his line, my family—the Barry clan—and the

Austermains—Freddy and Lucy's family. The more I thought about it, the more convinced I was that the king would name Freddy as his successor.

Freddy's father, the Duke of Manton, was known and respected by nearly everyone. Their territory was not the most populous or profitable, but it was well-managed. They had no enemies I could think of.

As for Freddy, he was well-liked by his peers. I could not imagine anyone would dislike him. In addition, he was married to the daughter of one of the biggest merchant trading houses in the kingdom. Through them, he would have a network of contacts within the merchant class.

The idea of assisting Freddy as an informal advisor pleased me. I began to consider how I would be of most use to him. Very quickly, I decided that hiding away in the eastern March would be counter-productive. Though I still wished to manage the March effectively and efficiently, there would be time available to travel.

I wondered if Lucy discussed this with the queen. They shared many confidences, so it would not surprise me. Lucy would certainly enjoy the opportunity for us to work more closely with Freddy and Greta in the future.

It took us a week to reach Reedsford. During the journey, I was pleasantly surprised that the king expected Fenwick and me to share his quarters in an enormous structure His Majesty jokingly called the "canvas castle." Of course, Houlsin and Chafter were always at hand. They made sure they were rarely out of sight of the king.

There were already many soldiers encamped on the plain when we arrived. Scanning the different groups, I came up with roughly thirty thousand men. Fenwick agreed with me. The high ground where we stood had been saved for His Majesty. Looking at the camps, I saw the flags of the Duke of Manton and Duke of Gulick. I asked His Majesty for permission to pay them a call.

"Please do," he replied. "And alert them that we will be calling a meeting as soon as the soldiers erect the pavilion we brought for that purpose."

Andy and I rode down, calling on my father-in-law first. Noel was there with Lucy's older brother, Alexander. While we were still exchanging greetings, Freddy and his father, David, wandered over. I never saw Freddy clad in a breastplate before, and I don't think I would ever have imagined it. Yet he seemed as comfortable in it as he did in a dressing gown, lounging on the sofa.

They had heard about the perilous adventure Fenwick and I shared and wanted to hear the story. I obliged them by sharing a condensed version and glossed over how we were found as Fenwick did when we told the king initially. When I finished, I warned them about the king's impending meeting. Freddy then pulled me away.

"You must see how I am armed," he said eagerly.

Freddy was not a fencer. The nuances of swordplay escaped him, and he looked awkward and clumsy with a blade in his hand. As a result, a few years back, I gave him a walking stick with a heavy gold knob on the end. I figured he could bash someone in the head more effectively than trying to duel with them. Freddy loved it, and twice put it to good use in my presence.

Freddy was an excellent equestrian, though. He was as comfortable on a horse's back as he was on his own two feet. This ability kept him alive once when his swordsmanship was not up to the task.

"What do you think?" he said.

He showed me a stout wooden shaft about three and a half feet long, topped by a studded iron ball. Demonstrating, he swung it about. Freddy's horsemanship, combined with this lethal club, would make him a fearsome foe in battle.

"It's perfect!" I said with a broad smile.

"I think so, too," he agreed.

He put his club away, and when he turned back to me, I noticed his expression was no longer so excited.

"What's wrong?" I inquired.

"What do you think about all this?" he asked, waving his arms to encompass the entire plain.

His question caught me unprepared. From the time when snow-covered Fenwick disturbed my peaceful evening, I had not given much objective consideration to the issue. Instead, I had been responding to one problem or challenge after another.

"Honestly, Freddy, it's been such a whirlwind for me; I will confess I haven't given it much thought. At least, not in the way that I think you mean. I suppose the word that comes to mind is 'unfortunate.' Just when I thought I might be settling into the life of a country gentleman, like you, Fenwick snatched me away and thrust me into the middle of this. It's also unfortunate from the standpoint of the kingdom, while His Majesty addresses the problem of succession."

"I will agree that 'unfortunate' is a good word in these circumstances," Freddy said. "Do you think the Rhetians are doing this because of Albert's death?"

"Yes and no," I replied. "From what we saw, they clearly have been preparing for a long time. Albert told me while we were away that he believed we were overdue for something like this. His death, though, might have been what pushed them to move now."

A bugle blared from the king's pavilion on the small hill. Freddy's father returned, and they mounted their horses. I went and untied Andy and climbed into the saddle. I rode up with Noel and Alexander.

In the meeting, I saw Earl Montgomery and his son, Quint Pompeo—Lord Tulley. Quint had been a long-time friend of Prince Albert's. He was the only one Albert retained after the debacle when Prince Wim tried to discredit his brother.

In those days, I was still assisting people in retrieving lost items. Quint later came to me for help in recovering a huge amount of money that he had lost to a swindler. Like Albert, the prospect of disaster forced Quint to mature in a hurry. He became a friend, and I actually introduced him to his wife, Siobhan.

After the council, I sought them out. Both were pleased to see me. In thinking about the king's desire for me to play a bigger role in the political realm, I realized Quint would be someone on whom I relied heavily. Between Freddy and him, they knew everyone.

The next two weeks saw the arrival of the rest of the soldiers. One of the last groups was the soldiers supplied by the Duke of Wickburn and Lord Chafter. The difference in them was substantial. Only the upper half of their brightly colored uniforms remained. They wore them as jackets, over a boiled leather jerkin and quilted vest, with a woolen shirt underneath, along with woolen trousers. Their weapons, though still an assortment, were at least of modern manufacture. As they settled in, I was pleased to see a great number of canvas shelters erected.

Houlsin and Chafter pitched a fit when they saw them, and immediately demanded someone to fetch their sons to come and explain what they saw. By this point, the king's patience with these two was nearly used up. Before their sons arrived, they demanded an explanation from His Majesty and threatened to take the men back to their territories.

The two of them rode down to where their troops were camped and summoned them to order. As the soldiers were assembling, the king arrived. Houlsin and Chafter's sons went to stand with him and not their fathers. The three of them stood impassively while Houlsin and Chafter ordered the men to strike camp and prepare to depart. While the soldiers were wondering what to do, the two sons stepped forward.

"Men of Wickburn and Klamach!" they bellowed, seizing their attention. "You are free men. If you choose to follow the orders of our fathers, you may. If you do, you may take with you only those items you had with you when you arrived at the capital. Your new clothing, weapons, shelters, and other equipment, which were provided to us through the generosity of King Mark, will be needed for the defense of our kingdom. Or you can stay, as the two of us intend to do, and join us in the fight to come. You will keep the items we provided to you. Speak among yourselves and let us know your decision."

Houlsin and Chafter began screeching in protest, trying to shout at the men that they must leave, and screaming at their sons, cursing their disloyalty. Their soldiers ignored them, for the most part. It was interesting to watch as small groups formed around certain of the men—obviously the most respected and influential members of the group. Then those men looked for others like them and gathered to talk in small groups. After about twenty minutes, six of them separated and approached the king. All of them bowed. One stepped forward a pace.

"Your Majesty, we would like to stay, but under the command of the men who have taken care of us these past two weeks," he said, nodding at the younger Houlsin and Chafter. "Is that possible?"

"Yes," the king replied.

"Then we choose to stay."

Overhearing this, Houlsin and Chafter seemed about to explode. Fenwick then approached them and spoke quietly. Their red-faced anger quickly paled. They returned to their quarters without another word.

"What did you say to them?" I asked Fenwick later.

"I presented them the choice the king instructed me to offer," he answered. "They could stay and be listed among the king's advisors—though I assured them no one would listen to their imbecilic ideas—or they could leave, in which case I hoped they would make it home safely, these being such dangerous times and all."

"It appears they have decided to stay," I said.

"They still may face difficulty in reaching home after this is over," Fenwick said. "They have been so annoying I may just use my own initiative. The king feels confident that their sons are prepared to take control if the unthinkable happens."

The last group to arrive, just after this episode, was the men of the March, under our family banner. While I must admit to some bias, our men were an impressive sight. Unlike the rest of the army's foot soldiers, who resembled farmers with some rudimentary training, the men of the March bore themselves as soldiers. They approached in step, with packs on their backs and their halberds resting on their right shoulders. You heard them before you saw them, as they were all singing that horrible song about me as loudly as they could.

I quickly found Lucy as she and her team of healers were erecting their canvas shelter. As always, her presence lightened my soul. It seemed like we sooner embraced than I heard the bugle summoning me to another meeting.

"Which of these is yours?" I asked, pointing at the shelters. "I want to know in case I come back after dark. I don't want to enter the wrong one and frighten someone."

"Caz, my naughty husband, what if I share with two others?"

"You don't, do you?" I asked, as my hopes crashed down from a very great height.

"No," she said, laughing at my dismay. "Majors and Minors, you're easy to tease."

"That was cruel."

"But funny."

23

After the arrival of the men of the eastern March, the king summoned the nobles to another meeting, which Houlsin and Chafter did not attend. The king welcomed my father. His Majesty also shared what happened with the Duke of Wickburn and Lord Chafter, though he did not hint at the threat Fenwick made. Though I sensed some concern from a few regarding the king's heavy-handed treatment of the two men, there were also sighs of relief from those who had been in camp with them the longest.

His Majesty then gave us the latest intelligence. I already knew it, as he and I discussed it earlier. We had agreed on the next steps.

"The Rangers have just confirmed that the Rhetians are using Musser Pass," he said, pointing to the map resting on an easel. "The Rangers are assembling at Pine Spring, here," he pointed, "and will do their best to interfere with the Rhetians' progress. We will leave Reedsford in the morning and move to outside of Biscayville. Once there, we will have one day, no more, to establish a fortified position athwart the Rhetian line of advance."

"Will that stop them?" came a voice.

"Majors and Minors, no!" the king responded. "If we are able to hold our position until nightfall, we will consider it a great success."

"If we don't intend to hold the ground, why go to the effort of fortifying it?"

"Because it makes it easier for our men to kill Rhetians," I answered, "without suffering equal losses. The Rhetians will outnumber us. Our challenge is to reduce their numbers as much as we can at every opportunity. Once we have whittled them down, then we will stand chin-to-chin if needed."

From the time we arrived in Reedsford, I spent a good portion of each day examining the king's excellent maps of the region. There were three different passes through the mountains the Rhetians might have used, and we prepared responses for each route. The Musser Pass, which they chose, would be the easiest for them to traverse. It also provided us with the greatest number of places, like Biscayville, where we could set our forces, inflict casualties, then fall back to the next position.

When I first started studying the maps, I purposely did not activate my link to Bellona. It took nearly an entire day of close examination of the area where the Rhetians would exit the Carmen Pass (if they chose that route) before I found what I felt was a good spot to draw up our lines. Even then, I was not certain I had picked the best spot.

The next day, I opened my connection with Bellona before looking at the maps. This time I looked at the area we were now discussing. Not only did I immediately identify the location near Biscayville as being well-suited, but I also knew how to position our different units. I could hardly write quickly enough to keep up with my thoughts. By noon, I had the location and a detailed deployment plan prepared.

Just to double-check myself, I looked at the area from the day before. With Bellona's guidance, I chose the same spot. Instead of hours, though, it took me only minutes. In addition, I understood precisely how to arrange our forces—something I did not have time to do the day before.

The king looked in on me from time to time on both days. On the first day, he came and looked over my shoulder. When he saw me scribbling hastily the second day, he watched briefly, then departed.

On both days, when I finished, I met with him to review what I determined. After the first day, I had only a location. After the second, I had a location, plus sheaves of notes on the disposition of our soldiers.

The morning of the third day, the king was a bit red-eyed when I saw him. He left me alone, and I used Bellona's assistance again. At no point did he look in to see what I was doing.

When I met with him later, he said, "We stayed up most of the night reviewing your ideas. If there are flaws in what you compiled, we couldn't find them. This is part of your 'gift,' isn't it?"

"It is."

"Then, by all means, continue to make use of it. Who knows, by the time this is over, perhaps we will look at the supernatural differently," he said.

Each noble's forces brought their own healers. Within a few days of the entire army being assembled, they had all gravitated to Lucy. As far as I knew, they never took a vote or even held a discussion along these lines, but Lucy became their leader and spokesperson. We learned later we were truly blessed by their care.

It was a seven-day trek to the place outside of Biscayville I chose. Along the route, we encountered the residents of the town heading the other way along the road. The king had sent messengers ahead, warning them of the Rhetian advance.

From the Musser Pass, the forest peeled away, leaving a grassy sward that provided a natural outlet for an army descending into Aquileia. On either side of this long meadow, the forest remained. Our position was atop a low rise at a place where the grassy area narrowed to roughly a furlong wide. Behind us, it opened back up.

Most of the army we left at the position we would defend after this. The lack of space meant we could deploy only a fraction of our forces. After breakfast, the morning after we arrived, we sent the wagons with our baggage back to the main body. We kept only enough wagons to carry the picks and shovels, and the cooking implements we used to make our dinner. We slept on the ground that night, without our canvas shelters. Breakfast in the morning would be bread, cheese, and smoked meat.

We dug a trench ten feet wide and eight feet deep just below the top of the rise, folded back at the edge of the trees. We heaped the shoveled dirt onto the higher side. Those who weren't digging were rolling logs over the loose earth to pack it down. When we finished, the rampart we created rose another six feet. The Rhetians would need to climb fourteen feet from the bottom of the trench to reach the top of the berm. To discourage them from trying to leap across, we planted sharpened sticks onto which a leaper would land.

We had a bit more than four hundred men equipped with long pikes. They would be our first line of defense. With them, we positioned halberds and poleaxes. Behind the fortification, we had scores of archers. Our last line was two hundred of heavy cavalry from the Castle Shield, prepared to run down any Rhetians who snuck through the trees on either side.

As the day ended, I spied my father standing on top of the rampart, watching the sunset. I climbed up next to him and stood quietly. He turned to me and laid his hand on my shoulder.

"Caz, this is magnificent," he said softly, then departed.

I wondered what he meant. My mind was on tomorrow's battle. I hoped what we prepared would be effective enough. The proof would come tomorrow.

Rain woke me just before the sun rose. From a light drizzle, it grew to a steady downpour. It would make it more difficult for the Rhetians to scale our wall, but it would also loosen the bowstrings for our archers.

Our scouts reported that the Rhetians were an hour away. Shortly after they returned, we spotted riders in advance of the Rhetian formation. They approached our rampart closer than they should, and we greeted them with volleys of arrows until they pulled out of range. We killed one. I thought it was a good beginning.

Through the rain, I saw the head of the Rhetian column. Reaching within myself, I opened my connection with Bellona. Almost as soon as I did, I realized I overlooked something. I ordered two groups of soldiers, a hundred each, armed with halberds, to move into the woods fifty yards deep from the edge of the forest. They were to hide themselves and lay in wait. Two short blasts of the bugle would summon the group on the left, and three for those on the right. When they heard the signal, they would advance and, I hoped, pin against our ramparts any Rhetians trying to sneak through the woods to get around our position.

The Rhetian army stopped just short of the rider's body. After a brief wait while they decided what to do, we heard orders shouted, and the front of the column broke into a run toward us. Our archers fired blindly over our entrenchment, but the Rhetians were packed together so tightly our arrows had no difficulty finding flesh in which to bury themselves.

Dozens fell—perhaps even hundreds. Still, the Rhetians kept coming. Their first men reached the ditch and tried to jump at a full run. They screamed as they landed on the sharp sticks we left for them. More followed, now sliding down the side of the ditch, then trying to climb the steep wall. Our pikemen leaned over and stabbed and stabbed until the first Rhetian arrows flew.

We were prepared for this.

"By sections!" I ordered with a bellow.

Like a complicated piece of clockwork, the pikemen flattened themselves atop the rampart while arrows whizzed overhead. Then different sections would jump to their feet and clear the wall in front of them of climbers before dropping again. The officers were calling out numbers according to a schedule I devised with Bellona's guidance. It made it difficult for the Rhetians to know which group would pop up next.

I heard two sharp blasts from the bugle, then a few seconds later, three. Our archers continued their hail of arrows the whole time, and Rhetians continued to fall. I saw the Castle Shield run down five men who emerged from the woods on the left, skewering them with their lances.

A deep-throated horn sounded from the Rhetian side, and they pulled back out of range of our arrows. I examined our position. We lost some men whose bodies were being loaded into one of the wagons. It looked to be about a dozen so far. There were about twenty men who were wounded, receiving aid from two of the healers. I peered over and looked into the trench.

I realized that our very success might abbreviate the length of time we could hold this position. The ditch was already half full of Rhetian bodies—over a thousand dead, I reckoned. Another assault like the last, and we would have only our rampart to protect us—the trench would be filled.

We heard the Rhetians shouting orders again, and the front charged for us. More of their men were able to put their hands on top of our rampart. Others were scrabbling at the dirt, trying to make the front crumble. More of our pikemen fell to arrows. Our men in the woods protecting our flank were called into action more quickly this time.

The deep blast of the Rhetian signal intoned again, and the enemy retreated. Our trench was now full of corpses. I called the nearest officers to me and informed them we would remain for the next attack but then would retreat. They passed the word along to their neighbors, along with a signal letting me know they understood. Section by section along our fortification, the officers acknowledged my command.

The Rhetians came screaming forward again. My halberdiers now joined the pikemen, skewering and hacking the Rhetians who reached the top of the fortification. Sensing trouble, I sent a hundred halberdiers to each flank, where Rhetians were emerging from the woods.

The Rhetian archers slowed their fire, as now some of their men were reaching the top. My bowmen continued without pause, firing over the wall into the packed ranks of our enemy. We held the enemy off, but they now had an easier route to the top, climbing over the bodies of their fallen comrades.

The Rhetian signal resounded again. My men quietly climbed down from the rampart and began to move briskly away. I went to where I left Andy tied to a tree and climbed on his back. Our men in the woods reemerged and joined us. I gave the signal for speed march. This was six paces at a brisk march, followed by six paces at a jog. When the Rhetians climbed the fortification we abandoned, we were nearly a mile away.

Some of them began to pursue us at a run but were called back. Unfamiliar with the land, the Rhetians were wary of rushing into a trap. We made it back to the rest of the army untouched. We arrived after dark. I immediately went to report to His Majesty.

"You've returned before you expected," he said with a concerned look. "Did we face a setback?"

"Your Majesty, fifty-seven of our soldiers died in the battle. Another seventy-eight were wounded, though none seriously. In return, I estimate that we killed nearly five thousand Rhetians."

"Majors and Minors!" he gasped. "Five thousand? Are you sure? That seems unbelievable."

"I found it difficult to believe myself," I said. "But I base the figure on the volume of our trench. We dug roughly seven hundred feet, eight feet deep, and ten feet wide. We more than filled the ditch. I reckoned the size of the human body compared to the size of the trench. The bodies filled it. That is why we needed to abandon the position before nightfall. The ditch was no longer an obstacle. They were able to climb on the bodies and reach the top of our fortification. We had to retreat. My estimate does not account for the Rhetians who fell before reaching our entrenchment. Hundreds fell to our arrows."

"When do you expect them to arrive here?" he asked.

"By nightfall tomorrow."

"Not earlier?"

"We kept a speed march pace the entire way back, Your Majesty," I said. "An army of that size will not be able to match that pace. If the Rangers are still attacking their baggage train, that will slow them further. If they are able to move more quickly, our scouts will provide a warning. Plus, the Rhetians insist on burying their dead. That will take time."

"Very well, Caz. If you see your father, please let him know we wish to see him."

I left the "canvas castle" and went looking for Lucy. On the way, I informed my father of the king's request. I found Lucy by the fire with the large group of healers. She rose with her usual uncanny grace to meet me as soon as she saw me.

It is difficult for me to describe how Lucy's presence restores me. One minute, my nerves were a jangled mess from the stress of the battle and the horror of seeing so many dead—even though they were our enemies. The next minute, I am in her arms, and feel soothed and calm. She took me to bed and held me through the night.

In the morning, I examined our position. We were in a fortified camp, to the northeast of Lake Mago. The fortifications were identical to those we dug near Biscayville. To reach our camp, the Rhetians would need to follow the road. For nearly four miles, the road passed between a lake and a heavily forested hill.

Given what we did the day before, I expected the Rhetians to arrive in the evening and pitch camp short of where the road went between the hill and the lake. All day, I checked with the different units of our forces. Those who had not taken part in the first battle, like Freddy, were eager to have their chance to close with the enemy. I promised them they would get it.

Late that afternoon, we saw Rhetian advance riders approach our camp. They reined in out of bow range. After lingering and assessing the size of our forces, they wheeled and rode away. Our scouts reported in later that the main body of the Rhetian army pitched camp where I thought they would.

When darkness fell, the men who took part in the first encounter had a specific assignment. They were to keep all the fires in our camp blazing brightly through the night. I reckoned the Rhetians would send men to spy on us and wanted to give them something to see.

The rest of our foot soldiers departed camp quietly, without torches, guided by local farmers who knew the area well. They arranged themselves in the trees on the hill beside the road. The light cavalry, which included Freddy and some of his men, and all the armsmen from the eastern March, took an animal track behind the hill and circled all the way around. They, too, were guided by locals who hunted in these woods. The cavalry would remain concealed until the foot soldiers made their attack.

When morning arrived, a thick mist rose from the lake. In the distance, I could hear the sound of the Rhetian army beginning its day. Not long after, our scouts reported the enemy was on the move, heading toward us.

When the head of the Rhetian column emerged from the mist, it was an eerie sight. I opened my link with Bellona and drew forth the tiniest tendril of her essence. When the Rhetians were almost within bow range, I nodded to the bugler. He sounded out the signal that others along the hillside repeated.

When the bugles stopped, there was a moment of utter silence, as though the entire world was taking a deep breath. Then, through the mist, I heard thirty-nine thousand of our men screaming as they began to charge down the hill into the side of the Rhetian column. The Rhetians in front of us were frightened and confused. Because of the mist, they could not see what was happening behind them.

While they were frozen in fear, the Castle Shield wheeled out of our camp and formed up on the road. When our men lowered their lances and spurred their mounts, the Rhetians tried to run away. They did not get far.

On the other side of the battle, four miles away, our light cavalry raced from concealment and smashed into the side of the Rhetians on the road. Then they turned and rode into the enemies who were trapped between our foot soldiers and the lake. The part of the Rhetian army that had not been attacked dropped their weapons and ran.

The mist cleared shortly after the screaming of the Rhetian soldiers stopped. I severed my connection to Bellona. The king gestured for me to join him. I climbed on Andy's back. We went forward only a few yards before Andy refused to go further. The road was covered in bodies, and he refused to step on them. I could not blame him. We turned around, and I slid from the saddle, looping his reins over a tree branch. The king's horse was no braver, and His Majesty tied him next to Andy.

The shore of the lake was soaked in blood. The water was predominantly red. I looked over at the king. His expression was one of stunned disbelief. We did not make it very far before the coppery smell of blood and the stench of death-loosened bowels overwhelmed us. Our soldiers began to pass us, returning to camp. The fronts of their clothes were covered with blood, but almost all sported grins that went from ear to ear.

All of a sudden, I heard what could only been a group of militia from the eastern March. They were singing that damned bawdy song, having made up new verses. When they reached the chorus, they saw me standing with His Majesty. They increased their volume and knuckled their forelocks as they passed by.

"Quite a catchy tune, don't you think, Lord Oritur?" the king remarked a moment later, maximizing my embarrassment.

24

We broke camp as soon as the last unit reported their men had returned. For the day, we lost a hundred and seventy killed with another two hundred ninety-six wounded. The Rhetians lost at least fifteen thousand.

"At what point do you think the Rhetians will give up?" His Majesty asked as we rode that afternoon. "They lost over twenty thousand men in the first two engagements and haven't even given us a bloody nose."

"Even with the casualties, they still outnumber us," I said. "It's now less than two-to-one, but just. I don't expect them to give up until we outnumber them so that even their fanatical minds must accept that victory is impossible."

"So, we need another three victories as horrible as this one," the king said.

"Unfortunately, yes, or one that is enormously awful for them," I stated.

We pitched camp that afternoon after a difficult crossing of what the locals called Hamil Creek. Swollen by spring rains and melted snow from the mountains in the distance, the creek more resembled a river. Even at the ford, the water was four feet deep, icy cold, and carried enough force to sweep an unwary man off his feet. We set up guide ropes for the men and towed the wagons across at great speed with dozens of horses hitched to them.

We continued on to the next place I had identified as suitable for battle, five miles from the creek. When we arrived, we began fortifying our position. Just after night fell, two of our scouts arrived. The king called me to his quarters to hear their report.

"The Rhetians are straddling the creek," the one said. "They got less than half their men across."

"How much less than half?" I asked.

"I reckon they have about eighty thousand men, from the length of their column," the first one said. "They got maybe thirty thousand over to our side today. That about right?"

"Near as I can figure," the second one agreed.

"Thank you, men," I said. "This is valuable information. You are doing great work. Please keep it up."

"Um, excuse me, milord, but are you Lord Oritur? Like in the song?" the first one asked.

"He is!" the king said gleefully.

"It's a right catchy tune," the second one said. "Everyone is singing it."

The king laughed uproariously as they departed. I put aside my feelings of embarrassment and quickly touched my link to Bellona. My initial thought when I heard the report of the scouts was to move immediately and strike their camp tonight. With my connection to the Goddess engaged, it seemed like an even better idea. How to approach the enemy camp was clear. I closed the link.

"Your Majesty, we need to muster everyone immediately," I said. "Having the Rhetian forces split by the creek is an opportunity too good to pass by."

"Are you sure, Caz?" he asked. "The men are near exhausted. That was a difficult crossing, and then we put them to work on the camp."

"Your Majesty, you have asked me to advise you during this campaign. My advice, based on the information we just received, is to mount an immediate attack." Changing my tone, I added, "You are my liege lord. If you wish for me to be quiet and go to sleep, I will do so without complaint. I never wish to overstep my bounds, especially with you, who have been so generous to me."

The king looked at me thoughtfully.

"Wake the bugler," he said. "Summon the council and get those scouts back here."

I found the scouts before they left camp and brought them back to the pavilion where we would meet. The members of the nobility trickled in. Curiosity at a summons so late marked their faces. When enough of the group assembled, His Majesty looked at me and nodded, indicating I should begin.

Usually, the king opened these meetings. His action caught me off guard. I rallied quickly, clearing my throat to give me another second to compose my thoughts.

"The scouts reported the Rhetians' position to us a few minutes ago," I said. "They had difficulty crossing Hamil Creek. By the end of the day, they succeeded in getting less than half their army over. They are currently split into two camps, one on either side. We have the opportunity, if we strike quickly, to enjoy the advantages of both numerical superiority and surprise. I propose setting out immediately to attack the smaller camp on our side of the creek."

"You want us to rouse the men, march five miles back to the creek in the dark, then mount an attack?" A voice whined. I could not see who it was.

"Yes," I stated firmly. "This is an unforeseen opportunity. The Rhetians made a mistake. When they saw how difficult the crossing was, they should have pulled back or completed it. They did neither, and we should make them pay for their error."

"You are confident of our success?" Freddy's father asked.

"I am. We will suffer casualties, though," I warned. "Unlike our first two encounters, we will not enjoy the advantages of fortification or terrain. We should, however, catch them by surprise. That will provide us one advantage. The other advantage will be numbers. We will have three men for their two."

"If we don't attack, what will happen?" Earl Montgomery asked.

"Then we face their combined force of eighty thousand or more, most likely the day after next," I said.

"And how many made it across the creek?" the earl inquired.

I nodded to the scouts. "Around thirty thousand, milord," the one said.

The nobles began talking and arguing among themselves. I looked to the king, concerned. He shook his head slowly and waved his hand slightly, indicating I should let them continue.

After ten minutes, the hubbub died away. A stout man with blond hair stepped forward. I recognized him as Lord Manafort.

"How do you propose we go about this, then?" he asked.

This was a question I hoped I would be asked. Bellona had helped me determine exactly what to do. I went to the map of the area that was resting on an easel.

"The foot soldiers will proceed along the direct route that we followed from the creek. We will form up here, behind this rise, and out of sight of the enemy camp. The cavalry will split off from us earlier, at this point," I indicated it on the map, "and one of the scouts will guide them to these trees just to the north. When the foot soldiers come over the rise, I expect their sentries to spot us and raise the alarm. We will still hit them, as they will be unprepared and disorganized at first. It will be important for our men to maintain formation since, within a few minutes, the enemy will regroup and form ranks to oppose us."

"And the cavalry?" someone asked.

"Once the enemy forms ranks," I said, "our line and their line will be locked together. The cavalry will then sweep down and hit the enemy flank."

Grunts of approval rose from the group when they heard this. All of them understood how devastating such a maneuver would be. Outflanking an enemy was a goal in nearly every battle but one not often achieved.

"When do we start?" Noel, Lucy's father, asked.

"As soon as we muster the men," I answered.

"Then let's not waste any more time," I heard a voice comment. "Give us our orders."

"Very well," I commented.

Using the map, I indicated where I wanted the different groups of men to be positioned. The meeting broke up. The Duke of Wickburn and Lord Chafter stayed behind. As far as I knew, this was the first meeting they had attended since the king dressed them down.

"Your Majesty, may we please speak with you?" Chafter asked.

"Of course."

Chafter and Houlsin both looked pointedly over at me, clearly not desiring my presence.

"Anything you need to say, you may say in Lord Oritur's presence," the king instructed. "We can assure you of his discretion."

From their expressions, I knew instantly that their purpose was to speak against me. The sly smile I thought I saw at the corner of the king's mouth hinted that he knew that as well. Houlsin sighed deeply.

"Your Majesty, we speak on behalf of a group of your loyal subjects," Houlsin said, "who are concerned about the amount of authority you have granted someone of such ignoble birth."

I knew instantly that there was no "group" beyond these two fopdoodles. No one with any hint of intelligence would choose these two to present a grievance to His Majesty, given their current status in the eyes of the crown. I waited to see the king's response.

"And though our first two actions against the enemy were successful, they could hardly have turned out otherwise," Chafert continued. "In both, we enjoyed all the advantages prescribed by Manat, Rollair, Gilliver, and Fagles, the generally acknowledged masters of military strategy. We possessed the benefits of both a fortified position and favorable terrain. But now we fear this man has exceeded the limitations of good fortune and common sense."

"Rollair and Manat state very clearly that night operations are to be avoided," Houlsin said. "Gilliver and Fagles also advise against them, except when the entire army has been well prepared for such action and is completely familiar with the ground."

"We, and the other members of our group, are convinced this attack is foolhardy and will fail utterly," Chafter said. "It will result in the destruction of your forces and hand victory to the enemy."

"We beg you to reconsider this reckless and ill-advised attack," Houlsin added. "It would be our pleasure to show you the passages by the authors we mentioned that address what this man has suggested."

The king nodded sagely, then asked, "Are you finished? Is there anything else?"

"We would appreciate it if you would restore to us the command of the forces we have contributed to your army," Chafter suggested. "The other members of our group are concerned that you may do the same to them at some point in the future. We would be distressed if this caused instability to your reign."

"Really?" the king said. "You do not feel your sons are doing well? I disagree. They are showing themselves quite capable. And who are the other members of your group? We would address their concerns directly."

"We are not at liberty to say, Your Majesty," Chafter replied. "They asked that we maintain their anonymity for fear of reprisal. We hope you can understand our need for discretion."

"Of course," the king stated. "Our reputation must be more fearsome than we knew."

The two men had grown more confident as the king allowed them to prattle on. These two clodpates believed the king was finding their arguments convincing. I had a suspicion they might have just commissioned their own demise.

"Thank you for bringing your concerns, and those of your anonymous partners, to our attention. Let us consider your points one at a time. You are concerned about Lord Oritur's ancestry? Interesting. You must have forgotten that we issued a royal decree nearly three years ago whereby Lord Oritur's birth was legitimized."

"We have not forgotten, Your Majesty," Chafert said hastily. "But a royal decree cannot change the actual circumstances of his origin."

"His mother was a housemaid," Houlsin added. "His family sent him away."

"Yet the other members of this company have accepted our ruling on the matter," the king replied. "Grudgingly, in some cases, with pleasure, in others."

"The other members of our group—" Chafter began.

"Please," the king snapped. "Let us dispense with play-acting. You speak for no one but yourselves. None of the others would be so dimwitted as to choose you to represent them."

The two men stood silent, their mouths opening and closing like those of a fish out of water.

"You say anyone could have produced the extremely lopsided victories in our first two engagements," the king continued. "It was Lord Oritur who chose the ground. It was Lord Oritur who directed the fortification. It was Lord Oritur who saw the advantage of favorable terrain. It is to Lord Oritur that we owe our success thus far. All the reading you have done is no substitute for a keen eye and intelligence. Both of you possess neither. Fortunately, your sons do not seem to be cursed with your imbecility. That you are here to speak against this night action convinces us utterly that it is precisely the right thing for us to do. You have banished all our remaining doubts. The only decision we have left to make is to decide what we shall do with you. Because we prefer to enjoy a reputation for benevolence, we present you with a choice. You may fight with your men tonight—not in command of them, but by their side."

"Or?" Houlsin asked fearfully.

"Or be disgraced, stripped of your titles and positions," the king said calmly. "All of you serve at our sufferance. It is within our power to replace any of you at our whim. If you ride with us this evening, we will know your answer."

The king gestured dismissively at the two. With a parting glare directed at me, they exited the pavilion. His Majesty sighed heavily.

"Did you enjoy that, Caz?" he asked

"No."

"Because of their insults?"

"What bothered me more was their arrogant stupidity," I said. "They forced you to deal with them harshly and showed they learned nothing. The insults about my birth are something I have lived with, and they have diminished in number and intensity. Your decree of legitimacy, much as I appreciate it, is meaningless to people like these. My actions since returning to the March, even though few understand the depth of the challenges we faced, have done more to silence that sort of talk."

"How do you feel the nobles view you now?" he inquired.

"I have supporters among them now," I answered. "Men who are respected for their families and their character. Their opinions have weakened preconceived notions to the point where most others are willing to evaluate me on my merits and my person, not my birth."

"Not to mention the soldiers sing songs about you," he teased.

"I would imagine that is held against me, if anything," I replied as my cheeks reddened.

"Don't be so sure," he said soberly. "Now, go kiss your wife goodbye, then return, and we will see about killing some more Rhetians."

I did as His Majesty ordered. Perhaps I spent a bit more time with the kissing than he intended, but who could fault me? I donned my armor and mounted Andy. Something nudged me mentally, and I collected two of the lances our armsmen used and tucked them under my thigh before we rode to the pavilion.

The king was there, along with Fenwick, my father, and Earl Montgomery along with Quint, plus two men I did not know well—the Duke of Chaldic and Lord Hepworth. I was somewhat surprised to see Houlsin and Chafter in front of their men. I noticed they would not speak to their sons and tried to pretend they did not exist. The rest of the soldiers were now assembled. Led by the two scouts, we set off into the dark night.

After covering three miles, the one scout took the cavalry off to the north. The king and our group stayed with the foot soldiers. When we drew within a mile, the word passed for the men to remain silent. All the muttered curses and good-natured joking stopped.

At about a half-mile away, we topped a small rise and could see the watchfires of the enemy camp. We had made it this far under the cloak of night, and I considered every pace we took from here without discovery to be a gift. I opened my portal to Bellona and felt the heightened awareness and strength that she provided flow through me.

When we ascended the last small hillock before the camp, their sentries spotted us and began shouting the alarm. Our buglers sounded the signal to attack. With shrieks and yells, our soldiers began to run downhill to the enemy.

In the light of the enemy's fires, I saw two figures on horseback charging well ahead of the rest of our men. When they drew close to the light, I recognized Chafter and Houlsin. Swords drawn, they hacked their way into the enemy, but it was only a matter of moments before they were dragged from the saddle and disappeared from view.

They were arrogantly stupid to the end, I thought. I don't know whether they thought their charge would inspire us, or whether this futile and foolish action would somehow redeem them. To me, it just seemed sad and useless.

25

Our soldiers crashed into the enemy camp, engaging in bloody slaughter at first. I could see as their forward progress slowed, and knew the enemy rallied. We rode closer, to see what was occurring.

The two lines were engaged, and a bitter fight with halberds and pikes was taking place. The men in the front stood on the bodies of the fallen. Our soldiers were still pressing forward, forcing the Rhetians back, step by step.

The fires of the enemy had spread to the canvas of some of the shelters. A blaze of light when one caught fire showed a small gap that opened in our lines. I urged Andy forward to meet the Rhetians who started to surge through. In the seconds I had, I opened my conduit with Bellona wider, allowing more of her essence to fill me.

I withdrew my first lance and spent it on a soldier whom I caught unaware of my sudden arrival. The second lance went through the chest of a man who was swinging his poleax at me. Then I sensed more than heard a mighty crash just behind me to the right. I whirled Andy around and saw the king's horse down. His Majesty's right leg was trapped underneath it.

I leapt from the saddle, leaving Andy to escape the carnage according to his own desires, while I drew my blade. From his back, the king parried one blow, then another. By then, I reached him and stood over him.

Touching the tan-zyan ring on my finger to the diamond in the pommel of my blade, I allowed the store of numinous energy to flow without restraint. My appearance changed as before, making me seem huge, but I could not spare it a thought. The enemy was straining forward, trying to reach the king.

Fenwick landed beside me. The two of us moved as fast as thought, our blades flashing in the firelight. Behind us, I heard Chaldic and Hepworth summoning men to close the gap in our line.

My father was to my left, protecting my side as I danced between and along the shafts of the pikes and halberds, slaying those wielding them. Montgomery and Quint were on the other side of Fenwick, keeping his right side free from harm. Our soldiers quickly filled the gap in the line, and the threat to our king was ended.

I tightened my control over my flow of divine energy, and my appearance dropped back to normal. Fenwick did likewise at almost the same moment. My father, Earl Montgomery, and Quint heaved at the corpse of the king's horse and managed to free His Majesty. In front of us was a pile of slain enemies.

At the moment, I did not spare it a thought. I heard our buglers sound the cavalry charge. Our riders swooped into the fray, and the Rhetian line crumbled and broke. The enemy panicked, and their soldiers tried to run from the fight. Most did not get far before our horsemen cut them down. Some, I learned, threw themselves into the swift, cold waters of the creek.

The gray of false dawn was illuminating the sky as we picked our way through the camp, searching for any survivors. There were not many to find. The king approached me. Clasping me by the shoulders, he embraced me for a long moment. I was slightly stunned by this, but before I could react, he moved to Fenwick and spoke in his ear.

Fenwick wandered off, returning after a few minutes with a large piece of pale canvas and a broken pike shaft. He attached the canvas to the splintered wooden pole and approached the edge of the creek. He called out in the Rhetian tongue, holding the makeshift flag.

Several minutes later, someone wearing a uniform dripping with gold braid stepped through the Rhetians on the other side and answered Fenwick. Their conversation began in angry tones but eventually softened. When they finished, Fenwick returned to the king and spoke in his ear, then crossed to the bugler.

The notes to summon nobles to a council meeting sounded out. While they were gathering, the king took a horse from a member of the Castle Shield and climbed into the saddle. When he judged enough had gathered, he raised his hand for quiet.

"We will take our dead and wounded from the field," he announced. "Then we will depart and allow our enemies to do the same. There will be no more fighting for ten days, while both of us tend to the fallen."

We assigned different groups of soldiers to the various tasks. Some were sent into the forest to chop down coniferous trees for funeral pyres. The resinous sap of these trees will cause them to burn despite the greenness of the wood. Others were detailed to begin collecting the bodies of our fallen. As unpleasant a task as it was, it would be far worse for the Rhetians.

Just over five thousand of our men died in the battle. The Rhetian losses were almost six times more. Our religion allows the cremation of the dead. The Rhetians' god insisted on burial.

Disposing of five thousand bodies seems a monumental task. We had nearly thirty thousand men, though, to do the work. By the end of the second day, we had built over a hundred huge pyres. The bodies were placed in them and on them. As the sun began to set, the king ignited the first. The others followed, and many of us kept vigil through the night for our brothers in arms.

By morning, the fires were no more than smoldering ashes. Only the bones remained unburned. With hardly a sound, we trudged back to our camp.

When I arrived, after I had tended to Andy, I looked for Lucy. She was with her group of healers, treating the more seriously wounded. Some of her golden hair stuck to her face with sweat. There were streaks of dirt and blood on her face, and more blood had splattered the apron she wore. She saw me, and nodded, but had no time to talk.

I found a quiet piece of grass and stretched out. Sleep claimed me as soon as my eyes shut. I felt a soft kiss on my lips, and thought I was dreaming. When I opened my eyes, Lucy was kneeling next to me, her face only inches away. She was dirty and disheveled, but still the most beautiful woman in the world to me.

"You look frightful," she commented.

"I do?"

"The front of you is covered in dried blood." She poked her finger below the edge of my breastplate and pried it up to see underneath. "It even soaked around the edge of your armor. Did you bathe in it?"

"No. Things did get a bit desperate for a minute or two," I said.

"Was this when you defended the king against a hundred foes?" she inquired with a teasing tone.

"A hundred? No. It wasn't that many. Who is saying—"

"It was thirteen," Fenwick announced, flopping down on the ground next to me. "Clearly, I must have dispatched seven of them. There is no way you outdid me."

I was confused. I turned to Lucy. "How did you hear about the king? Where did this nonsense about a hundred come from?"

"The song, Lord Blockhead," Fenwick snorted. "They've already written new verses. Still no mention of me. My feelings are quite hurt."

"Majors and Minors," I muttered in disgust.

Lucy laughed. "I think it's hilarious," she said.

"His Majesty enjoys it, too," Fenwick added. He began to whistle the tune.

"Please stop," I begged. "Tell me what you discussed with the Rhetians."

"They are such unpleasant, humorless people," Fenwick commented. "First, I asked if they were ready to surrender yet. They were indignant that I even suggested it. I reminded the man that he had lost half his army in a week and told him I thought it would be a shame to lose the other half as well. He did not appreciate my sentiment."

"That explains why the dialogue sounded so harsh at the beginning," I said.

"He then asked me if we wanted to surrender to him. You should be proud of me for not laughing in his face. Instead, I suggested that if we had suffered losses as severe as theirs, we would definitely be pondering the question."

"Did you insult him?" I asked.

"Oh—I truly wanted to," Fenwick said. "But I was speaking for His Majesty, so I thought I had better play the dip-lo-mat. His Majesty later advised me that I should have instead suggested the man perform an action he would need to be extraordinarily well-endowed to accomplish."

Lucy laughed robustly at this.

"Then I brought up the matter of a truce to attend to the dead. It was relatively easy to get him to agree. They wanted two weeks. We offered one. The compromise was ten days. I suspect they will need more time. They need to dig a horribly big hole."

"I imagine so," I said.

"Now, much as I enjoy passing the time in the company of your lovely bride, I fear that duty calls," Fenwick said. "He sent me to fetch you."

"The king?"

"None other."

With a sigh, I heaved myself up. I bent over to give Lucy a brief kiss, then followed Fenwick. He began whistling that awful song again.

When we arrived at the king's pavilion, His Majesty was finishing a conversation with a half-dozen nobles whom I knew only slightly. As they exited, they greeted me with friendly nods. That was something new.

"We are exceedingly grateful to you both for stepping forward when we fell," the king said. "Without your protection…"

He blew out a sharp breath and shook his head.

"You have our thanks and, I hope, the thanks of the entire kingdom."

"They added a new verse to the song, Your Majesty," Fenwick chirped, "though I am conspicuous by the complete lack of recognition of my exploits."

"Don't worry, Fenwick," the king replied, pretending a conciliatory tone, "We are sure your day will come. Now, to business. We have some time to prepare for our next encounter with these people."

I accessed the merest puff of Bellona's energy. Looking at the map, I considered the situation. One location stood out.

"Here," I said, pointing at the map. "Farsall—two days' from here. We will occupy the high ground here. It is not a steep slope, but it is long."

"How long will it take to fortify our position?"

"No time," I said. "Other than the area where we will park our baggage, I don't intend to improve the ground at all. I want to encourage them to close with us."

"Why?"

"If we dig in, Your Majesty, they will avoid battle if they can," I explained. "The country here is more open. They enjoy much greater freedom of movement. Rather than attack us where we are dug in, they will try to slip past, moving to one side or the other. That will pull us out of our position and force us to react to their movements in order to prevent them from reaching the river."

"And this place? Farsall?"

"As I said, the slope appears non-threatening, but the length of the slope will take a toll. They will not understand that until too late. If we deploy near the top, I am confident they will respond. They still outnumber us by a handful, and nothing they have suffered to this point has deterred them," I explained. "They will engage us."

"And then?"

"They have not been able to employ their cavalry in any of our encounters so far," I said. "This will offer them an opportunity. They will attempt to flank us, but they will not be successful."

"Why not?"

"Because we will be prepared," I said. "We will draw their horsemen into a trap lined with steel. Our cavalry will pretend to leave the field. The Rhetian horsemen will wheel to roll up our line. As soon as they do, the halberdiers and pikemen I will position in the tall grass will emerge. We will destroy their cavalry, and ours will regroup to counterattack, downhill, and flank the enemy instead."

"And do you base this on…?" the king inquired.

"On what Fenwick and I observed while we were held prisoner by the Rhetians," I said. "Their foot soldiers seemed to be conscripts. Their cavalry was not. I think that their horsemen come from the ranks of the landed and consider themselves superior in every respect. They will demand that the battle be put in their hands."

"Do you agree, Fenwick?" the king asked.

"Lord Oritur's observations regarding the Rhetians match my own," he said. "What he says makes sense to me. I had not been thinking of things in those terms."

"You are confident, Caz?"

"Yes, Your Majesty."

Over the next week, the king required my presence in many different discussions. All of them centered on issues outside of the war brought forward by different nobles. I knew none of the people well, but I listened diligently and wrote down copious notes. After the first such meeting, I offered to surrender my scribblings to the king. He chuckled softly.

"Our secretary over there takes all the notes we need," he said. "Your notes are for your use. For instance, what did you think of Lord Walchick?"

"He struck me as blunt and straightforward."

"Go on."

"His main complaint was regarding the import tariffs on iron ore," I said. "He claims that, even with transportation costs, he can obtain iron ore from Nagah more cheaply than from mines in Aquileia. The tariffs increase the cost of ore from Nagah to the point that there is no cost advantage. He would like you to remove the tariff."

"Does he have a solid argument?" the king asked.

"Well, that depends on one's point of view, doesn't it?" I offered. "If we consider only his territory and his people, his argument is sound. When we expand our view to include Aquileia as a whole, his position is weaker. Aquileian mines provide work for our citizens. Those workers may actually buy some of what is produced in Walchick's area. And if we open up our view even more broadly, we encounter other potential issues."

"Such as?"

"I'm not well-versed in the countries on the southern continent, Your Majesty, but I seem to recall that Nagah has a reputation for still using slave labor—particularly in dirty, dangerous work like mining," I said. "If that is indeed the case, buying iron ore from Nagah supports slavery while weakening the position of our own people. From a moral standpoint, Walchick's argument fails."

"You are correct. Nagah still uses slaves in certain areas. Do you think Walchick has ever considered that?" the king asked.

"If he has, he probably discarded those issues as a problem that does not involve him," I suggested.

"So, how do we resolve Walchick's complaint?"

"We don't, Your Majesty," I said. "I imagine you have tried to explain the larger issues to him on several occasions without success. He either does not wish to understand or is incapable of taking into account things outside his own territory. I suspect it is a bit of both."

"Now, Caz, throwing all that aside, did you like Walchick?"

"I was introduced to him for the first time today, so—"

"Did you like him, on the basis of this one interaction?"

"I did."

"Would that influence you to try to help him?"

I thought carefully. Yes, I liked Walchick immediately. Then I considered how I would treat Freddy, or Quint, or Ratty Hawkins in a similar situation.

"I would like to say it would not," I replied. "Even more, I would hope that a friend would not put me in such a position. But it is the nature of your office, isn't it? The office and the man reside in the same person."

"Our friends tend to be those who ask for nothing," he stated. "Your father is one such man. Manton, Gulick, and Montgomery are others that you know. Chaldic and Hepworth, you have just met. There are still others."

"This is my political training," I remarked.

"Have you guessed why we believe it is important?"

"I presume it is to mold me into that sort of man," I replied. "One who asks for nothing except for the opportunity to be of service to his king. Someone who can provide an objective point of view and be more than a lickspittle."

"This was a good start, Caz," he said with a smile. "We have kept you long enough today."

The meetings with the various nobles were usually on the dull side, I found. My conversations with the king afterward were of the most benefit. Most nights after dinner, I rehashed the topics with Lucy, my father, and Fenwick. Our discussions were fascinating.

Near the end of the week, we broke camp and moved everything to Farsall. Our scouts kept us informed of the Rhetians' progress in burying the dead. They required two days past our agreed-upon truce to finish. We had no intention of attacking them in this place or at this time.

26

The main feature of the land at Farsall that attracted me was the broad, gently sloping ridge—if one could even call it a ridge. We encamped on the top of it. The slope facing the direction from which the Rhetians would come was a broad meadow. Last year's dead grass remained, standing over three feet high. I marked with twine and stakes certain areas where no one was to trample the grass.

The Rhetians arrived three days after we did, in the mid-afternoon. They pitched their camp a few hundred yards from the foot of the hill. We watched one another for the rest of the day.

The following morning, we roused our men just before sun up. We made sure everyone ate a hearty breakfast and had time to attend to his personal needs. An hour after sunrise, our bugles sounded, and we drew up our battle lines. Our front line stretched nearly a mile, with men lined up four deep. The cavalry, both light and heavy, was split between our flanks.

In the days leading up to this moment, I coached the cavalry carefully on their role. When challenged by the enemy's horsemen, they were to provide just enough resistance to convince the enemy they were in a fight. The cavalry would then pretend to panic and bolt.

Hidden in the tall grass I protected from trampling, two thousand halberdiers on each flank crawled on their bellies into position. They formed a thick line just behind the cavalry and at an open angle to the front line. These were the soldiers who would win the battle for us.

When the Rhetians saw us form our lines, they hurried to do the same. We heard the shouted orders as the enemy matched their formation to ours. As they marched to the foot of the slope, I could see their ranks of foot soldiers were thinner than ours, only three men deep. Their cavalry, relatively untouched in the previous engagements, were more plentiful than ours, though, with half again our number. The play-acting I wanted our cavalry to employ might not be so difficult.

I touched open my connection with Bellona and felt her gift flow into me. Seeing the array for the battle to come, I was more convinced than ever that my analysis of the Rhetians was accurate. I tried, and failed, to keep a grin from my face.

"That is an ugly look on your face, Caz," Fenwick commented.

"Why?" the king asked. "He's smiling. That's not unattractive."

"You're not a Rhetian, Your Majesty," Fenwick cracked. "They would rightly see that smile as a threat."

"Perhaps he is thinking of what new verses they might add to his song," my father joked.

I ignored their banter. Instead, I watched as the Rhetian line started up the slope toward us. The deep-throated Rhetian horns sounded, and their foot soldiers began running toward us, yelling and hollering. Our men stayed where they were, following my instructions. They were not to close with the Rhetians until the distance between them was down to fifteen yards.

The Rhetian soldiers were no longer a straight line across the ridge. Individuals had either forged ahead or fallen behind, as the long shallow slope sucked the wind from their lungs. Their yelling had ceased. All we heard now was their panting and gasping. Their uneven first line drew near, and our foot soldiers moved forward as a solid mass, with a shout to shake the heavens.

We pushed the exhausted Rhetians back fifteen, twenty, thirty yards. I dared now glance at our flanks. Our cavalry appeared to be breaking, abandoning the field of battle in a panicked retreat. The enemy horsemen on both flanks regrouped and dressed their lines, preparing for the charge they knew would bring them victory.

At nearly the same moment, the Rhetian horse charged on both flanks. Just before they smashed into the end of our battle line, my hidden halberdiers jumped up from the tall grass. Their vicious implements of war were designed for just this purpose—to stop cavalry charges, and slaughter horses and riders. There was no escape for the Rhetian horsemen. The riders in the rear forced those in front of them onto the slashing blades of our soldiers.

In minutes, three-fourths of the Rhetian cavalry was lying on the ground, staining last year's grass with their blood. The remainder were heedlessly galloping downhill. Our halberdiers raised a savage victory cry, a keening that sent a shiver up my spine.

Our cavalry had wheeled around and now did to the enemy what they had hoped to do to us. The Rhetian lines broke like a sudden summer thunderstorm. Their men ran down the slope, their weapons discarded since the useless weight slowed them down.

Our horsemen cut many of them down as they ran. The men of the Castle Shield kept cooler heads and began to herd the fleeing soldiers toward the Rhetian camp. The Castle Shield circled around the camp and prevented anyone from escaping, drawing a tighter and tighter circle around the fifteen thousand or so who survived.

I closed my link with Bellona, but not before I sensed the oddest feeling of satisfaction radiate through me. It reminded me of my boyhood when my grandfather would praise me for mastering a difficult task. I wondered if the Goddess was pleased with me or if I was simply happy that it was over.

"I suppose we ought to go talk with them, Your Majesty," Fenwick said.

"Let's just enjoy this moment a little longer, Fenwick," the king replied. "This is something that will be in all the history books, which is a gratifying thought, but even better, we were all witness to it today. The men who fought with us will be honored for the rest of their lives. Just think of it!"

"What do you think you'll do with them?" Fenwick asked.

"Well, first, we'll make them clean up their mess and bury their dead," he said. "After that, we'll escort them to the Musser Pass and send them back. We'll give them a message that we would prefer to be friends instead of enemies, but they won't listen. They never do."

Fenwick approached the enemy, who were corralled in by the lowered lances of the Castle Shield. He called out, and the man in uniform marked by the plentiful golden braid stepped forward. Fenwick's tone was imperious. This was not a negotiation.

The Rhetian's first response was oddly defiant. Fenwick answered with a dismissive tone, gesturing with his arm at the Castle Shield who surrounded them, and then at our army just behind. When he finished, Fenwick began to walk away.

The Rhetian called him back. In this exchange, he was far less aggressive. When the dialogue ended, Fenwick returned to us. Orders were being shouted among the Rhetians, and their soldiers began moving.

"They will surrender their weapons, piling them over there," Fenwick informed the king, pointing to a spot. "The cavalry will surrender their mounts. Please instruct the Castle Shield to allow them to proceed."

The king gestured with his hand, and one of the officers relayed the order. Some of the Shield's members pulled their horses back to create an alley for the Rhetians to proceed. The enemy filed out and began to drop their remaining weapons in a heap. When the foot soldiers were finished, the remaining cavalry and officers rode out and surrendered their horses.

"I informed him of the terms of surrender," Fenwick reported to the king. "The idiot then said they would all die gladly for their god. I told him we would be delighted to kill them, but we would leave their bodies unburied. That was enough to change his attitude."

"Thank you, Fenwick," the king said.

We observed as the Rhetians laid down their weapons. When they finished, our soldiers supervised them as they began burying their dead at the foot of the slope. Our men separated our dead from the Rhetians, and teams were already dragging wood from the nearest forests to build our pyres.

We lost another four thousand men that day. Nearly thirty-five thousand Rhetians fell. It was a terrible waste of human life, all because one people could not tolerate views that differed from theirs.

It took more than two weeks for the Rhetians to finish burying the bodies of their countrymen. In that time, there were two days when they refused to work, claiming it was their holy day, and labor was forbidden. While we waited for the Rhetians to finish, we cremated our fallen, and sent our wounded back to Reedsford. Lucy and the healers went with the wounded.

It gave me the opportunity to spend time with Freddy, Quint, and Lucy's brother Alexander—whom I did not know well before this. Freddy, as urbane and charming a man as you would ever meet, adapted to military life far better than anyone could have expected. Quint shared that the men of Manton loved Freddy and had even come up with a song celebrating his battlefield exploits, though it was not nearly as popular as the one about me that made me cringe.

His Majesty continued to meet with various nobles, attending to the administration of the kingdom. In some of those, my presence was required, and the king and I discussed what I saw after every conference. A few men tried to bring forth their sons as candidates for the succession. The king curtly informed them that this was not the time or place for that.

There were other meetings in the "canvas castle," to which I was not invited. I reckoned those were the discussions regarding the succession. Elsewhere, Fenwick was kept busy as a translator, and as he was the only person in our party who spoke the Rhetian language, I could not probe him for information.

The Rhetians finally finished their sad task. Through Fenwick, we issued orders to set out for Musser Pass. Our army escorted them, though in some ways, it seemed unnecessary. The Rhetians were as dispirited a bunch as I think I ever saw.

"Their common soldiers are almost afraid to return," Fenwick reported to the king on the second to last night before we reached Musser Pass. "They fear they will be blamed for the failure of the invasion."

"Perhaps we should offer them the chance to resettle in Aquileia?" I suggested.

"That is a kind and generous thought, Caz," the king said. "But we doubt any would accept the offer. Certainly, any with wives or children will not stay. Still, it will reflect well on us to make the attempt. Present that to them when we part, Fenwick."

When we reached the foot of the pass, Fenwick presented the resettlement offer. I could tell some of the Rhetians were tempted as they looked around nervously. Several of their officers noticed and barked at them. None stepped forward.

"What happened there?" I asked Fenwick.

"The officers threatened eternal damnation to anyone who stayed behind," he replied.

We encamped there, watching as the Rhetians straggled away. The mood among our men was one of exhilarated relief. They were singing as they went about their chores.

"They changed the chorus," Fenwick remarked. "Listen—"

> Under Oritur's firm command,
> They died by thousands at our hand,
> With halberd, pike, and horseman's lance,
> they saw us come and shit their pants.
> The king fell, Oritur stood fast
> None of our foes beyond him passed.
> Rhetians lay in mounds of dead,
> The grass underfoot soaked blood red.

"Majors and Minors," I muttered.

"I'm so glad they kept the soiling of the trousers bit in," Fenwick teased.

"It is the best part," my father agreed.

"Without question," the king added.

"Still, not a single stanza about me," Fenwick complained. "It's sad."

"We prefer it when no one knows of your exploits," the king commented. "Remember?"

"True," Fenwick said with a dramatic sigh.

"Rest assured, we appreciate your work on our behalf," His Majesty added.

"Consolation enough," Fenwick announced.

"Duncan, the ranks of the Rangers are quite thin after all this," the king stated, shifting the subject. "Do you think any of your armsmen would be interested in joining? It occurs to us that you might not need nearly as many."

"We will ask," my father said. "There are some who quite enjoy the life. Others are looking forward to a more relaxed existence, though. I will present it to them."

Word reached me later that evening that some men were looking for Fenwick and me. A few minutes later, eight Rangers approached the fire where I was sitting. I recognized them immediately and jumped to my feet.

"Majors and Minors!" I gasped.

"Hello, Lord Oritur," they said. "Where is Mr. Fenwick?"

It was the eight men who escaped from the fort with us. We greeted one another with back-slapping hugs. Someone who learned who they were fetched Fenwick and brought him over to our fire.

They wanted to know what happened to the two of us, and we shared our story. As usual, we attributed the appearance of the Traval ship to luck. We then asked for their tale. By now, the crowd around the fire had grown large. The one they called Ken seemed to be the spokesman for the group.

"After we left you, we kept on heading north along the road for about two leagues," he said. "We knew our job was to lead the Rhetians on a merry chase, so you two might have a chance. We kept going until we saw a small creek. We reckoned the water would wash away our hoofprints, so we turned off and went northwest. Plus, we figured by then we'd done all we could for you. The creek didn't head in the ideal direction, but we hoped the Rhetians wouldn't notice we left the road. Even better, the creek bed was a couple of feet lower than the ground on either side, so that would make us harder to spot."

"There weren't no cover to be found," another named Marty commented.

"We turned north after the creek disappeared under some rocks," Ken said. "For the rest of the day and all night, we headed due north. By morning, we reached better country—grassland instead of that dusty plain. We kept going and ran into some cattle. That made us nervous since we reckoned we would run into their owners. We weren't wrong."

"So, there's two fellers riding along, and they called over to us," added Marty.

"We don't speak Rhetian," Ken resumed, "so we just waved, friendly like, and kept going. Since we weren't taking any of their stock, they just waved back and let us be. We rode for a few more hours, and then we were all used up—

horses too. We stopped by another creek and, after we all got a drink, we slept and let the horses graze. Just before nightfall, we started up again, heading north. We rode all night and found a good spot to lay low for the day. Kept that up for another three days. The only people we saw were far away."

"But then—" Marty said.

"But then we reached the foothills of the border mountains," Ken continued, "and we came across a road. Might have been the same road we started on, a lot further along. Hard to say without a map. Anyway, we didn't dare follow the road. Sure enough, we saw a company of soldiers marching north not long after. We kept an eye on 'em, making sure they never saw us."

"Wasn't that dangerous?" one of the listeners asked.

"Well, we reckoned if we kept up with them, we wouldn't run into others by surprise," Ken said. "Maybe it wasn't the smartest idea, but we were all pretty tired. It worked out alright, though."

"Until we hit the trees," Marty added.

"When we reached the forest, there were more soldiers," Ken said.

"A lot more soldiers," Marty commented.

"They were corduroying a road," Ken explained, "and there were all sorts of people. By now, we sort of knew where we were—heading to the Musser Pass. It was pretty clear that was the path they were going to use when they attacked us. So, we decided to head for the Carmen Pass, and hoped enough snow had melted so it was clear."

"You went straight through the forest?" an onlooker inquired.

"Followed game trails as much as we could," Marty replied. "As long as they pointed in the right direction."

"Anyway, it was mighty slow going, but we got to the Carmen Pass, and there's one of their skirmisher camps right there," Ken resumed. "The pass looked to be open, but to reach it we needed to get past five or six dozen men."

"How did you get around them?" I asked.

"Didn't," Marty said. "Went through."

"We watched for a whole day," Ken explained. "And we noticed they were pretty relaxed. I think they reckoned they pushed the Rangers far enough away that they didn't need to worry like normal. So, we snuck into camp in the middle of the night, cut their horses loose, and set the whole place on fire. We galloped down the path for a league and then pulled off into the trees. When the skirmishers recovered their horses, they came tearing after us."

"Remember, it's the middle of the night," Marty commented.

"The ones chasing us ran into some of their own people in the dark and started killing each other since they both thought the other was the enemy. While they were fighting, we went around them. The next thing you know, the sun is coming up, and we meet some Rangers."

27

The following morning we began our return under a pouring rain. Despite the weather, spirits remained high. The war was over. We were returning home, and most people would be back at their farms or shops just before the end of the month of Harpa, when spring turned into summer throughout Aquileia.

In the eastern March, there should be time for those in the militia to plant a late crop if their relatives and neighbors had not already plowed and sown their fields for them. Not all of our men were returning, though. We lost a hundred and fifty-seven members of the militia and seventeen armsmen. My father and I had already agreed to provide relief to the families of the fallen.

I did not see much of my father during the journey back to Reedsford. He spent his time with the king, the dukes of Manton, Gulick and Chaldic, Lord Hepworth, and a few other nobles in what seemed to be a council meeting on horseback. The group stayed out of earshot, and when anyone approached, they all fell silent. Though I had no way of knowing, I was convinced they were discussing the plans to choose the king's successor.

After arriving outside Reedsford, the army started to disband, as the different nobles led their people home by different roads. Lucy and I said our goodbyes to her relatives. It had been so good to see Freddy. Even though our duties had taken most of our time and attention, we still had found moments here and there when we could sit and swap stories for our mutual amusement. It was also the most time I ever spent with her brother, Alexander, and I enjoyed getting to know him better.

Two days later, as we were riding back to the capital after leaving Reedsford, I told Lucy, "I think Freddy will make a good king."

"Freddy? King?" She laughed.

"Why are you laughing?" I protested. "I'm quite serious. Your family and his, the Austermains, are widely respected and have no enemies. You are neither too powerful nor too weak. Freddy is liked by everyone who meets him. Through marriage, he is connected to one of the two biggest merchant traders in the country, which provides connections the typical noble does not have."

"Those things are all true," she replied, "but can you truly imagine 'Lord Compote' as our sovereign?"

Her comment made me burst into laughter. At three different points in my earlier adventures (which I have already committed to the page), Freddy adopted the dim-witted, self-centered, socially oblivious, and often obscene persona of "Lord Compote." Originally the character was based on a former classmate of ours, but Freddy had evolved him into his own unique person. As I remembered different outrageous moments, my laughter grew.

"I don't know, my dear," I said when I recovered, "perhaps 'Lord Compote' might be a very good king. His reign would definitely be entertaining."

"What brought this whole idea to your head?" Lucy asked.

"Just wondering who His Majesty will choose," I said. "I suspect the meetings he has held where I have not been invited are discussions of possible candidates, as was the group that was thick as thieves all the way to Reedsford. He probably mentions several names to see how the different nobles react to each one."

"He doesn't need to make an immediate decision," Lucy observed.

"Eh—the longer he delays, the more anxious people will become."

"Do you trust his judgment? Lucy asked.

"I do. I'm just curious. That's all."

"It's probably someone you haven't thought of," Lucy remarked. "Not Freddy. Though your analysis of the family situation is good."

I shrugged in acknowledgment. "Alexander, perhaps?"

"Where Freddy is perhaps too social and not serious enough, Alex is not outgoing at all."

"I've always found him friendly," I commented.

"You are a rare exception."

I sighed. Freddy had seemed the right choice, but Lucy's observations were correct. Though he was never known for licentious behavior, neither was he seen as someone who was especially serious.

"I wonder what the next crisis will be," I said a few minutes later.

"Fenwick's wedding," Lucy replied quickly, then stifled a laugh.

"I entirely forgot," I admitted. "It is fast approaching—at the solstice. Thank all the heavenly beings that it can proceed as planned."

"He will need your support, dear," Lucy advised. "By the day of the event, he'll be one nervous twitch after another."

Later on the journey, my father asked me to ride with him. We made common chitchat for a mile or so. Eventually, he broached the subject he wished to discuss.

"When we return to Easton," he said, "I will marry Ariana. We would like you and Lucy to stand with us."

"We would be honored."

"I should have done it before we departed," he said. "I have been worried about her ever since—it would have been a horrible thing for her if I had fallen in battle."

"From what Lucy and I have seen, your death would have been no less painful to her if you were married."

"Perhaps," he admitted. "But marriage is a commitment to another made in the presence of the Gods. If I did not return, she would at least have that knowledge in her heart."

"That's true." A moment later, I grunted, "Huh!"

"Huh—what?"

"I'll have a stepmother again," I remarked. "I hope this one won't try to have me killed."

My father recognized I was joking with him. He playfully tried to shove me off my horse. When that failed, he began singing the song that tormented me in his off-key voice. The men nearby picked it up and, thankfully, drowned him out. I still had to listen to it, though.

Nineteen of our armsmen decided they would like to join the Rangers after my father spoke with them and extended the offer. All of them were single. They admitted that, without the threat of the nomads, they would find the job of being a roving constable around the March dull. They were returning to the March to settle their affairs and gather their belongings, then would head back west.

Lucy and I rode with my father and our soldiers as far as the capital. The men seemed slightly downcast at our parting. I believe that was due to their not being able to torture me any further with that damnable song. The entire way back from Reedsford, they sang it at least once every day. What was even worse was that my father and Lucy knew all the verses and would sing along—as loud as they could. Adding to my discomfort—my father couldn't carry a tune if you packed it in a rucksack for him.

The king and the Castle Shield had ridden ahead of us, beginning at Reedsford. Fenwick went with them. They were all mounted and reached the capital in half the time it would take us. Despite my strong desire to get home, I stayed with my people. I owed them at least that much.

Lucy and I planned to spend a couple of days in the city before returning to Easton. We both were looking forward to sleeping in a familiar bed and a couple of days out of the saddle. When we returned to the March, our stay would be limited, as we needed to return to the capital for Fenwick's wedding.

We arrived in mid-afternoon. I delivered Lucy to the house and left our bags, then took the horses to stay under Jerry's tender care at the Foaming Boar. When I arrived, Jerry was brushing out his horse—the massive coal-black gelding named Thunder. You can imagine my dismay when I heard Jerry humming the tune of the song about me.

He turned when he heard Bella nicker. Leaving Thunder, he rushed over to embrace Bella and Andy. It was a tender enough sight that I nearly forgave him for humming that awful ditty.

"Mr. Caz," he exclaimed after caressing the two beasts, "two members of the Castle Shield taught me a song all about Lord Oritur. That's you, innit?"

I sighed and rolled my eyes.

"Did you really do all the things they say?"

"The song exaggerates things a little bit, Jerry, but yes, for the most part, I did those things," I admitted.

"Cor! You're famous, Mr. Caz. I'm hearing it all over the city now," he said.

I groaned at this news. It got worse. Jerry began to sing the chorus in a beautiful clear tenor.

"Jerry, you have a magnificent voice," I said when he finished. "It's truly a gift. But please, don't sing that song around me. The soldiers tormented me by singing it all the way here."

"Why not, Mr. Caz? It makes you out to be a hero like in books. I'd love it if someone sang a tune about me like that someday," he said.

He took a breath as though he would start again.

"Thank you for taking care of Bella and Andy, Jerry," I said before he could begin. "We'll see you in a couple of days."

I hurried home, not stopping to see Carl, the inn's owner. A couple of days of rest, enjoying peace and quiet, with only Lucy and our housekeeper for company, was what I wanted most. Naturally, when I walked to the door of the house, Fenwick's beautiful piebald gelding, Davy, was tied up out front. Fearing the worst, I opened the door, spotting Fenwick sprawled in an armchair, with his legs dangling over the arm.

"Oh, the wolf in the story," Fenwick remarked upon seeing me. "Hello, Your Famousness. Her Loveliness and I were just chatting about you."

"You're lucky I see a smile on my wife's face, Aloysius," I replied, barely suppressing a snarl. "That tells me you are not here as a harbinger of another errand to faraway lands that might get me killed."

"Nothing that fun, I'm afraid," Fenwick drawled. "Your lovely and charming wife has just invited Julienne and me to dinner tomorrow evening. I'm glad you arrived, though. If you were ten minutes later, she would have put me to work drawing the water from the well for your bath."

"You came by just to wheedle a dinner invitation?"

"Sadly, no," he answered. "I come bearing dispatches from my employer."

"Do they involve foreign travel?"

"No."

"Great risk to life and limb?"

Fenwick shook his head.

"Then you might be forgiven."

"It's just a request for a report on the state of the March. He is most interested in crop estimates—jute, in particular. He also requests the presence of both of you for a meeting on the twenty-ninth of Skerpia which, may I remind you, is two days before my wedding."

"Well, we are heading back to the March in a few days," I said. "I will need to write ahead to ask people to compile the figures. Do you know the subject of the meeting?"

"I don't have the foggiest idea," Fenwick replied as he stood to leave. "Wish me well. Tonight, I have an obligation to attend dinner with my future in-laws. Herbert, as you know, is a genial sort. Madam, however, I prefer to take in small doses, spread well apart."

"Did you ever hear about the time Freddy and I called upon her?" I asked.

"No, I haven't. That was before my time. Save it for tomorrow evening, and we can all share a laugh," he advised.

In the morning, I opened the letter from the king. As Fenwick intimated, it was a request for crop estimates. His Majesty was especially curious about the jute crop. His concern was that the rough sacks needed to store grain would be available in time. I shared those worries and suspected we would need to buy the sacks from Mooresa again.

Of course, that might provide an excuse for another adventure with Freddy in his role as Lord Compote. Thinking about his behavior on the last venture nearly made me laugh out loud. Lucy saw my smile and slid into my lap, draping her arm over my shoulder.

"Something amusing?"

I explained what I had been thinking.

"I doubt Freddy can get away," she said. "Perhaps your father should go?"

"With Ariana?"

"Exactly. Julienne can point them in the right direction and give them letters of introduction, if necessary."

"Won't it be a bit dangerous?" I asked. "We are, after all, establishing our own jute plantation. Surely the Mooren will be upset about that?"

"Chances are they know nothing about it," Lucy said with a shrug. "The only clue they might have is Mr. Balboa's departure last year, and his employer did not value him much. Otherwise, Balboa might not have come."

The more I considered Lucy's idea, the more I liked it. My father would enjoy a new sort of challenge and would get to travel. I resolved to mention it to Julienne at dinner.

The remainder of the day, I spent copying out letters to the mayors and heads of the towns within the March, asking for their crop estimates. I would have preferred to call on them personally, but I would not have the time before Lucy and I needed to return to the city. When we reached Easton, I would give the letters to some of the armsmen to deliver, as they would be quicker than the Royal Post.

28

My father was away when we returned to Easton and the manor. Ariana informed us he was already visiting the families of the soldiers who died. She expected him back in two days. When he arrived back in Easton, we would go to the Temple of the Three Major Gods, where Lucy and I would witness Ariana's marriage to my father.

The six armsmen who spent the winter in the rooms above our stable were still at the manor. Four of them would be leaving soon to join the Rangers—I was fortunate they had not departed already. Before they went west, I asked them to help deliver the letters I had written to the towns and villages, asking for crop estimates. They all agreed to help.

The day after my father arrived, we went to the Temple. The head priest was waiting for us and conducted the simple, brief ceremony uniting my father and Ariana as man and wife. We returned to the manor for lunch, and while we were waiting for our food, I noticed the two of them holding hands. They had been careful not to display their affection so openly before this. Seeing them both looking so at ease with one another made me smile.

"Father, do you think we will be able to supply the grain sacks needed this year?" I asked. "I'm worried about the timing. If we can't, we need to make other arrangements."

"You might be right," he said. "We should visit and find out from Balboa what he thinks. That's another one of those details we did not put to rest."

"If we need to buy the sacks from Mooresa again, Lucy and I thought it might be a good task for you and Ariana to take on," I suggested.

His eyes flickered with immediate interest, but he chose the safest path.

"What do you think?" he asked his new bride.

"I would love to visit my homeland and show it to you," she said.

"My only concern is the risk of a hostile reception," my father said to me.

"I doubt whether they know we are establishing our own jute production," I said. "The only clue would be Mr. Balboa's disappearance, and if you remember, his previous employer did not think highly of him. Plus, they have no way of knowing he is working with us. I will ask Julienne Traval when we return to the city if she has heard anything. She may also be able to provide you with contacts."

"We will need those," my father agreed.

The following morning, my father, Ari, and I set out for Port Charles. My most recent visit was in the middle of the night at the end of the wild river ride Fenwick and I went on. I was glad to not repeat it. My last visit during daylight hours was more than six months earlier.

The view of the town center was tremendously different from the empty scene I remembered. Fenwick's inn and the accompanying stable were built. Other structures on the lots we'd sold were framed and roofed. Riding to the harbor front, the area where Hawkins Trading Company was building their warehouse and wharf was a hive of activity. Traval & Company was busy expanding its operation on the other side of the harbor.

We decided to stop by the inn first since it seemed to be the most completed of the newer construction. Penfrew met us at the door. We could smell sawdust and paint from within.

"This building is still a month away from completion, except for the kitchen," he said. "That was one of the first things we finished, and we've been feeding all the workers in town since. As soon as we got the stable building under roof, we've been renting sleeping space to a number of people. It's nice to be able to show a profit before the buildings are even finished."

My father and I then went to the bridge over the Pheas River. As Fenwick had told me, there was a large wooden bridge. In the center, there was a section on either side, currently raised in the air. Between them was a space large enough for a riverboat to pass through.

I was impressed with how simple the bridge mechanism was to operate and how well-constructed it appeared. The raised sections were counter-balanced and easily lowered or raised. The nearer just required a strong push, and it began to fall. The tip of the further section was connected to a stout rope that was tied to a cleat on the side. Pulling the rope caused that section to drop.

There was another rope connected to the end of each section, passing through a sturdy frame above, terminating at a winch on either side. It was easy to figure out that turning the winch handle would pull the section up. I gave it a try to see how difficult it was. It did require some strength but was well within the capability of nearly any adult.

There were small landings on the river below the bridge with stairs leading up. I reckoned that was in case a boat came along and found the bridge sections down. A man would then get out of the boat and raise the bridge with the winches.

We rode across and quickly reached our plantation. The massive barn and the cottage for Mr. Balboa were the two structures already completed. Work was underway on the large house my father commissioned, the manufactory building, and other cottages for our tenants who would work the farm. In the fields, everywhere, one could see the shoots of the jute plants.

Mr. Balboa saw us from a distance. He came jogging over. A noticeable smile adorned his face.

"Hello! Hello!" he called as he drew closer. "Is good see youse! Look! Look! Everywhere is good."

Mr. Balboa's grasp of our language was tenuous, but his excitement was understandable even so.

"Things are going well?" my father asked.

"Dan, dan," Balboa replied.

Ari whispered to me that "dan" was "yes" in Mooren.

"Soil very good. Weather very good. Rain good. Warm. All good. See?" he said, waving his arm at the fields.

"I'm glad you are satisfied," my father said with a smile.

"Will be good crop," Balboa stated.

"That is good news. When will you harvest?"

Mr. Balboa needed to think of the correct words.

"Two munt more, tree munt less," he said, using his fingers to show.

"Between two and three months from now?" my father asked.

"Dan."

"That puts us at the end of Heyannir," my father said to me.

"How long does it take to process the plants?" he asked Balboa.

Balboa did not understand.

"Soak?" I offered.

"Crop so big, soak nudder two munt more, tree munt less," Balboa replied, understanding my inquiry.

"We will need to go to Mooresa," I said to my father.

"Ari, ask him about the manufactory," my father requested. "I remember Mr. Balboa had drawings of spinning machines and looms that needed to be made. How many people will he need to convert the harvest into the finished sacks by harvest time next year?"

Ari and Mr. Balboa began conversing in Mooren. He clearly understood what we wanted to know. He gestured to the barn and then to his cottage.

"He has engaged three tenants to do the work so far," Ari explained. "They are living in the barn loft until their cottages are finished. Then they will bring their families. When it is not growing season, the tenants and their spouses will work in the manufactory. In addition to the tenants, he will need three other workers. Unlike the tenants, where he prefers to have families, the workers should be single. He recommends women because their fingers are smaller. They should have quarters, too, but not individual cottages. One building to share, he says. He has the drawings of the spinning machine and the looms. There is no one here to build them, so he will need to go to Easton soon to have that done."

We checked in with Mr. Pruitt, the builder we engaged. He showed me the plans for the main house, which my father approved. I had not seen them before.

"Everything that you see underway should be complete by the end of Twiman at the latest," Pruitt said. "We are behind schedule because getting materials from the capital was a bottleneck. The sawmills in the March are now shipping material downriver, and that is speeding things considerably."

"We will need at least one more building before you leave the area," my father said. "Mr. Balboa needs a residence suitable for housing three single women who will work in the manufactory."

"I can draw up plans for the residence quickly," Pruitt said.

We took our leave from Mr. Pruitt and Mr. Balboa, and returned to the inn in Hillstead. I was delighted with the progress we saw in bringing Port Charles back to life. I wondered what I would see in a few months.

By the time we arrived back in Easton, responses from the heads of the towns and villages were already waiting for me. The armsmen I sent to deliver the requests for information stayed to collect the crop estimates. I began compiling the figures, measuring them against what was delivered the previous fall. Even with the militia being called away, the numbers showed an increase of just over ten percent in the amount of land put in use. I was certain the king would be pleased to learn this.

Even better, some of the responses included notes to the effect that there was still more land lying fallow. While farmers had increased their planting, they did so by a conservative amount. I could not fault their prudence. If the prices they received for their crops remained stable, I was sure they would put more land into play next year.

I joined my father on the remaining visits to the families of those who were killed in what was now known as the Fifth Rhetian War. In addition to the parents or spouse, we also met with the mayor or head of the village to ensure that the community would continue to assist the family of the fallen man. Of course, those families who lost a husband and father needed more support, and we were assured they would receive it.

My father informed the wives who had been married to one of our tenants that they would owe no rent for at least three years. Those who owned their land would pay no taxes during that same period. We also provided each family with a hundred ducats. My father was careful in how he presented this gift.

"This is not compensation for the loss of your husband," he said. "There is no amount of money that would be enough. This is to prevent difficulties from reaching your door. If something happens and more is needed, please let me know, and we will make sure you do not suffer."

"Has anyone ever taken advantage and abused this?" I asked later.

"Once," he replied. "Even then, I did not quibble. The man died under my command. I was responsible."

The time came for us to return to the city and Fenwick's wedding. I was looking forward to the event with pleasure. Lucy, my father, and I had almost accepted Fenwick as part of our family, given how involved he had been in our lives the last few years—for both good and bad. We all liked Julienne a great deal and were happy for them both.

The event would also be Ariana's social debut as Lady Easton. I had no qualms about her ability to carry herself well. She was attractive, poised, and well-spoken, and she and my father clearly doted on one another.

My first task in the capital was my appointment with His Majesty. I had the crop estimates provided by every town and village in a leather portfolio. I assumed they would be the topic of our meeting. In addition, I would inform him of our need to buy the grain sacks from Mooresa again this year. The previous year we made a tiny profit on them, as we sold them to the trading houses, who then supplied them to the farmers. The minimal cost of each sack was factored into the price the traders paid per modium for the different types of grain and produce.

We returned to the city three days in advance of my meeting and the wedding. We entertained every evening. First, we invited Julienne and Fenwick for dinner. The next night, Ratty Hawkins and Inger Fairchild, Linc and Nellie Ellsworth, and Quint and Siobhan Pompeo came. On the third night I was surprised by the arrival of Freddy and Greta.

When I parted from Freddy at Reedsford, he told me he would not be returning for the wedding. Apparently, he assumed his father would want him home in Manton. To his surprise, his parents insisted he come to the wedding since Freddy and Greta had been key components in several adventures with Fenwick. There was no time to write to warn us, though I suspected Lucy knew somehow since we cooked plenty of food that night—enough to accommodate two extra servings easily.

During those three days in the capital, I had an odd feeling that there was something I should know to which the others were privy. That sensation actually started when we left Easton together. Once we arrived at the house, it grew stronger.

I became convinced that every time I left the room, I was suddenly the topic of conversation. When I would return, there would be an awkward pause before someone picked up the thread of what was being discussed when I left. I told myself I was imagining things. Yet, when I was sent away to school, my illegitimate birth made me an easy target for more cruel jokes and embarrassing pranks than I could remember. Those feelings of loneliness and insecurity reared their ugly heads within my psyche. But these were the people for whom I cared the most, and I felt guilty for harboring even the slightest suspicion regarding any of them.

Still, on all three nights, Lucy found a reason to send me out of the dining room to find something for her. She and her students had concocted a skin cream that included a subtle glamor, and Lucy brought jars of it with her. Each evening, they were in a different place in the house, requiring me to hunt them down after not finding them where Lucy "thought" they were. She even had enough to give Greta a jar, plus one left over that I reckoned Lucy would give to the queen.

There was no one with whom I could discuss this odd sensation without appearing either crazy or overly mistrustful of my family and closest friends. I tried to think of what they might be planning, or what they might be hiding from me. It came to me in the middle of the night, before my meeting with the king.

Lucy must be pregnant, I thought. *That explains why she seems to be keeping some happy secret. They haven't told me yet because…*

That point stumped me. I lay awake the remainder of the night, trying to solve that riddle. The best answer I could dream up was that Lucy was planning on making an announcement at Fenwick's wedding and surprising me. There were flaws in that guess, but it was the least unsatisfactory solution.

When the sun came up, I gave up trying to sleep. Lucy felt me stir. She insisted I bathe before seeing the king. Somewhat grumpily, I went to pull the water from the well. Roberta was already awake, preparing breakfast.

In my currently baffled state of mind, I started to think her lack of a reaction to seeing me drawing water so early was another sign of what was being plotted.

And yes, dear reader, I even used the word "plot" in my mind. That is how dark my thoughts were that morning.

I must confess now, looking back, I was behaving like a child. I stomped up and down the stairs, not caring if the noise woke my father and Ariana. When I lifted the water buckets with the hoist, I made sure the pulleys squeaked as annoyingly as possible. I threw the water into the tub, not caring about how much sloshed over the side and how big the puddle was that I created.

When finally the bath was ready, I dropped my nightclothes in a heap in the middle of the floor of the bedroom for someone else to pick up. I slammed the lavatory door behind me. Then I sat in the tub and sulked.

My brooding lasted until I noticed the water cooling. Then I figured I'd better wash before it cooled further. When I finished and climbed out, I slipped in the water I had left on the floor and nearly fell on my butt. That was when I realized I was acting stupidly.

I composed myself as best I could. Though I was still on edge, I resolved not to let the others see it. I cleaned my teeth and combed my still-short hair, then returned to the bedroom.

Lucy left clothes for me on the bed. For whatever reason, she chose my most formal suit. I thought my meeting with His Majesty to review crop estimates hardly called for such an ensemble. Then I reckoned it was all part of the scheme—that whatever the joke they planned to pull on me would be made funnier to them if I wore this outfit. This outfit also convinced me that my guess about Lucy's possible pregnancy was wrong.

With a grim smile of satisfaction that I was getting closer to figuring out how they planned to have fun at my expense, I dressed. The rest of the household was already eating breakfast. None of them commented on my clothing, which convinced me it was part of the joke.

29

B ecause of my attire, I needed to find a hackney. Riding Andy would have ruined the white stockings I was wearing. I found one in the market square nearest our house.

Delivered at the bridge to the castle, they were expecting me at the guard house. A page was already waiting and took me across. The seneschal was also prepared for my arrival and took me inside.

"I apologize, milord," he said as we entered the castle. "There has been a slight hitch in His Majesty's schedule this morning. He asked me to have you wait."

He took me to a small drawing room and ushered me inside. *Of course, there's a problem*, I thought. *It's all part of whatever it is they're planning. They'll probably make me sit here the whole day. Ha. Ha. Ha.*

I chose a comfortable chair and sat down, my leather portfolio with the crop figures on my knees. Enough time passed, that the dark mood I was in crested and broke. After boiling to a seething rage, I had a sudden moment of clarity. I realized Lucy would never, ever, subject me to ridicule like this. She might tease me or poke fun at me, but always gently.

On the one hand, I felt like an idiot for even entertaining such horrible thoughts. On the other, I now was completely baffled by what was happening. That *something* was taking place, I had no doubt.

I wondered if this had to do with my father's stated intent to step aside at some point in the future. Perhaps I would take my oath before the king and become Lord Easton today. If that were the case, I could certainly forgive Lucy and my father for their little deception. Yes, they were having a bit of fun with me, but only in the mildest way, in what was a happy circumstance.

It was easily an hour or more later when I heard a soft knock on the door. It snapped me out of my pondering. The seneschal opened it without waiting for my response.

"They're ready for you now, Lord Oritur," he said.

They, I thought. My meeting was to have been with the king. Even though he referred to himself in the plural (as was Aquileian custom), no one else did. *They* meant there were others I would see. I was now convinced I guessed correctly, and I would soon be swearing my oath to the king.

The seneschal took me in a direction that did not seem familiar. We were near the Throne Room, I suspected. We reached a door, and the seneschal opened it, gesturing me inside.

I was still wearing my sword. If I were going to see the king, I needed to surrender it before entering. I began to unbuckle the beautiful sword belt Fenwick had given me, but the seneschal put his hand on my forearm to stop me.

"Not today," he whispered.

As I rebuckled it, with my portfolio tucked under my arm, I glanced into the room. There was a table made from a massive piece of wood. Seated around the table, I saw the Dukes of Chaldic, Caurus, Manton, and Gulick, Earl Montgomery, my father, Lord Hepworth, Lord Pilaro, and Lord Shames. The last two I knew only by name.

Fenwick was sitting next to my father. I wondered briefly why he was there but did not give it more thought than that. They were all dressed as formally as I was, even Fenwick.

At the head of the table, in full regalia, sat the king and queen. At the end of the table opposite Their Majesties were two seats. Lucy occupied the one on the left. She, too, was dressed formally, her hair up. I smiled, now convinced I knew what was to happen.

"Welcome, Lord Oritur," the king greeted me, "though this might be the last time we use that title to address you. Please sit and join us."

I took my seat, guiding my sword out of the way. Lucy reached over and clasped my hand. Her eye twinkled at me and, in my heart, I instantly forgave her for the oddness of the last few days.

"Do you know why you are here?" the king asked.

"I believe so, Your Majesty," I replied, then took a deep breath. "My father has mentioned his desire to step aside from his duties as Earl of the Eastern March. This meeting is for me to swear my fealty to you as the new Earl of the March, and these distinguished guests are present to witness my oath."

The king smiled broadly—the biggest grin I ever saw on his face. Without looking away from him, I tried to see the others to judge their expressions. From what I could see, they were also grinning. Suddenly, I realized I guessed incorrectly.

One of the things I learned when I went away to school was to keep my emotions from expressing themselves in my facial expressions. It was a defense against the bullying and torment. I pretended all the jibes and insults did not affect me. My ability to present an impassive demeanor later proved to be quite a valuable asset when playing cards—especially when the stakes were high. Both the king and Prince Albert had remarked on my lack of discernible reaction in the past. At this moment, my bafflement was so profound, I could not keep it from my face.

"Ha!" the king crowed. "Do you see that? Do you see that, dear? He is utterly flummoxed!"

"I can see, dear," she replied as she smiled at me in a kindly way. "How much longer are you planning to tease him?"

"Just a little bit more," he told her. "I don't want to torture him—well, not too much—but I am having fun."

"Not too much, then," she said.

"You are partially correct that these guests are here to witness an oath of fealty from the new Earl of the March. But not from you," the king said. "They are more than guests, however. They serve as our advisory council. We have been delighted to welcome your father into this group, though you may not—"

"Not too much, dear," the queen reminded him.

"You're right, Lily," he said with a sigh.

I was hardly listening. If I were not to be named Earl of the March, the only one in the room who did not already hold land in the king's name was Fenwick. My eyes darted over to him. His face was impassive, betraying nothing. He kept his glance fixed on the table, refusing to look at me.

"We have a different role and title in mind for you," the king resumed. "You were present at Albert's death. You risked your life to try to save him, only to find him dead. As a result of his passing, the line of succession was broken."

He gestured with his arm, taking in everyone seated at the table.

"These men have met with us many times since as we grappled with the question of finding and naming an heir. In the midst of this, the Rhetians launched an invasion that we suspect they had been planning for several years. Our fear was that the war might delay our deliberations. Instead, it provided clarity. Everyone who was present in the western March reached the same conclusion, independently and separately. Some of them had only those events on which to base their judgment, but they were convinced. The rest of us have seen your other contributions to the welfare of Aquileia, and for us, it was an even easier decision."

I could not breathe. The king was preparing to name me his heir. In all my wildest imaginings, my most fevered dreams, I could never have conjured this. Lucy squeezed my hand, sensing my exhilaration.

"There remained only our closest advisor's opinion," the king said, "and she agreed before we even finished extolling your fine qualities. It is our intention to adopt you and name you as our heir. What say you?"

Did I want to accept? Of course. But the decision was not mine alone to make. If I agreed, Lucy's life would change dramatically, and perhaps not for the better. With adoption, my father technically would no longer be my father—the king would. My decision would also affect his plans for the future. In examining both their faces, I saw similar expressions, both urging me to seize what was being offered.

"Your majesty, you honor me more than I can fully comprehend," I replied. "I accept, though I have one small request."

"Which is?"

"When you adopt me, would it be possible for my name to be 'Casimir FitzDuncan Barry Gau?' Both the FitzDuncan and Barry names are important to me."

"So it shall be," the king said, waving his hand in acceptance. "Is there anything else?"

"I do have one concern I must mention," I said. "My birth. I fear my bastardy will hurt the kingdom."

"That is the question all of us at the table have wrestled with," Lord Pilaro said. "Lord Shames and I were the last to oppose your candidacy because of that, and that alone. Some at the table have known you for many years. Others are more recently acquainted. All share the same stellar opinion of you—"

"Preston," my father interrupted, "tell him what really convinced the two of you that his illegitimacy will not be an issue."

'It was the song," Lord Pilaro said, blushing. "Lord Shames and I were wavering. We know you the least well of all of us. You are an impressive man, and your accomplishments in the war are nothing short of miraculous, but your birth could be held against you. The Duke of Manton and Earl Montgomery convinced us to offer you our conditional support. If, once we returned home, we heard people singing that song the soldiers love so much, we would accept that people cared more about your deeds than about your parentage. On the third day after our return home, I heard them singing it in the common room of an inn."

"It was the second day for me," Lord Shames volunteered. "We wrote His Majesty immediately, removing any conditions from our earlier acceptance."

"There are some formalities that we need to address," the king said. "Please approach and give us your sword."

The king rose. As he did, so did everyone else. I went to him and handed him my blade, hilt first. He gestured for me to kneel. When I did, he laid the flat of the sword on top of my head.

"Do you, in the presence of all the Gods, Major and Minor, and these witnesses, renounce any and all claims to your hereditary position as Earl of the Eastern March?"

I looked at Lucy and my father. They both nodded ever so slightly. I gulped. "I do."

"Do you absolve Duncan Barry, Earl of the Eastern March, of any and all obligations to you and your descendants?"

"I would hope he would continue to advise me and that our personal relationship not suffer," I protested mildly.

"Good point," Earl Montgomery said. "Your Majesty, perhaps 'financial and hereditary obligations' would suffice?"

"Do you absolve Duncan Barry, Earl of the Eastern March, of any and all financial and hereditary obligations to you and your descendants?"

"I do."

"Do you swear to honor the Gods above all things, and the Three Major Gods above all others, and renounce all the works of the Lord of the Seven Hells?"

"I do."

"Do you promise to defend this realm against all enemies, foreign and domestic to the limit of your ability until death shall claim you?"

"I do."

"Will you love the king, your sovereign and father, and the queen, your sovereign lady and mother, and defend them and their rights to the utmost as long as they both shall live?"

"I will."

"You may stand," he said.

When I reached my feet, he gave my sword back, and I sheathed it.

"You are not yet our son, Casimir," he said. "There will be a ceremony immediately following Mr. Fenwick's wedding where we will formally claim you as our son and successor to the throne, in the presence of the Three Major gods and the people. At that point, you will become His Royal Highness Prince Casimir, and your wife will become Her Royal Highness Princess Lucille. Unfortunately, until that moment, you are without title or parentage."

"Your Majesty, I lived without a title until you granted me one," I said. "This is no hardship."

The king nodded at my words. I stepped backward, then found my way back to Lucy. She clasped my hand eagerly.

"Mr. Fenwick, Lord Easton," the king called.

My father and Fenwick approached. The king took Fenwick's sword and bade him kneel. He put the blade on his head as he had mine.

"Do you, Duncan Barry, Earl of the Eastern March, in the presence of all the Gods, Major and Minor, and these witnesses, accept Aloysius Fenwick as your son and heir?"

"I do."

"Do you freely accept any and all financial and hereditary obligations to him and his descendants?"

"I do."

"In the presence of all the Gods, Major and Minor, and these witnesses, we now declare Aloysius Fenwick as the true son and heir of Duncan Barry, Earl of the Eastern March," the king announced.

"Your Majesty," my father said, "as we have discussed, it is my desire to allow my son and heir to assume the title of Lord Easton, Earl of the Eastern March. I swear to provide him guidance and direction all the remaining days of my life, if you would release me from my oath of fealty to you and Her Majesty. My loyalty to you shall remain ever steadfast, and I will continue to serve you to the best of my ability all the days of my life."

"Are you, Aloysius Fenwick Barry, willing to assume the duties and privileges inherent with the title of Lord Easton, Earl of the Eastern March?"

"I am."

"Do you this day pledge fealty to the Crown of Aquileia, pledging to provide arms in times of war, counsel in times of peace, and service whenever called upon by your sovereign, according to the laws of this realm?"

"I do."

"Do you swear to honor the Gods above all things, and the Three Major Gods above all others, and renounce all the works of the Lord of the Seven Hells?"

"I do."

"Do you promise to defend our kingdom against all foes, foreign and domestic, to the limit of your ability until death shall claim you?"

"I do."

"We call upon all the Gods, Major and Minor, to behold this oath of fealty in front of the witnesses here present, given in good faith and of free will. Keep this oath, Lord Easton, upon penalty of death and eternal damnation."

The king allowed Fenwick to rise and handed him back his sword. Fenwick sheathed it and returned to his place at the table. He still would not meet my gaze.

When the king took his seat, we all followed suit. I wondered what else there could possibly be for us to discuss. The king did not wait long.

"Please pass the crop estimates to me, Caz," he asked.

I handed the leather portfolio to Fenwick, who then passed it along.

"Rather than waste everyone's time while I examine these, please share the summary."

"Land under cultivation has increased by just over ten percent," I said. "With fair weather, yield should increase by slightly less than that amount."

"Why less?" Fenwick asked.

"The most fertile fields were already being worked," I explained. "The additions will come from less productive pieces of land. I would not expect yields from them to be as bountiful."

"Anything else in your report?" the king asked.

"We will need to obtain the jute sacks from Mooresa again this year. I apologize, Your Majesty. In planning, I overlooked the fact that the jute plant does not produce fully formed sacks. There are other steps involved in their manufacture, and we did not estimate the amount of time they would take."

"Better to figure that out now than at harvest," Lord Shames commented.

"If I might make a suggestion, Your Majesty?" I asked.

He nodded.

"Please send my father—er, Duncan—along with his new bride to Mooresa to negotiate the purchase. Ariana Barry is a native of Mooresa. If Julienne Traval can provide an introduction, I am confident Duncan and Ariana will be successful."

"How do you feel about this, Duncan?" the king inquired.

"We would like to do this, Your Majesty," he said.

"Very well. Fenwi—excuse us, Lord Easton—will you ask your bride-to-be for her assistance with this?" the king asked.

"She has already done so, Your Majesty," Fenwick answered. "The topic came up at dinner a couple of nights ago. I will provide them to Duncan."

"Good," the king grunted in approval. "Last item."

"Ahem," the Duke of Chaldic cleared his throat. "If history is any guide, following their devastating defeat, we should expect a surge in pirate activity coming from the Rhetians. That was certainly the case in the most recent conflict. Aquileia responded by issuing letters of marque and reprisal to counter this. Led by Sir Samuel Krum, our privateers were so successful that the Rhetians begged us to sign a treaty where they agreed to refrain from piracy and open certain ports for trade, upon the condition that we recall Krum."

"Was the treaty a success?" I asked.

"Only in part," Chaldic replied. "The Rhetians did allow our merchant ships to dock in three of their ports but refused to buy anything from us. They did avoid attacking Aquileian ships on the open seas, but that ended when they learned of Krum's death. At that point, they also closed their ports again. Still, it is the only treaty ever signed with the Rhetians in recorded history."

"The only treaty?" I asked.

"The only one," Chaldic confirmed. "The Rhetians consider themselves to be at war with all non-believers. Since we are the only country that shares a border with them, it affects us more seriously and more often than any other country."

"But they trade with countries on the southern continent who don't follow their bizarre religion," I protested.

"I never said they weren't hypocrites," Chaldic smirked. "Again, having an ocean to separate you seems to lessen friction."

"What exactly is a letter of marque and reprisal?" I then asked.

"It's a license issued by the government allowing the bearer to engage in—well, piracy—against ships of another country," Lucy's father, the Duke of Gulick, explained. "The idea is to set pirates to catch pirates, but unlike true pirates who attack anyone, privateers—as they are called—are limited by their sponsoring government to restrict their depredations to specific enemies."

"Anything else?" the king asked.

"Subsidies," Lord Hepworth mentioned. "In Sir Samuel Krum's day, the crown offered subsidies to cover the cost of ship-building."

"What form did these subsidies take?" the king asked.

"The government 'lent' the money to captains who stated that the purpose of the ship was to attack the Rhetians," Hepworth explained. "The loan was repaid by applying the crown's share of revenue from the prize court to the unpaid balance."

"Prize court?" Fenwick asked.

"When a privateer captured an enemy vessel, he would try to bring it to an Aquileian port. Once there, a magistrate appointed by the crown would rule whether the ship was a legitimate prize of war. If so, the ship and its contents would be sold at public auction. The crown would get a quarter of the proceeds. The owner of the ship kept the rest for himself and his crew," Hepworth said. "Several of the privateers became quite wealthy, with Krum being the most successful."

"Are there any other questions?" Hepworth asked.

No one mentioned anything.

"Do you all support the idea of issuing letters of marque?" the king inquired.

A chorus of "aye" rang out.

"Now, whoever shall we appoint to oversee this operation?" he mused.

King Mark, now legally my father, turned his gaze slowly to me and lifted an eyebrow. Then I noticed everyone else at the table was staring at me, including Fenwick—or should I say Lord Easton—who wore a bemused smirk on his lips. I swallowed hard, almost feeling the nausea caused by ocean travel rising from my stomach. But, dear reader, that is a story for another day.

ABOUT THE AUTHOR

John Spearman (Jake to his friends and colleagues) is a Latin teacher and coach at a prestigious New England boarding school in addition to writing. When school is not in session, he lives in coastal Maine. He began writing because his wife challenged him.

This book is the seventh of the FitzDuncan series. Spearman has three other book series, all in the category of military science fiction. The first was the Jonah Halberd series of four books. The Sandy Pike series is set in a different universe from the Halberd books. His newest series, featuring a female hero named Perseverance Andrew, is related to his first four books, the Jonah Halberd series. The Andrews books take place in the same universe as the Halberd series, though over three hundred years earlier.

If you enjoyed reading this book, please consider leaving a positive review on amazon.com or goodreads.com. It will help other readers like you find books they might enjoy. To learn more about the author's different works, please visit www.johnjspearmanauthor.com